Night in N

Bizarre Beats from the Big Easy

A FunDead Publications Anthology

Edited by Amber Newberry & Laurie Moran

To New Orleans:
beloved and misunderstood, truly a sister to our dear Witch City.

CONTENTS

ACKNOWLEDGMENTS

We'd like to thank Creative Salem and John Andrews for the constant source of inspiration and support.

THE LAST BALLAD OF NIKKI STONE
By J. Benjamin Sanders Jr.

When Nikki Stone sang, she could reach down into your soul, take your emotions and play with them like they were her personal toy. With the power of her voice she could make you laugh, cry, writhe in sexual release, or collapse in a drug fueled stupor with just a few well-honed lyrics. She owned you, and could make you delight in that ownership.

She stood in the wings with the rest of the band while they waited for the concert to start, dressed in her usual costume of a white wife beater, vest, and skin tight pants. She peeked around the curtain to get a look at the shifting mass of people out on the floor, singing under her breath while she shook her thin arms to loosen up. Her layers of wrist bangles rattled like castanets as she tried to calm the butterflies in her stomach.

Nikki was tiny, an elfin figure with dark close-cropped hair with dark over-sized eyes, and thin, in an anorexic chic sort of way. Several rings ran across her brow above eyes smeared with a dark shadow to give them a hollow look, and a matching lipstick slashed across her thin lips.

The sounds rising from the crowded floor washed over her in a rolling wave as thousands of voices echoed hollowly about the arena, reached the rafters, and tumbled down again to crash against the stage. She glanced over her shoulder at Joe Miller, the band's bassist, with his guitar slung by his side, its neck pointed down so he looked like some old west gunslinger, dressed in a leather duster and wide brimmed hat, ready to draw and smash his foe down with the pure sound of his weapon. Jack Engles held his axe by the neck, choking it beneath his white knuckles as he swayed from side to side, his eyes burning feverishly in anticipation. Bobby Moon stood back in an attitude of pharmaceutical calm, drumsticks twirling through his nimble fingers like miniature batons. All of the band members were ready to go, waiting for the announcer to bring them out.

"Take this, Nikki." Alice Hoyt passed over a bottle of water. Alice had

1

been hired to be her nanny, the guys insisted that she have someone there to take care of her, and Nikki agreed as long as they let her choose the person. She chose Alice, who had started her life as a Big Easy Soul groupie, until Nikki elevated her to the role of personal assistant. She wasn't worth a shit at her job, but Nikki liked Alice, so the rest of the band tolerated her.

"Thanks. Why don't you go and have some fun, and meet me back in my dressing room after the show?" Nikki squeezed Alice's hand and turned her attention back to the stage.

The lights went down, and several spots popped on and swept across the stage in a spill of rainbow lights. The noises from the floor slowly died down as the people rushed to find their seats, and Nikki could see Terrence, T-Man, Morales as he ambled across the stage to the microphone stand in the center.

"How you doing tonight, my babies? Are you ready for some hot sounds straight out of the Louisiana swamps?" He called out to the crowd and waited a few minutes until the excited roar died down. "I'm T-Man, for all you fans out there, the engineer that drives the night train of hot hits on the Big Q, where from midnight to five every night I take you to visit all those exotic and far off lands around the world, from Kashmir to Shamballa and beyond. I have been given the great honor to come out here and introduce one of the most creative and stimulating, as well as one of the best, new bands to come down the pike in a long time. Of course, I'm talking about that little girl with the biggest voice going in music today, Nikki Stone, and her band, Big Easy Soul, with their mixture of hot driving rock and voodoo bayou rhythms, spread across the world by the sheer force of her will and refusal to fail. So, let's give a big welcome home to Nikki Stone and Big Easy Soul!" T-man stepped away from the mic and began to clap, but his ovation was swamped by the deluge of applause and whistles that came from every corner of the arena, the sound building until it thundered back from the rafters and washed over the stage. Nikki stepped out onto the glossy boards and found herself caught by a white spot that escorted her across the stage in a pool of liquid light. She reached the microphone, and then smiled out at all those adoring faces, before the stage floods flashed on and blinded her. The other band members found their spots and began a last minute instrument check.

Nikki grabbed the microphone with both hands, leaned closer and spoke with a deep sultry voice that stretched out in a long drawl. "How y'all doing?" She released a wicked laugh. "We're certainly glad to be here and hope you enjoy the show tonight. We're gonna start off with an upbeat and easy one, then get into the grittier ones later if y'all got the time."

She looked back over her shoulder at the band and saw they were ready, so she raised her right arm and used it as a baton to count down. "One, two, three, hit it." The band started to play. The music flowed across the stage, hot and sweet as jalapeno jelly. Nikki began to sing with a deep soulful voice that burned its way into their hearts and brains.

Stormy weather
When we're together.
Rain keeps falling
Down on me.
Stormy weather
Whatever you want,
You know that you
Can get it from me.

La de da da, la de da
La de da da, da le da

When I embrace you
And see your eyes.
I see nothing
But cloudy skies.
You bring the rain
Like falling tears.
To wash away the pain
Of all my years.

La de da da, la de da
La de da da, da le da

For the next tune her voice went deep and rough, so that it sounded like she had crawled through a gutter clogged with filth and sewage. It soaked into her clothes, smeared across her flesh, slipped past her lips, and filled her mouth with its rancid taste. It was this feeling of near emotional rape and subjugation that she gave to her audience.

I was used and abused, and beaten on down,
Molested and tested all over this town.
Hit on and spit on 'til my life was fog,
Defeated and treated like a mangy old dog.

Her voice blended with the music and wormed its way into the listeners' hearts and souls, so each and every one of them could feel the loneliness, abuse, and pain she sang about on those hard and indifferent streets in that nameless and pitiless town. Nikki closed her eyes and reached up to wrap her hands around the stone that hung about her neck on a leather thong, letting her fingers caress the oily smoothness while she relived the memory of the night it came to be hers.

* * *

The hot torpid city of New Orleans could be a cold hard place at times, especially for a young singer trying to break into the music business. Nikki had gone door to door for every audition she could find, and so far, every one of them had been slammed in her face. They usually turned her away before she could even finish her first song, and most of the band members weren't very kind when they critiqued her abilities. They ranged from gentle letdowns, to being downright savage.

"Can't sing worth a shit, love."

"Sorry Nikki, but we're looking for someone with a bit more range."

"Maybe if you had some bigger boobs some of the fans could overlook the way you sound."

"Come back when your voice changes, and when you can carry a decent tune."

"Have you considered waitressing? You ain't got the tits to be a dancer."

She heard it all, and after several weeks of failure, Nikki had reached her breaking point. She went out to get good and drunk in a place where she could sit down and listen to the house band play, with their overweight and under-talented chanteuse.

A couple of hours of steady drinking pushed her ever deeper into that deep pit of depression. Nikki stood and staggered outside to leave the neon beer lights and the blue smoky haze behind. She tried to clear her head by breathing in the recently rain scrubbed air to push out the growing alcohol buzz that rattled around in her brain.

Leaning against the dirty brick walls, she could feel her gorge rise. She pushed off and reeled into the alley, the air redolent with the stench of rotten garbage and rancid grease. She dropped to her hands and knees, and vomited. She emptied her belly of everything that she had eaten that day, the beige puddle filled with formless chunks, and her mouth awash with the bitter bile. She puked again, and sent the burning fluid pushing through her sinuses so that it dripped out her nose and trailed liquid ropes of mucus. Her stomach convulsed until her muscles ached as they locked up and tried to push even more of the sour semifluid contents from her belly, but she had nothing left to give.

That's when she started to cry, a bare trickle of tears that washed down the side of her nose and dripped into the rancid puddle beneath her face, and then the dam broke. She was so wrapped up in her self-pity that she never noticed the cautious approach of the stranger.

"What for you cry like dat child? You sound like your heart be breaking." The soft voice with the trace of a Caribbean lilt intruded upon her moment of desolation. Then a hand resting comfortingly on her shoulder forced Nikki to look at the figure that knelt beside her through her tear blurred eyes.

"Git up now gurl. No sense for you to wallow in de filth of dis alley now, or your own sickness neither." She was a large woman with skin so dark it seemed to have a purple sheen, and a smile as white as bleached linen. She wore a colorful bandanna of red and yellow over her close-cropped hair, layers of beaded necklaces circled her neck and hung over the impressive bosom hidden beneath her calico blouse. Nikki was mesmerized by the way they slithered and rattled when the strange woman moved. Strong hands helped the girl get to her feet. She leaned into the unknown woman and seemed to absorb some of the pulsing vitality until she had the strength to move along.

"Tis' a good t'ing for you dat Mama Flora jess happen to be here. Too many people out at dis time of de night would be up to no good, and would take liberties wit' a pretty young white gurl like you. Why don't you come wit' me child, I have a little place around de corner here where you will be safe enough." Mama Flora helped steady the drunken Nikki, and led her away from the alley and back out to the street.

"Thank you," Nikki managed to croak out.

Mama Flora led her down the street to a small shop whose glass front had been filled with an assortment of dark goods, stuffed swamp creatures, thick books with wood and leather covers, dried plants, jars filled with colored powders, and a collection of odd-and-end bones. The dark-skinned woman opened the door and led Nikki inside, passing through the front that looked like an old-style apothecary, with a lot of antique canisters and jars that lined the glassed-in shelves.

They passed through the cluttered shop and pushed through a thin curtain that led into the back, which she had converted into a simple but comfortable living quarters. Mama Flora lit the small gas stove, and put on a kettle to boil.

"Have a seat me gurl, get yourself comfortable while I brew us some of me delicious tea. It will soon set you to right, den you can tell Mama Flora what it is dat be ailing you." She pointed to the small table covered with a blue checkerboard cloth, then reached into the curtain covered cabinets to fetch down a couple of mismatched cups. As soon as the kettle started to whistle, Mama Flora dropped in several pinches of dark leaves and set it aside to steep for a minute. When it had sat long enough, she poured them both a steaming cup and set one in front of Nikki. The mysterious woman then took the seat across the small table from her guest.

"Now tell Mama why you were out der on your knees in dat alley, all sick like, crying and such. Has life been treating you dat bad?" The woman sipped from her cup and waited for the young girl to speak. Nikki tasted the tea, and let its soothing flavor rinse the bitter bile from her mouth. Its heat soon unwound the heavy knot that lay in the middle of her belly and made her feel light-headed. The tea seemed to be almost mystically calming, at least calming enough to get Nikki to talk.

"For as long as I could remember, all I've wanted is to sing. To stand up on the stage in front of the lights and the crowds and be able to tell the people in the audience how I felt, and get them to know how I lived through my songs. I wanted to share with them my pains, my joys, the good times and the bad, but it seems that nobody but me believes I can be that type of singer." Nikki went on to explain what she had been going through for the past few weeks, the cruel comments, the put downs, the propositions and suggestions that she might be able to get what she wanted, if she would just give in a little and cooperate. It just spewed out of her while the woman listened, made sympathetic noises, and nodded sagely.

"I have somet'ing here dat will help you, I t'ink. It's a gift from Mama Flora." She rose from the table, went to an old chest that sat against the far wall, and rummaged through it until she found what she had been searching for. She carried it to the table and laid it in front of Nikki: a smooth stone with a small hole carved in it, through which a narrow strip of leather had been threaded. Nikki reached out to touch the stone, and felt an electric spark. She caressed the stone's surface and could feel several irregularities, as if it had been covered with near invisible carvings.

"What is it?" Nikki asked curiously, and noticed that the black woman wore one identical to it around her own neck.

"Dis what we call a soul stone. You wear dat when you sing and de people won't hear just your voice, but dey will be feeling whatever it is dat you be feeling."

"It's real?"

"As real as you or me, as real as your desire to be up on dat stage and singing to all de people out der dat listen to you, as real as your dreams." Mama Flora assured her with a wide smile when Nikki looked up. "Put it on and from dis day forward never take it off again."

Nikki slipped the leather strap over her head and let the stone fall down to settle in the wide valley between her small breasts. It felt cold at first, but quickly warmed as it lay against her flesh. Feeling a wave of weakness, she didn't notice how a matching stone around the old woman's neck flashed, or the way the wrinkles at the corner of Mama Flora's mouth smoothed. How the crow's feet at her eyes seemed to lose a toe, or how her eyes seemed to have an unnaturally hungry glow.

"What can I give you for this?" Nikki asked, her voice touched with wonder.

"It be a gift, dis for you, gurl, and jess for you. You take it and go out der and show dem what you have in your heart. De stone will show dem, yes it will surely show dem, and dat will be me reward." Mama Flora flashed Nikki a mysterious smile from across the rim of her cup as she took another long sip of her tea. That look could have been chilling if Nikki had been paying attention. "De only warning I give you is to be careful with dat t'ing. Its power can seduce you as well, if you not be careful, and end up stealing your own soul."

Nikki looked around at some of the obvious antiques scattered around the room, and got the sense that the woman had a personal attachment to many of them. "Have you been here long?"

She chuckled softly. "For longer den you can imagine chile."

Nikki finished her drink and thanked Mama Flora. She left, filled with a new determination to find a band that needed a singer. She stepped out into the mid-morning sunlight as it tried to peek through the gray cloud cover of the overcast sky. It shocked Nikki to see the sun up. It had been around two in the morning when Mama Flora had picked her out of her pool of vomit in that filthy alley. That meant eight or nine hours had passed while she rested in the little shop.

It took her most of the day to find what she wanted, but Nikki knew she couldn't hook up with just anybody. She found what she had been searching for in a little out of the way club called the Voodoo Lounge, and a trio who called themselves Big Easy Soul. The lead guitarist also sang as well, but the group felt they needed a female singer to front the band if they were going to take that next step. Nikki met with them and talked to both Jack and Joe, while Bobby stayed back and nursed a dark drink in a highball glass. They agreed she would return that night and do a set before a crowd, so the band could gauge how the audience would react to her voice.

That night when she walked into the packed Voodoo Lounge, every square inch not taken up by hot sweaty flesh had been filled with the blue gray cloud of smoke. The band stood on the stage in the middle of their first set, the music loud enough to drown out every conversation short of a scream. Jack had left word with the bouncer, so he escorted Nikki behind the bandstand by making his own path. He shoved and pushed the men and women out of his way with hands and elbows. The bouncer was big, black, and bald, with a perpetual scowl on his face, and those that turned to scream out complaints let the words die on their lips when they saw who did the pushing. He seated her at the band's table with a couple of thin, bleached girls.

Neither bothered to acknowledge Nikki, they just continued to stare at the three men on the stage while they played on to the delight of the crowd.

After about fifteen minutes the band took a break, stepped off the stage, took seats around the table, and poured drinks from the iced pitcher in the center. Joe even filled her glass. She sniffed it carefully, overly cautious since she didn't really know the guys yet.

"Relax, it's just Coke. Band rule, we don't drink when we work, it makes you sloppy," Jack assured her. Joe and Bobby lifted their glasses in a mock toast in her direction before they gulped their drinks down. She took a careful sip, and realized they had told her the truth.

"Think you're ready for this? You can go up with us on the next set and show us what you've got, okay?"

Nikki nodded. None of the guys bothered to introduce the girls, and the girls couldn't have cared less. They sat with their heads together and whispered and giggled, and did their best to ignore her.

"I'm ready, what do you want me to sing?" They discussed several options, but finally offered the lyrics to one of the band's own songs. She glanced over them and nodded. "Sure, I can do it, how does the tune go?"

"Just follow us, and you'll be fine. Let's go guys, it's time to earn that big paycheck Marv is gonna give us tonight." They groaned, pushed away from the table and headed for the stage. Jack took the microphone to announce the change.

"Thanks for coming out here tonight to support our band. Right now, I want to announce that we have a special treat for you, a female vocalist that wants to join us for the next set. Ya'll give a Big Easy Soul welcome for Miss Nikki Stone." He stepped back and passed the microphone over. There were a few yells and whistles at the announcement. Nikki looked out at the crowd, and her belly did flip flops.

"One, two, three." Jack screamed while Bobby beat time with his sticks, and they jumped into the song. Nikki grabbed the stone around her neck and held on to it while she waited for the right time to join in. Her voice, deep and husky, told the story of the harsh burden of her life in song, and spun it out into an emotional bludgeon that stunned all those that heard it for the first time.

> *Dreams of cocaine, I feel no pain.*
> *Snorting those narrow white lines.*
> *Get so high, I feel I can fly.*
> *End the frustration that leaves me blind.*
> *I do it twice, it can feel so nice.*
> *Then the need is gone for just a short while.*
> *'Til the next day, when the pain comes to stay.*
> *I will sell my soul for a snort and a smile.*

When she sang, the conversations tailed off, the yells and laughter falling to soft, barely heard whispers. The crowd turned their attention to the bandstand, and the four people that stood under the harsh white spotlights. They listened as they had never listened before. She wove the pattern of her song into a razor-sharp stiletto that pierced the aching conscious of the listeners, like a metal tipped scourge she used to flail away at their bodies, peel away the outer flesh and expose the raw boney core beneath. Nikki's soulful voice made them feel all the desolation and pain that flowed from her music.

She could see people start to cry with want, or shiver and moan from the harsh ache of withdrawal. Some went numb as their eyes grew hollow and bruised. Most of the crowd sobbed with relief when the song finished, and after a moment of stunned silence, they rose and showered Nikki with thunderous applause that quickly grew to a tsunami of adoration. She could feel the intensity of the emotions that swept through the audience as they heard the sheer power of her voice.

"Goddamn girl, you didn't tell me you could sing like that." Jack said when the applause finally trailed off.

"Man, oh man, I think we have a keeper here, Jackie Boy. What do you say, Bobby?" Joe turned to look at the drummer.

"I say hell yeah." He accented his words with a rim shot, and finished with a crash on his high hat.

"Welcome to the band Nikki, the job's yours if you want it." Jack slapped his big hand on her thin shoulder, and she could only nod her head, her throat closed with emotion as tears dewed her eyes.

"Let's give them something else so they don't think it was just a fluke, how about Voodoo Woman?" They were on stage until past closing, and nobody dared leave the bar while they played. The bouncer had to turn people away as the sound of their music leached through the doors and out onto the street, and began to draw everyone within hearing range toward the club.

* * *

Jack watched Nikki worriedly as song after song rolled across the sea of undulating and writhing bodies stretched across the arena. She stripped bare their emotions and exposed each and every flaw they might have. Nikki sang soul burning songs of drugs, pain, abuse, and loneliness, divulged her own inner weaknesses for their benefit, and made them feel what she felt, hurt how she hurt, and dream what she dreamt.

The Big easy wasn't so easy for me,
The dirty French Quarter is where I went to die.
My soul was lost like a ship at sea,
But it's where I could live my lies.

He said he would always be true to me.
But he never really tried.
I thought we would be together you see,
But now he's gone, all I do is cry.

Nikki poured her soul into her music, and Jack could see how it affected those people in the front row. He could hear the soft sobs and see the glisten of tears as they flinched away from the painful lash of her lyrics; she scourged their emotions raw with false memories so fresh it was as if they had personally lived through them. Song after song lifted them to the peak of sweet glory, and then plunged them down to the searing borders of Hell. Nikki became drenched with sweat and drained of more than just energy, it felt as if she put her life-force into each and every song, and seemed to sap a bit of Jack's own.

Love can be such a lovely thing,
But I know the pain it can bring.
When you foolishly give him your heart,
Always believing you will never part.
He said he loved me and like a fool,
I believed what he said was true.
But before long I could see he was so vain,
And the one-way love drove me insane.

When they were done with the third encore of the night, Nikki was so weak that Jack and Joe had to help her off the stage and back to her dressing room. Each held an arm as they carried her off and could hear her soft voice still singing under her breath. She crooned a song meant for her ears only as she smiled beatifically off into the distance.

"How much longer can this go on man? This'll end up killing her," Joe said to his friend, and they could hear the crowd as they called for still another encore, whistling and clapping as they called out Nikki's name.

"Don't you think I know that? I've tried to get her to take some time off, but she won't. She says only the music is important, and the people have to hear her sing. Whenever I try to cancel a gig, she goes behind my back and reschedules it. If I thought just walking away from this whole damned thing would stop her, I would do it," Jack explained angrily.

"Can't do that Jack. They need me. I need them. I have to sing, that's the only time I feel alive anymore." Nikki panted and tried to get her feet under her so she could walk unaided, but she collapsed. "Let's go back out and do one more song."

She tried to suck in more air to her overworked lungs, and sounded as if she might be suffocating.

"No Nikki, that's enough. Maybe after we get you back to the dressing room, Joe, Bobby, and me can go out there and play another set. That might satisfy them." Jack sounded damned sure she was done for the night, no matter how badly she might want to go back out there.

"Bad idea dude, remember what happened last time we took the stage without Nikki. We almost had a riot on our hands, like those people couldn't live without hearing her voice." Bobby spoke from behind them, and then slipped past so he could beat them to the door.

They carried her inside and set her slumped body in a large padded chair. Jack looked at her pale face covered with sweat; her clothes were soaked, and her skin felt clammy to the touch. He laid his fingers alongside her throat and held them there for a moment, and could feel the thin, rapid beat of her heart. She never stopped singing though, he could see her lips moved, though her voice was no louder than a whisper, and even at that he could still feel the power of her song as it dragged on him.

I love my love, my love loves me.
I know just how happy we will be.
To taste his kiss and feel his caress,
Fills me with hope, I must confess.

"Shit, it's getting worse man. Help me get her out of these clothes and into the shower. Where the fuck is that bitch, Alice? She should be here right now."

"Probably out banging some roadie, or getting stoned somewhere behind the stage," Joe offered.

"Fuck and double fuck. We can't wait for her to show up. Bobby, see if you can grab somebody out there to give us a hand, there's bound to be some female fan that would give her left tit to help us with the famous Nikki Stone." He and Joe sat her up and stripped the sodden wife beater and vest off and tossed it on the floor. Jack grimaced when he saw the way her ribs stood out starkly against her body. Her small breasts were no more than flaccid bags, and her flesh was covered with dark bruises.

"Dammit, that bitch Alice is fired, I don't care what Nikki says. This is how she takes care of her?" Jack spit out angrily.

"Calm down man, I'll go get the shower started." Joe slapped him across the shoulder, and stepped into the private bath, and soon he could hear a hissing spray.

"Make it a damned hot one," Jack called out. The door opened and Bobby stepped in, dragging a wide-eyed girl behind him.

"This is Angie, she said she would help."

"Good. If you run into Alice anywhere, tell her she's fired, pass the word among the crew. If I see her around after this, I'll fire and replace every son of a bitch out there."

"About time. That stupid bitch is all but useless," Bobby said.

"Oh, wow. This is really Nikki Stone. I thought that might just be an excuse to get me in here for a gang bang," she gushed. She looked at Nikki and her eyes went wide with surprise. "Is she high?"

"No, it's just the music. She's like this after every show, and that goddamn cow that's supposed to be here to help her is off doing God knows what. Are you sure you're cool with this?" Jack turned to look at the girl, dressed pretty much as Nikki, a groupie, only this girl had a little bit more meat on her than the real Nikki did.

"Sure, I can handle it, but somebody has to help me get her into the shower. Move out of the way while I strip off her jeans." Jack stepped aside, and Angie dropped down to her knees and quickly shucked the jeans off the unresponsive Nikki, until she sat in nothing but her birthday suit and that ever-present stone around her neck. Angie stared at it, and then reached a tentative hand toward it, her trembling fingers stretched out. A big hand slapped down on her wrist and jerked her back.

"Don't. That's Nikki's pride and joy, and she will come unglued against anyone who touches it. I've seen her come scratching and clawing her way out of a coma when an intern grabbed it to get a closer look, and that poor boy looked like he had been tossed into a cage of pissed off wild cats when she finished with him. I'm telling you that for your own good," Jack warned her, his voice much gentler than his grip.

"What the fuck do you mean I can't go in there? Do you know who I am you piece of roadie shit? I'm Nikki Stone's personal assistant, and she'll have your balls if you don't get out of my way." Alice's screeching voice came through the door.

"He what? Jack Engles! You mother fucker, you can't fire me. None of you can fire me. I work for Nikki, you sorry piece of shit. Get your hands off me, don't touch me. Nikki, Nikki, they won't let me in. Nikki, I need help!" Her voice became hysterical, and they could hear the scuffle out in the hall.

"Bobby, that's your cue. Get rid of that worthless slag, and I don't care how you do it. Take her to the cops with a bag of smack or ice and tell them you caught her trying to deal it to the fans if you have to, just get her gone. And tell her if we ever see her around where we play again, I'll make sure she disappears for good, and make her believe it."

"Sure thing man," Bobby flashed a joyous grin and slipped out the door. The sound of a loud slap followed by a scream of outrage came through the door a moment later, another slap, then came the crying.

"She's singing. Why is she still singing?" Angie asked from where she knelt between Nikki's splayed legs.

"She never stops. I don't know why, but she never stops. She didn't used to be that way, but it's getting worse. It's almost like an addiction eating away at her. Now let's get her into the shower and cleaned up." Several hands reached out, pulled Nikki to her feet, and steered her toward the bathroom door. A moment later they heard Angie's scream.

"Oh my God. Jack,! Jack, she's not breathing." The three band members burst through the door and found the girl on her knees beside the sprawled body, her gaze turned pleadingly toward them.

"Oh shit," Joe cursed when he saw Nikki with her eyes rolled back, her chest not moving.

"Shit is right man. Come on Bobby, I need you to help me. I'll supply the air; you work on her heart. Somebody call nine one one, tell them to get here as fast as they can."

They were still working on her when the paramedics showed, but it was too late, Nikki Stone was gone. They loaded her on a bed and covered her with a sheet, but while the others were distracted, Angie slipped the stone off and put it around her own neck. She stood there with the rest of the band when they took Nikki through the door and down the hall, and she began to sing a song of farewell.

Death rides in on a pale steed,
To bear away your soul now freed.
Your last breath, burns like fire,
As with a sigh, you gently expire.
You go away, and leave us alone,
To sing the ballad of Nikki Stone.

Jack and the rest of the band looked at her in shock, unable to speak for a minute, until Bobby managed to get out in a strangled voice. "My God, she sounds just like Nikki."

LOSING YOUR MARBLES
By Klara Gomez

"Your turn, Tommy." Danny's voice comes across as a threat. He looks confident in his prediction of winning every game this week, and now he stands taller than the other two boys, rolling his prize-stash of marbles in an old, rusty can.

Four marbles remain on the floor, and Po-boy here flicked my navy shooter out of the circle, which means I'll probably go home empty-handed. But I can always refill my own stash by playing my little cousin. He'll whine and whine after losing, and I'll probably get blamed and be punished for it, but I'll get my hands on some marbles by the end of the week, one way or another. Whether it be winning them fairly or stealing them.

"Hey, you're stepping over the circle," I tell Danny, pointing at his foot.

"I am not!" he replies, smearing the line under the sole of his sneakers. He picks up the chalk and draws over what he erased, except he makes the circle narrower on that end—another trick to get me to lose.

I scowl at Danny. "Step back or I'll aim my shooter at the sack between your legs. It'll hurt so much that you'll drop your marbles, and believe me, Po-boy here will not think twice. He'll take your marbles and make a run for it."

"He knows better," Danny says, crossing his arms and fixing Po-boy with a naughty smirk.

"And so do you, Tommy," Po-boy adds looking my way, his eyes filled with concern. He's afraid of Danny. Everyone is, including me. I've just gotten good at bluffing.

"Po-boy, whose side are you on?" I ask and watch him shrug.

As I aim my shooter at Danny's red marble, I can't help but think how quickly Po-boy got used to his nickname. It all started a year and a half ago, in first grade. Danny, Augie, and I were in the school cafeteria, eating whatever nasty lunch they were serving that day, when we noticed this kid eating the juiciest po-boy I'd ever seen. We soon learned that his mother, Mrs. Leblanc, had bought a hotdog cart and turned it into a po-boy cart. She had set her wheeled shop on Decatur Street, by Jackson Square. A few weeks later she appeared on TV—her son standing next to her with a toothless grin, his head pushing against his mother's roundness so that the camera could show his own roundness—and the woman who spoke from the microphone called Mrs. Leblanc ". . . a true innovator," and her po-boy cart ". . . New Orleans' best-kept secret." And yes, we still call him Max in front of his mother, especially when she treats us to free food.

My stomach growls as my nostrils detect the smell of a freshly cooked meal. It isn't a po-boy, it's definitely crawfish étoufée, coming from a nearby kitchen. For a second I'm more interested in eating than winning Danny's red marble.

Augie crouches next to Po-boy, his spider-like fingers open as he speaks. "We're playing for keepsies, you guys. If Danny wins, we'll just have to improve our game."

"Shut it, Augie," I tell him, sticking my tongue out and biting it. I knuckle down and scowl at Danny's red marble. "You're coming home with me," I whisper, feeling my shooter shift slightly over my sweaty fingers. I grab it firmly, take a deep breath, lean lower, and...

"What are you guys doing?"

My shooter flies out of my hand with great speed and misses the red marble, rolling out of the circle and meeting a slope on the concrete floor that makes it change its course.

Danny applauds, nodding his head at the freckled face that peeps at me with wide-open eyes.

"Gertie, what are you doing here?" Augie asks, with both hands over his head. His face is like hers—long, skinny, and white—like one of those glass milk bottles from the old days. Thankfully, Augie's face is not as freckled, and not as annoying to stare at.

"Why did you tell your stupid sister about our new playground?" Before I finish my question, Augie is shaking his head.

"He didn't tell me anything," Gertie responds with a smile. The sun makes her freckles pink and sore like fire-ant bites.

"Sure," I answer, rolling my eyes at her.

Danny's voice comes from afar, "Good luck hitting anything but your pride." He's crouching low, laughing at my piss-poor game, and I hear the rattle of marbles in his can. He's a few years older than the rest of us, and for some reason, he talks a lot about *pride*. He's tried to explain it to us, and I think we're starting to get it. Although when I tried to explain *pride* to our school counselor—who had punished us for getting into a fight with two third graders who were calling us names—she just shook her head, and called Danny a bully. But I don't see it that way. I think it's wise to have a friend who is taller, bigger, and scarier on your side; even if that means having to give him your snack money every once in a while.

"This game is over, guys," I announce as Danny returns. He drops my shooter in the palm of my hand and collects the four remaining marbles. No one dares to complain.

"Let me guess," Augie tells his sister. "Your invisible friend told you where we were?"

Gertie narrows her eyes on Augie, and then looks upon something dark she has been carrying in her arms. With a tilt of her head, she shifts her position, and I notice her fingers stroking the black curls of a doll.

Augie turns my way, with eyes bulging out of their sockets. "Believe me, I'm no snitch. She didn't hear it from me, and she was still asleep when I left the house. I'm sure she didn't follow me."

"Alma told me," Gertie says in a whispery tone.

"Who's Alma?" I ask Augie.

"That would be Gertie's invisible friend," Po-boy responds, placing a hand over Augie's shoulder. "If I ever get a sister, I will surely leave the house."

But Po-boy wouldn't know anything about having siblings, which is probably the reason why his mother packs his lunchbox with such delicious sandwiches. I have two brothers in diapers, which means I qualify to get free disgusting lunch at school. Dad tells me one day I'll be third in command, but for now, I am only good for helping around the house. And it stinks!

"Gertie," I call, doing my best to look menacing. "Girls are not welcome on our turf. Girls only bring bad luck. *You* made me lose all my marbles."

"Well, Tommy," she replies, hugging her doll a little tighter, "don't blame girls for your condition. If you're losing your marbles, you need a shrink. I hear Mr. Mitchell, our next door neighbor, used to work at a looney bin. Maybe he can help."

The boys burst into laughter, their fingers pointed at me.

Even though she likes to play with her dolls, Gertie has the brains of a middle-schooler. Must be all the reading she does. She is definitely sharp and has ridiculed me in front of my friends more than once. I think that's the word—*ridiculed*. My mom told me it's used when someone embarrasses you in public. She explained it once, when we got invited to a birthday party, and I pulled down my older cousin's pants in a room full of girls. According to Danny, *being ridiculed* is the opposite of *being proud*.

"Gertie, you're stupid and crazy. If anyone needs a shrink, it is you . . . talking to invisible friends," I scoff.

Gertie's face turns sweet as she tugs on the sleeve of my T-shirt. "Tommy, don't be upset. It really was Alma who told me you'd be up here."

"Whatever." I walk to the edge of the rooftop as my friends break into a wave of '*Ooobs!*' and '*Aaabs!*', hiding my embarrassment under my long, brown bangs while making time for the joke to wear out.

The rooftop to Po-boy's building is slightly higher than the rest around the block. It is filled with old TV antennas, two big cisterns, clotheslines draped with white linen, and it features a great view of New Orleans's geometric-shaped rooftops. Po-boy brought me here a few nights ago when he realized Magda Larieux, a seventeen-year-old girl who lives in my building, had been sneaking up here with Jimmy, her boyfriend. Po-boy and I came up the stairs, laid chest-down over the floor, and crawled close to the cisterns until we could hear the strange sounds Magda and Jimmy were making—their silhouettes swaying together to a fast-paced zydeco song that played on someone's radio. I don't understand why, having such great open space, they'd choose to wedge themselves between the concrete tanks to dance. Or why they moaned and called God repeatedly. This is no church. For crying out loud, it's Po-boy's rooftop. Anyway, Po-boy and I ended up getting tired, and we crawled back to the door and headed downstairs, calling it a night.

Gertie's little brown eyes are fixed on mine. Her strappy dress shows all her bones. She looks like she could lift in flight with a flock of pigeons and disappear behind the gabled rooftops.

"Anyway," she says, as I rejoin the group, "I only came to tell you that I'll be spending the rest of the week at Dad's." Gertie's eyes shift to her brother, and I feel a sudden relief at knowing she's no longer picking on me.

"Dad's coming for us?" Augie asks.

"He's coming for me. Mom's not letting you go. You're grounded, remember?"

Augie lowers his gaze, bites his lips, and kicks a little pebble with the tip of his boot. "Well, I'm not planning on studying anyway. It don't matter if I'm at Mom's or at Dad's. Plus, Dad don't care about my grades. He only cares about his new girlfriend . . ."

"Wife," Gertie reminds him.

"Yeah, whatever! He only cares about that witch and their new baby. He forgot about us."

Gertie purses her lips and brings her doll forward to show him. There's a chubby black face under all that curly hair. Her little white dress has a lot of detail—ribbons, flowers, and other silly, girly stuff.

"What's that?" Augie asks, glancing at the doll sideways.

"It's a gift from Liza," Gertie responds.

17

Augie's jaw slowly drops, his scowl intensifying. "That evil witch got you a gift?"

Gertie nods with a half-smile. "See, our stepmother actually likes me. In fact, she loves me."

"She does not," Augie replies.

"She even told me she won't mind Daddy spending all the time he wants with me. And she apologized for being so rude at first, and for wanting to keep him all to herself. That's why she got me this doll," she says, bringing the little black thing close to her neck, "to say sorry, and to let me know how much she loves me."

Augie's face is red, his eyes are about to burst into angry tears.

"Your stepmother is stupid," I snap at Gertie, wanting to protect my friend's pride. "All girls are stupid."

"That's right." Po-boy comes to the rescue, stepping closer to her.

"Yeah," Augie adds, advancing towards his sister. He rubs his eyes with the back of his hand and hides his clenched fists in the pockets of his shorts. "Stupid Gertie," he whispers as the red-haired girl takes a step back.

"Stupid Gertie," Po-boy adds, and the rest of us follow.

"Stupid Gertie, stupid Gertie, stupid Gertie . . ." We continue chanting and huddling around her. Gertie is on the brink of crying. She backpedals and stumbles, but Danny is standing right behind her. He hooks his hands under her armpits until she regains her balance. My heart begins to pound loudly as Danny gives Gertie a little push, sending her forward towards her brother.

"Stupid Gertie," Augie whispers, his face inches from hers. He pushes her towards Po-boy.

"Stupid Gertie," Po-boy tells her, nudging her towards me.

"Stupid Gertie," I call, as my knees begin to shake. Although I'm afraid of what might happen to her, I know I can't be the one to defend her. I put on my ugliest face and give her a little shove, sending her back to Danny.

Gertie is losing it, and part of me feels really bad. I only hope we scare her enough that she will leave us alone once and for all. Her eyes keep swelling as tears wash the pink out of her freckles. Her orange brows curl up. "Promise I won't look for you again. Now, please stop," she begs.

"Stupid Gertie," Danny calls her, thrusting her small body down towards the floor without much effort. Like a ragdoll, Gertie's body falls, and I'm praying she doesn't get hurt or bruised. Danny picks her up by the arms and makes her stand.

Gertie holds her doll tight and takes a deep breath. "Alma," she whispers, "make them stop."

A *swoosh* lifts a wave of dust from where we stand and sends us all backpedaling. My heart wants to leap out of my chest and take off running, while my eyes travel from face to face, looking for an explanation. But my friends are rattled, eyeballing Gertie with mouths agape like hungry hatchlings. Gertie's braids become undone as a whirlwind begins to form around her. Her eyes, bright and surprised, follow the ghastly ascension of her black doll, which rises a few feet above her head as the wind picks up. The clean linen that had been left to dry on the clothesline also comes to life, lifting in the air, floating above our heads, dancing like ghostly figures around the black doll.

"Unbelievable!" One of us says.

"What is happening?" Another one asks.

"Gertie," Augie calls with a frightened voice. "If Alma is real, she can tell you the truth about our stepmother. Ask her to tell you the truth about Liza."

The wind comes to a sudden halt. Gertie's hair, the doll, the sheets, and clothespins remain paralyzed in mid-motion for a few seconds before plunging like a frustrated exhale. All of us keep very still, our eyes fixed on Gertie. She kneels before the sheets and glances back our way.

My heart beats in the back of my throat, my breath comes out of my mouth in tiny drafts that seem to slice the dense air around us. I suppose all my friends are just as scared and curious as to what is happening. We step forward, joining her.

The doll's head rests on the blankets—a diagonal crack across the round smiley face. Gertie's lips quiver as she clutches onto her broken toy. She grabs the headless body first, cradling it against her chest. And as she picks up the head, brown dust pours out of its cavity, staining the white of the clothes.

"What's this?" Gertie wonders, peering through the dark opening. Her fingers reach inside the hollow head and pull out slowly, exposing a bundle of dried herbs tightly bound with a thin rope of red hair, identical to Gertie's.

"Voodoo?" Danny leans forward, his arms stretched over my shoulders and Po-boy's.

"I knew it," Augie says, crouching next to his sister. "Luanna Ferrant told me she spotted Liza in Madamme Pierroux's shop. I peeped inside that store once—some serious, heavy-duty stuff. Gertie, this is not a joke."

Gertie remains calm. Her hand dips inside the doll's head as if expecting to find more icky things. "Ouch," she flinches and carefully pulls out a small, folded cardboard paper. It is wrapped in black thread and covered with sharp sewing pins. She brings the paper to her mouth and bites the thread, loosening a strand. Her lips bleed as she pulls the loose end of the string, the paper unspooling like a yo-yo. Gertie cleans the blood from her mouth with the back of her hand, and straightens the paper.

"Holy Moly!" Po-boy says, as the five of us spot Gertie's school picture, a pin on each freckle, like a silver porcupine.

"Liza placed a voodoo spell on you, Gertie. What are we going to do?" I ask.

Gertie's lips turn into an unlucky upside-down horseshoe. She holds her breath while studying the herbs, the dust, and the pinned photograph. After a while, she lets out a sigh of relief. "Alma says she'll make it better."

"Alma is not real, Gertie," Augie insists. "What we just saw was caused by that devilish doll. It's evil. Evil voodoo. The bad stuff, you know? I say we torch that thing right now!"

"It's a beautiful doll, Augie. And Alma will clean it and fix its cracked head so we can play with her."

Po-boy slaps Danny's back, urging him to follow. "Let's go downstairs and grab the lighter."

Augie turns my way, bouncing on his heels. "Don't let my sister out of sight, Tommy."

"Promise," I say, and watch my friends quickly disappear behind the old wooden door. As I wait, I keep a steady eye on Gertie, who smiles at her broken doll as if it were as good as new. She tugs and pulls the little dress, runs her fingers across the curly head, and rocks the little body and severed head in her arms with the sweetness of a mother putting a newborn baby to sleep.

"Gertie," I call her, scratching my head. "I've heard that if you pee on the object that carries the bad magic, the spell is broken."

"Nonsense, Tommy. Why would I pee on my beautiful doll? Why would I let anyone destroy it? Why, when Alma has promised to make it all better?"

"You're crazy, Gertie. You're crazy. You're really losing your marbles, you know that?"

Gertie chuckles a bit, her gaze landing on her doll. "Just watch," she says.

A chill draft wraps around the two of us as the funnel we had seen earlier reappears. Gertie's smile widens as the doll drifts out of her hands and once again begins twirling in upward motion, the two pieces floating in the crisp air above us and coming together. Slowly, and mysteriously, the crack on the doll's face begins to repair itself. For a moment I think I'm seeing my grandmother's VHS rewinding a movie. My heart beats even louder than before, and sweat begins to drench the back of my shirt as I tune into Gertie's mad laughter. She lets out a little snort, her hands clapping in excitement as we both stare in complete awe. As the wind slowly dies, the doll begins to descend, zigzagging back and forth like a drifting feather, landing onto Gertie's hands.

"Guys, you won't believe this!" I tell Danny, Po-boy, and Augie as they come into view. They're out of breath from having rushed down and up four flights of stairs. They run our way, carrying a lighter, newspaper pages, and a metal bucket.

"What happened?" Po-boy asks, panting.

Gertie smiles, looking at our faces, and stretches out her arms to show her doll—not a single scratch.

Danny shakes his head and opens his mouth to speak, when we all catch a glimpse of something lifting in the air before us.

"It's not over," I say. "Just watch."

The bundle of herbs and the pinned photograph tumble as a thin cloud of brown dust lifts them into flight. All of it swirling in a loop. All of it circling above our heads. The boys and I step back cautiously and watch the whirlwind form before Gertie. The ingredients of the voodoo craft dissolve into a bright glow of golden waves that swirl upwards and disappear against the brightness of the sun.

"Holy cow!" I bring my hands close to my heart as I spot the golden silhouette of a girl about Gertie's height. She stands in the center of the whirlwind, flexing her arms and legs as if she'd just hatched from an egg.

"Alma!" Gertie's voice is a high shrill. She jumps on her tippy-toes and breaks into an excited applause.

Alma's see-through figure moves about in her cone of golden light until she begins to assume more vivid colors. I pull my bangs out of my eyes and feel the sweat dripping down my face. I do just like the others. I force myself to remain still—all of us, in shock, contemplating the apparition of Gertie's mysterious friend.

A hand reaches out from behind the moving wall of wind, and Gertie immediately kneels and reaches out to touch it. With smiles and giggles, Gertie snorts happily as Alma's hand goes from ghostly to solid—real flesh, bones, and the outline of tiny flexed muscles under the skin of her arm.

The wind slowly dissipates. Danny, Po-boy, Augie, and I remain imprisoned in a deep, deep silence. The two girls kneel face to face, their palms touching, their eyes locked, the two of them smiling at each other victoriously. I glance at the flawless doll inches away from Gertie and Alma, tucked in a comfortable crib made out of fresh linen that's kept in place by perfectly-positioned clothespins.

But the doll's dress is gone. The doll's dress is missing! And right before our eyes sits a plastic model of the female anatomy in its full nakedness. I look away and shut my eyes, feeling rather silly. Even though it's only a doll, I'm still embarrassed by the thought of a naked girl. With a half-open eye, I peek at Gertie, relaxing at the sight of her being fully-dressed. I look for comfort in my friends' faces but find them as stiff as statues, gawking at both girls.

And then I notice Alma.

"Oh, no." I take a step back, stumble, and quickly regain my footing. I cover my eyes with both hands, and hold my breath for a long minute, before finding the courage to take it all in.

Alma—the girl forged by magic and wind—does not seem to notice us. She is a pretty girl with chubby cheeks, a cute smile, and curly short hair. And her knee-length dress is all white, and glows brightly against her dark skin. And it is the prettiest of all pretty dresses—filled with ribbons, flowers, and other silly, girly stuff.

With a sudden movement, Alma shifts her head our way. We all gasp at the glossy-eyed girl who came from a mysterious place. "Want to play?" she asks with a surprisingly beautiful voice. Po-boy says, "A-ha." Danny nods his head with a dumb face. And I gulp loudly in reply.

Alma looks at her friend as if requesting approval, and there is a playful twinkle in Gertie's eyes as she nods.

Rising to her feet, Alma smooths the wrinkles in her dress. She looks straight at us, releasing a determined exhale as her arms relax on the side of her body. She blinks a few times, closes her eyes, and turning her hands, palms up, she begins to raise them slowly.

My heart thuds loudly as it goes from the back to the front of my throat. And although I've never heard of a heart coming out of someone's mouth, I keep my fingers glued to my lips just in case mine decides to jolt out and run away from all this madness.

No one dares to move as Alma's hands rise past her shoulders. Her gesture prompts tiny pebbles, sand, and chipped concrete pieces to levitate over our heads. She conducts the movement with her arms, making it spin faster and faster, until we find ourselves standing in the center of a larger, more powerful funnel. And with a quick snap of her fingers, Alma brings all movement to a sudden stop, and we all freeze for a minute or two, feeling an electrical charge lift the ends of our hair, our eyes set on the stillness of the whirlwind.

I hear Po-boy's laughter, then Danny's. As I glance around me I consider that maybe we've been sucked into one of those strange modern art paintings we saw during the field trip to the museum—the ones that show a perfectly normal place with something really weird happening in a tiny corner. My friends' expressions are hilarious. We all look like we've been hung upside down—our hair standing up like cartoon characters that have been struck by lightning.

Alma shares a look with Gertie, and both girls nod at each other. A louder snap interrupts the sounds of laughter, and we answer with a chorus of frightened gasps. The debris that Alma and the wind had summoned has been transformed into something else. Something beautiful. Something magical that begins to pour down on us.

Tiny colorful spheres bounce up and down the floor of the highest rooftop on the block. Alma and Gertie wrap their arms around their stomachs and laugh as they watch Danny, Po-boy, Augie, and I take off running in wide circles. And as I fill my pockets with a new, expensive stash, I consider there's no greater magic than the one we can create with our own desire. For I had always dreamed a secret dream, that one day it would rain marbles.

WELCOME TO NEW 'AWLINS
By Brad P. Christy

"Welcome to New 'Awlins!" boomed the deep, gleeful, James Earl Jones-like voice of a trumpeter leaning against the wrought iron fence outlining Jackson Park.

Cassie jumped and grabbed Deanne's arm.

"Jesus, Cassie," said Deanne, pulling her arm away.

Cassie held her chest and laughed. "Sorry. One too many café au laits," she said and gestured back across the street at Café Du Monde, where the girls had just come from devouring beignets.

"You think?" said Deanne. "At least wipe the powdered sugar off your face; you look like a coke-head with depth perception issues."

Cassie scowled at her best friend, then quickly wiped her cheeks with a napkin she had stashed in her pocket.

"And, you!" Deanne yelled at the trumpeter. "A little heads up next time?"

The trumpeter's bushy eyebrows—stark white against his dark skin—raised in surprise until they nearly touched the brim of his pork pie hat. Several artists and street performers also stopped what they were doing to see what the ruckus was about. The trumpeter kept his eyes on Deanne as he slowly leaned over to another older gentleman who was sitting on a milk crate beside him. The milk crate guy looked up from behind his Coke-bottle-thick glasses, and both men let outfits of roaring, raspy laughter.

Cassie hid her face in her hands.

"Did you hear that, Marv? She says she'd like a heads up next time," said the trumpeter to the milk crate guy.

"I heard it, Winston," said Marv, his voice sounding strained, as if he were being slowly strangled.

"Baby girl," said Winston, "This is New 'Awlins! You won't find anywhere in the world where you'll get less of a heads up!" He blew a few

24

notes through his trumpet to accentuate his point. "There's beauty and love and mystery just waiting to jump out from around every corner, under every street light, and riding every sweet musical note from Lake Pontchartrain to the Mississippi," he said with such passion and reverence that he might as well have been describing his all-time favorite dessert.

"You tell her, Winston," said Marv.

Winston blew a few notes and adjusted the Saints jersey he wore over his semi formal wear, which seemed a bit too warm to Cassie, considering it was a balmy evening in late September. "In a town where jazz reigns supreme, I'm afraid you ain't going to get no heads up." He went back to playing a lively tune on his trumpet while Marv drummed a set of spoons on his thigh.

"I thought Marie Laveau reigned supreme," said Deanne.

Winston abruptly stopped playing, and Marv dropped a spoon.

"Dee, shut up," hissed Cassie, looking around at the street performers who had also stopped what they were doing.

The trumpeter cleared his throat and smiled. "Not for a long, long while, baby girl."

"Yeah," croaked Marv. "Best be looking out for—"

Winston gently placed his hand on Marv's shoulder. "Now what in the world would a couple of pretty, young things like yourselves be doing looking for all that mess for anyhow?"

Deanne held up a neon green plastic cup. "Aside from Hurricanes," she loudly sucked the last drops of the notoriously potent beverage through a straw, "New Orleans is just a bunch of Voodoo shops and ghost parades, right?"

Cassie shushed her friend. "I'm so sorry, sir. She's been out in the sun all day. The Garden District is beautiful, by the way."

Winston chuckled. "You know what? I like you. You got as much class as your friend got gumption. I like that. But this ain't the Garden District. You got to be on your toes when the sun goes down here."

"Come on, let's get out of here," said Deanne.

Cassie ignored her. "Thank you for the advice," she said to Winston and dropped a couple of dollar bills into his trumpet case.

"Hey!" said Deanne. "That's cab and/or drinking money."

"Don't be rude."

"Don't feed strays."

"You're still being rude."

"All I'm saying is that every panhandler for a mile probably heard that money drop," said Deanne matter-of-factly.

Mortified, Cassie looked at Winston and Marv.

Winston took off his pork pie hat and wiped a handkerchief over the bald patch on his scalp, then blew a few notes through his trumpet. "So, what have you girls planned for this evening?"

"None of your—" started Deanne, but Cassie cut her off.

"We're taking a graveyard tour," said Cassie.

Marv let out a raspy chuckle.

"Bad part of town," said Winston.

"Real bad," echoed Marv.

"Best you get on board with a good tour group, one that'll make sure you come back the same way you went in. My nephew, Duane, runs a good one. Here," said Winston. He handed the Cassie a business card.

Deanne snatched it out of her hand. "Duane's Poppin' Ghost Tours?"

"Look on the back," croaked Marv.

She flipped it over, and read, "Every time a coffin thumps, a vampire gets its fangs." She lowered the card and stared at Winston. "Cute."

"It's like *A Wonderful Life*," croaked Marv.

"Oh I get it," said Deanne, tapping away on her phone.

"Because of the water table, right?" said Cassie. "The coffins get flooded, and the bodies hit the tops of the coffins."

"That's right," said Winston.

"Well, thanks, but no thanks," said Deanne. "Fang-SINating Tours has a 4.5-star review; your nephew has a 2-star review." She held up her phone so the two older gentlemen could see the screen. "Come on, Cassie," she said and pulled her friend down the pedestrian-only Saint Ann Street.

"I guess you can't help 'em all," Winston said to Marv.

"You tell 'em, Winston," croaked Marv.

"Good luck, girls!" shouted Winston. "And *lay-say le bon tom roo-lay*!" The older gentlemen went back to playing an upbeat jazz tune as the girls walked away.

"What did that guy call me?" asked Deanne.

"Why are you so defensive? He just told us to let the good times roll, Dee."

The pedestrian street was teeming with life. Groups of lively tourists decked out in tight clothes and gaudy beads laughed and shamelessly flirted with passersby. People snapped pictures of Saint Louis Cathedral and talked about historic sites or which bars to hit first, and largely they all tried to ignore the local artists and homeless that lined the dimly lit street.

Above the noise, a dog barked right behind the girls, making them spin on their heels. Standing a few feet away was a guy in a ratty Army uniform. He pushed aside his shopping cart loaded with trash bags filled with clothes, cans and bottles, and a terrier wagging its tail. The guy looked like he was in his early twenties, far too young to be the very high rank his jacket suggested. He scratched his mangy beard. After a shave, haircut, and a few baths, he might be considered attractive, thought Cassie.

He held out his hand. There was excessive dirt packed under his fingernails. "Help a Vet out?" he said, not in a pleading way, but in an impatient, demanding sort of way.

Cassie looked at the cardboard sign on the side of his cart that said the Army had kicked him out because of his PTSD. "Where'd you serve?" she asked. "My brother is in the Army; in Colorado."

"I don't need to explain myself to you!" he shouted. "You're greedy like all the rest! Ain't got time for a war hero, do you? You don't know what it's like in war!"

"Get lost!" yelled Deanne. "She didn't—"

The guy cut her off. "I have to live on the streets because your government doesn't care about Vets! Why should I think you would care enough to spare some cash?"

Cassie reached into her pocket. "I'm sorry-,"

"You're sorry?" said the guy with a sarcastic laugh. "Here I am on the streets, and you'll just spend it on drinking and whoring around!"

Cassie's jaw dropped, and she shoved the money back in her pocket. She grabbed Deanne's arms and stomped down the street.

Deanne yelled back, "And yes, yes we are!"

The shopping cart quickly rattled up the street behind them. "Oh, geez, I'm sorry about that. Wait up!" the guy yelled after them.

Cassie and Deanne picked up their pace for another block and took a left on Royal Street in hopes of losing him in the crowd. Now that the sun was fully set, the street was saturated with jazz and smells of beer and cigars, and was bursting at the seams with bead-flinging pedestrians. But still, the shopping cart guy kept up. Even ducking into the occasional bar to refill their Hurricanes didn't help.

Deanne stepped out of the bar and threw her hand in the air. "God! Leave us alone!"

"Yeah," said Cassie. "You're creeping us out!"

The shopping cart guy's dog, tail wagging, looked back at his owner as if looking for a response.

He looked back at the dog. "What?" he said rhetorically to the dog. "Fine." He turned his attention to the girls. "I just wanted to say I'm sorry. My condition…hey, I'm not that creepy."

"Yeah," said Deanne. "You are, and not the creepy we were looking for." She sucked the remaining frozen drink through her straw loudly.

Shopping cart guy snickered. "If you want *real* New 'Awlins creepy, you should go to Lafitte's Absinthe House on Bourbon Street."

Cassie was captivated by his mischievous, unblinking grin. "Why?" she asked, the word catching in her throat.

"Because that's where the dead go for a drink," he said.

"Whatever," said Deanne, tapping at her phone.

The shopping cart guy turned his cart around. "Don't take my word for it," he said as he vanished into the crowd.

"Freak," said Cassie, carefully watching in case he came back.

"Actually," said Deanne. "It sounds kind of cool. It says here that Jean Lafitte's Old Absinthe House has been operating for more than two-hundred years. Supposedly, Andrew Jackson and the pirate Jean Lafitte met there to strategize the Battle of New Orleans in 1815. It's also super haunted and…ooh, Oscar Wilde drank there."

Cassie grabbed the phone. "And Mark Twain; nice."

The girls refreshed their drinks, headed up to Bourbon Street, and took a left. Cassie thought Royal Street was crowded, but it was nothing compared to Bourbon Street, where life and laughter and debauchery flooded in from every angle. Music from bars competed with street musicians to be heard. History and mysticism clashed with souvenir shops. And the many strip clubs contrasted against missionaries holding signs that begged people to repent.

One does not simply walk down Bourbon Street, thought Cassie, you dance down it.

By the time they reached Bienville Street at the edge of the French Quarter, the rowdy crowds had thinned, giving way to a smooth jazz vibe rather than a celebration. Most of the tourists were on their way to the epicenter of the party. There, on the corner of Bourbon and Bienville, stood the unassuming Jean Lafitte's Old Absinthe House (since 1807).

"Wow," said Deanne as they looked up at the neon *Miller Lite* sign above the door. "Not exactly what I expected."

The Absinthe House was dominated by an enormous bar with towering mirrors and every alcohol imaginable prominently displayed on an island in the middle of it. An old jukebox belted out a Johnny Cash tune. Dusty football helmets, some autographed, were suspended from the unfinished ceiling. What could be seen of the walls through the thousands of tacked-on business cards looked old enough to be original, and the lights were turned down low.

Patrons sat huddled together around the bar, telling stories and jokes. Everyone appeared to be having a good time, thought Cassie, except for a group in the back that looked bored, if not somber."I guess not everyone's in the mood."

Deanne nodded. "Probably because they don't have drinks." She nudged Cassie and pointed out a couple of seats that had opened up, and ordered a round of house specialty Absinthe Suissesses.

Cassie took a sip and recoiled. "Oh, God! People actually drink this stuff?"

The bartender, who looked like a badly-aged Stevie Nicks, frowned at her.

Deanne, on the other hand, drank hers as fast as she could. "It might be the absinthe talking, but that's pretty damned good." She tipped the glass at the bartender. "Gonna drink that?"

Cassie slid her drink to Deanne and checked her watch. "We need to get going. The tour is going to leave without us."

Deanne wiped a bit of frothy drink from her lip. "Okay. I just need to pee first." She hopped up from the bar stool and stumbled her way to the restroom in the back of the Absinthe House. A few minutes later, she wobbled back and leaned against the bar rail.

"Are you alright?" asked Cassie.

Deanne wiped her forehead. "Yeah. Stupid absinthe. I'm good. Let's get out of here."

As fast as Deanne could manage, the girls rushed back to the north side of Saint Louis Cathedral, where people were gathering and staring up at the three-story shadow of Jesus being cast on the cathedral. Most of the group had tour books and drinks in their hands, but half of them seemed disinterested. Cassie recognized a few of the less-enthused members of the group as the nondrinkers from Lafitte's.

"Check it out," whispered Cassie.

Deanne stared at them blankly, then shook her head. "Oh, I almost forgot," she said and pulled a necklace from her pocket and handed it to Cassie. "It's a protection charm against evil spirits."

Cassie raised a brow. "When did you buy that?"

"Street vendor. Humor me."

"Fine," said Cassie, slipping the charm over her head, "but you know this stuff makes me uneasy."

A man dressed in all black Victorian attire complete with top hat and black eyeliner jumped into the group."Fangththoo all fo—!" He coughed and spit out a set of oversized, plastic fangs. "Sorry about that, folks. Even more so because it is very hard to pull off a Romanian accent with these in." He held up the fake fangs and most of the people chuckled.

"Ooh, tough crowd," he said. "Welcome to Fang-SINating Tours! My name is Lestat…" he paused for effect, "okay, not really, but it sounds better than Jim." The crowd became eagerly engaged. "When the bus gets here, we'll take off for Saint Louis Cemetery, the resting place of the Voodoo Queen Marie Laveau. Now, for insurance purposes, we can't allow you to bring your drinks on the bus, sorry about that. I'll be coming around to check your receipts and waivers so please have them ready."

Jim turned as Cassie was pulling up the proof of purchase on her phone and ran into her. He dropped his plastic fangs in the gutter, and she dropped her phone on the sidewalk. "Oh, geez, I'm so sorry," said Cassie, picking up her phone.

"No problem," said Jim, looking down at his muck-covered fangs.

Cassie knelt down to pick them up.

"No. That's alright," he said with a smile. "I am *not* going to put those back in my mouth."

Cassie let out a small laugh and smiled back.

As Jim went about checking receipts, Deanne whispered, "What's going on with you and Count Hottie?"

Cassie blushed. "Shut up, Dee." She glanced over at Jim, who glanced back and smiled. She could feel her cheeks get warm.

The tour bus pulled up and flung open its door. People either emptied their drinks or quickly drank them as they piled into the small bus. Cassie was comforted by the smell of bleach because it let her know the bus was at least clean. Jim announced some bonus sights along the way. He also gave out safety tips and a strict warning to not leave the tour group once they arrived at the cemetery for several reasons, such as the fragile nature of the above-ground graves, wildlife, and people up to no good. The driver set the radio station to a blues channel.

As the bus rolled down the street, Cassie looked out the window. Winston and Marv were watching them. Winston was playing his trumpet with one hand and waving to her with the other. The shopping cart guy was standing next to them, also waving, his dog sitting attentively, watching the bus with his tongue out.

"Oh my God, that's weird," said Cassie, her face against the glass.

Deanne was holding her head, eyes shut. "What?"

"Look," said Cassie, but the bus had gone too far. "That old guy with the trumpet was waving...oh, never mind."

About ten minutes later, the bus pulled up to the iron gates of the Saint Louis Cemetery. High, brick walls stretched out along the street on either side. Through the already open gate, Cassie could see silhouettes of the famous above-ground crypts and lit-up housing on the far side of the cemetery in the distance. The moon offered just enough light to make her nervous. The silence didn't help.

As the last of the tour group stepped off the bus, Jim reminded them all to stay close and not go running off. "Remember, this is a rough neighborhood," he said loudly. "There's more than just ghosts and goblins to watch out for in here."

After seeing the Homer Plessy tomb and the iconic oven wall vaults, the tour group was deep in the cemetery. Spanish moss hung from decrepit crypts, some busted open and some tagged with graffiti. Stagnate pools of brownish water filled graves and potholes along the walkways and roads. Pieces of concrete from broken statues and markers littered the area.

"Quit being coy," whispered Deanne.

"Stop," Cassie shushed her, even as Deanne shoved her up next to Jim.

"Enjoying the tour?" asked Jim.

"It's great. We actually were warned against this one." She didn't know why she said that.

Jim laughed. "Really? Why's that?"

"This will sound so stupid. An old trumpeter guy told us we should take his nephew's tour instead." Cassie laughed along with him.

"You mean Duane's Poppin' Ghost Tours?"

"Actually, yeah," said Cassie. A coffin thumped next to them, making her jump.

Jim held her. "You know what they say about coffins thumping?"

She smiled at him. The point ends of fangs peeked out from his lips. "Funny. The fangs are a nice touch. Do you buy them in bulk or something?"

"Just had the one pair," he said and opened his mouth wide. The fangs looked real.

Cassie pushed him off and quickly walked over to Deanne. Tourists screamed as the people from Lafitte's snatched them up and pulled them into the shadows. Gurgling cries echoed off of the crypts.

She grabbed Deanne's wrist. "Dee, we have to run!" The two of them ran back the way the tour had come, but it was a maze. They ducked from crypt to crypt, splashing through the standing water.

"What the hell is going on?" whispered Deanne.

"I don't know," gasped Cassie. Tears streaked down her cheeks. "Those poor people."

"That's why you sign a waiver," said Jim from behind the girls.

Cassie and Deanne jumped back. They were surrounded by leering faces smeared crimson in the moonlight. Deanne put herself in front of Cassie, who held up the charm to ward off evil spirits.

Jim as he furled his brows and hissed. He held up his hand to shield his eyes. "No!"

"Back!" yelled Cassie.

Jim laughed and dropped his charade. Strings of thick blood dripped from his chin. "Sorry, I couldn't resist. Is that supposed to repel me or something?"

Cassie felt her heart sink into her stomach.

Deanne turned around and looked her in the eyes. A set of ivory fangs extended in her mouth. "Now we really can be friends forever," she said and took Cassie by the neck.

As Cassie thrashed under her best friend's bite, Jim wiped his face. With a wide smile, he said to the girls, "Welcome to New 'Awlins."

THE HOOD
By Cassandra Arnold

The door swings shut behind me, and I step forward into the hallway behind my hostess and follow her to the foot of the stairs. Around me, I am aware of the tilted timbers of the house, of walls painted in a riot of colors, hung with artifacts and paintings, strings of Mardi Gras beads, and a pair of shrunken heads.

I hold onto the rail as I climb and drag my case up behind me. I was never a tall man, and now I am shrinking as I age, muscle mass vanishing as relentlessly as my hair. A spider scuttles to one side of the tread and jumps off the edge, letting out a wisp of silk as it seeks a safer home. The house certainly sounds like it was built in 1857. Every step has an individual creak. My rasping breath sounds more and more asthmatic and dangerous. The woman in front of me is gray-haired and wizened, her skirts tangling her skinny ankles as she climbs. We are both hauling ourselves up the treads as if our lives depended on getting to the top. Perhaps hers does. I'm sure she depends on Airbnb guests for her survival.

I stop to catch my breath. Staring at me from the wall is a faded sepia picture of a man. Perhaps the Ship's Captain that built the place when Fauberg Tremé still held the memory of being Louisiana swamp. He has the look of someone who has gazed far across the world, watching for whales and storms, bowing to no one but the work of his Maker. I tilt my cap at him, one explorer to another, take another step up, and then another.

The Turret Room is just as advertised.

I stand resting my hands on the iron rail of the double bed and let my heart quiet down. I blink slowly in the slanting light that fingers its way through the shutters and sets dust motes whirling in front of the windows in each wall. To the right of the bed are a tall armoire and a matching dresser, their dark polished wood reflecting distorted images as we move about the room. She points out the features of the rental in a voice as faint and cracked as an old 78 RPM record.

I nod to show I'm listening.

Which I'm not.

I'm swiveling my eyes to the left of the bed, where a nightstand holds an old brass lamp. The stem is formed of a wolf arching out a cleft in a giant tree. The shade is dark red with the remnants of gold tassels at the rim. Beneath it is a crystal glass holding—

She suddenly moves very fast for someone who seemed so old and swoops the glass and its contents into a hidden crevasse in the folds of her clothes. Her eyes meet mine for the briefest of glances. In the gloom of the room, her pupils have expanded to dark, wide pits, the irises a golden rim around the black.

Her look dares me to have noticed, dares me to speak. I swallow and walk to the window, pulling back one of the wooden shutters and leaning out. Below me, the potholed roads reach out in all directions. I look along the one that leads to the bank of the Mississippi River and I smile and mutter, "Beautiful. Just what the doctor ordered."

I know what was in that glass.

Teeth.

An hour later I am in one of the French Quarter restaurants that Trip Advisor recommended, poking a fork experimentally into a bowl of crawfish étouffée. It's cool on the balcony. Below me, decorated horse-drawn carriages are clip-clopping by and there is street jazz in three directions.

I am not visiting for the music.

Or the ambiance.

It is history that has drawn me here: one page, one drop in the maelstrom of forces and ideas and events that have forged this place of spreading Virginia Live Oaks, slavery, and Bourbon Street excess.

One event in one family.

The life of my hostess, Julie Trévigne.

I reach into my pocket and slip out a creased photo from the depths of my wallet. The man might have been me in my youth, except for his clothes and haircut and solemn studio portrait stare. I turn it over and silently repeat the words on the back:

"We are the music makers…
Remember me,
Godfrey."

I know the poem, its paraphrasing by heart. All nine stanzas. O'Shaughnessy simply called it Ode. He's famous for the first few lines, but the ones I can't forget for even a second come right after that:

"...world-losers and world-forsakers,
On whom the pale moon gleams."

When I get back, the house is dark. I slip my key into the lock, and the door creaks open. Forget the stairs, there is no part of this house that can be silent, as if it has stories it longs to tell, as if it is begging for a voice, a language to make the unreal real. I stand in the darkness, waiting for my vision to adjust. The damp southern air folds around me, slides into my ears and throat, settles on the collar of my jacket and the tops of my shoes.

I take a step toward the stairs, and the walls rustle and remember.

It takes me longer than it did the first time to reach the top. I have my inhaler in my hand, sucking at the relief it promises, but it doesn't help.

When I open the door to the Turret Room, I am dizzy and my vision is blurred. My pulse taps out a wild jazz rhythm, the beats fast and slow, hard and faint, with a logic all their own.

It takes a moment before I see the shadowy figure sitting upright on the bed.

The wolf lamp casts a dim glow across the floor, a red carpet from the door to her side.

The crystal glass is back in place. Empty and clean.

I lean against the door frame, my hand slipping into my breast pocket and pulling out the tiny image of my father as he was before I was born.

'Remember?' I whisper, the sound hardly born beyond my lips by the feeble movement of air that is all my lungs can achieve.

"Godfrey?"

My fingers clench into fists as a spasm of pain rocks my chest.

She reaches out a slender arm, the skin pale and unlined in the blood-tinted light and takes the paper.

"My father."

A giggle escapes her, as high-pitched as a girl's, horrendous in the sultry night.

She leans forward as if to see better and shreds the paper with quick motions of sharp ivory teeth. Fragments fall like confetti onto the cloth that covers the bed.

She giggles again, raising a hand to cover her face.

"I sent you away," she says, "to keep you—"

She stares away toward the window. The sun has long set. It is moonlight now that snakes and sneaks its way into the room, falling on the armoire and the dresser so that the wood is striped like the pelt of a great carnivore stalking in the night.

"Tyger, Tyger, burning bright..."

I wonder if I am remembering the right words, the right tale.

She turns back to face me, rising to her feet and gathering the cloak that lay on the bed around her skeletal frame.

The red folds and the hood wrap around her as if by the magic of long custom. But dust falls from the fabric, and I know I was right to return.

"Mother," I whisper, as she gathers me into her embrace, and I let go of the effort of standing, of taking one more agonized breath.

"Mother, I love you so."

IN THE TIME OF THE HONEYSUCKLE MOON

By Hillary Lyon

In 1987, the newly-weds gently bickered on their walking tour of old New Orleans. She was enthralled with history, art, and supernatural experiences; he was enthralled with booze, French cigarettes, jazz, and more booze.

"Oh, come on, Richard, it's *his* house!"

"Ugh, getting your picture in front of his house is such a touristy thing to do—it's so *déclassé.*"

"Oh for God's sake—I'm a fan! I've read everything Beauregard Michaud's written. It's not like he's even going to know what we're doing. Besides, I'm sure people do this all the time. C'mon, please, one snap, just me in front of his gate. We'll be quick."

Richard sighed with annoyance and resignation. "Okay, fine, but just one pic. I don't want to spend all afternoon here." He was already planning their evening trip to Club Gros Chien. Best experimental jazz in the South. Hanna wasn't crazy about jazz; too bad, Richard mentally snickered. Since he agreed to go on this dull walking tour to please her, she could spend a few hours in a smoky bar to appease him. Tit for tat.

Hanna pecked her new husband on the cheek and bounced over to the gate. She clutched her handbag tightly in excitement, and smiled the most sincere smile Richard had yet seen on her face. It nettled him. The clouds parted overhead, and through the magnolia trees, the sun dappled the area right in front of the ornate wrought-iron gate. Lush vines of honeysuckle twined around both sides of it. Hanna squinted, either from the bright sunlight or the sheer glee of getting her picture in front of her favorite author's home. It was a cute look on her, Richard admitted to himself. He snapped the camera's button and captured the moment.

"Okay, done, let's go," Richard insisted.

Hanna turned her back to him and held the bars of the gate, tilting her head to one side to get a better look at the large house. It was a two story affair, white with black shutters. Overgrown, blooming azalea bushes clustered along the front steps of the house's expansive porch. Wisteria climbed one of the decorative pillars. In the huge front lawn, trees wore mantillas of Spanish Moss, like southern widows forever in mourning. An old, uneven, cracked sidewalk led from the gate to the porch. Hanna took a deep breath and closed her eyes. Oh, to live in such a lovely, timeless place.

"C'mon, we're burning daylight. If you want to finish this tour," Richard waved a small map at Hanna's back, "let's get a move on." He folded his arms and licked his lips; why, he wondered, did she want to hang around here like it was some kind of shrine? He'd read, at Hanna's insistence, one or two of this guy's books—horror fiction about voodoo or hoodoo or whatever and vegetable zombies. Or was it enlightened plant people? Not his cup of tea. In exchange, he'd had Hanna read a couple of his favorite biographies of 1930's Hollywood stars. That was fair. But intelligent, articulate zombie-trees? Sentient talking weeds? Creeping flora worried over the fate of their eternal souls? Really? She held a masters in English literature and yet preferred horror fiction. When she argued the genre was legitimate as literature—had its great authors who showed brilliance in plot and language and characterization—he tuned her out. The classics were what the American Library Association approved and promoted, he claimed, regardless of what Hanna said. Her opinion was just that, and counted for nothing. He raised his chin and said in a patronizing, sing-song fashion, as if to a child, "Hanna, let's go."

Defiantly, Hanna plucked a single honeysuckle blossom, and with great flair, pulled the stamen through the little flower, producing a single, glistening drop of flowery sweetness. She then tilted her head back, opened her mouth, and dropped that little jewel on her tongue. Delicious! Even more so because the taste came from a flower on Mr. Michaud's property—or maybe from the fact that she was making Richard wait. Either way, such heady delight from one drop! Hanna felt just a little bit dizzy. Richard coughed theatrically, to get her attention. She closed her eyes and wished Richard would just disappear, just for a moment, so she might stay here just a little bit longer. She opened her hazel eyes and looked at the house. Was there someone looking out the French window? Was that Mr. Beau, himself? She thought she saw a shadow behind a sheer curtain; she thought she saw the curtain flutter. Maybe not. She turned away from the gate and walked over to her husband. She reached for his hand, and he gave back the camera. Instead of taking her hand, he went through his elaborate routine of lighting his cigarette.

They walked on, side by side but not touching, away from the beautiful old manse and all the stories breeding within it.

* * *

At the Club Gros Chien, later that evening, Hanna attempted to converse with Richard, but the music was too loud, and he was too immersed in his scotch and in the atonal stylings of the featured performer. When she said, at last, "I'm going outside for some fresh air," he nodded, having understood her perfectly. Funny how he heard that, but nothing else she'd said all evening.

Outside the club, the night air was damp and cool and comfortable. She stood directly under the club's marquee and people-watched. Tourists moved in clusters, drinks in hand and laughing. A few families wandered by on their way back to their hotel-homes, some couples held hands and whispered to each other. Seeing those couples made her heart tighten and crimp; what was she doing wrong, that her new husband was so bored with her? How could she fix this? She couldn't talk to her friends (they were all his friends) or to her family (they weren't in favor of her marriage to Richard in the first place). If she was a serious drinker, she thought, she'd spend most of her time on this trip drunk. Like he did. But she wasn't, so she didn't.

"Excuse me, ma'am," a raspy voice addressed her. "Would you happen to have a light? I seemed to have lost my lighter somewhere along the way this evening."

Hanna swam ashore from her thoughts and looked at whom the voice belonged to, an older gentleman; 'dapper' as her grandmother would have said, wearing a three-piece glaucous gray, natural sharkskin suit, complete with gold watch-chain, walking stick, and Panama hat. He was an old black man with perfect posture and neatly manicured nails. He wore a fresh honeysuckle flower in his suit coat's lapel.

"Uh, yes, I think I have some matches," she said as she dug around in her purse. She found the matchbook she'd taken from their hotel and handed it over to the old man.

"Oh, I just need one light, not the whole book," he said after lighting his pipe. The blue smoke that drifted towards Hanna smelled like incense, she thought, with a hint of cloves. It was a pleasing combination, one Hanna preferred to the charred-toast smell of Richard's Gitanes.

Hanna was fascinated by this man; he seemed larger than life, like a character out of a story.

"Ah, yes," the man read from the back of the matchbook, "*The Hotel Armand & Courtyard Dining. Finest Accommodations in New Orleans Since 1897.* Nice place to stay; matter of fact, I've slept there a more than few times in my long life," he added with a small laugh. "My name is Alphonse. And you are?"

"I'm Hanna. Pleased to meet you, Alphonse," she said, and actually meant it. He was the most interesting thing she'd encountered this evening.

"'Hanna," Alphonse began. "Now that's a lovely name, for a lovely young woman. I would bet you are a visitor to my fine city, yes?"

"Yes," Hanna blushed, feeling not just like a tourist, but out of place in a community she would love to belong to.

"Why are you standing by all your lonesome outside this noisy club? I can understand not wanting to be inside—that screeching going on in there ain't jazz—but why such a pretty thing like you out here by yourself?"

"My husband is inside, and I—I needed some fresh air and a break from all that cutting edge culture," Hanna laughed.

Alphonse handed the matchbook back to Hanna, briefly touching her open palm with the tips of his fingers. "I get that. Some of the most beautiful things in the night are found outside of 'civilized' culture." He made a sweeping gesture with his pipe. "Take, for instance, the comely presence of that full moon up there. I think of that as a 'honeysuckle moon,' on account of its rich color. Don't see that in big cities up north. Only find it here in New Orleans, and then only from certain, *enchanted*, locales. Can't you positively taste the sweetness of life, just by looking at it?"

Hanna looked at the moon, and smiled; she liked the idea of a 'honeysuckle moon,' full of beguiling sweetness. The very thought of it made her feel peaceful. "Yes, I think I do," she replied after a long pause.

"You should come visit me at my store—here's my business card—before you leave our funky town," he smiled. "It's walking distance from your hotel, and I'll give you a discount for being so friendly. So lovely." With that Alphonse bowed slightly and walked off into the humid night, and weaving in between crowds of tourists, quickly disappeared.

Hanna looked at the small card. The corners had gold flourishes, and the font was just as flowery. *Alphonse Delacroix*, it read, *Purveyor of Curios, Mementos, & Spells for All Occasions*. She giggled and slipped the card into her jeans' back pocket. I do love this town, she thought to herself before returning to the noisy interior of Club Gros Chien and her indifferent husband.

* * *

Mid-morning the next day found Hanna drinking coffee and eating beignets on the lush patio of the Hotel Armand. Richard slept in, as usual. From her seat on the patio, she could see the window of their room. As she sipped her cooling coffee, she watched that window. Before too long, Richard parted the curtains and looked down below; he spotted Hanna right away. She waved. He closed the curtains. Richard took his time getting dressed and coming downstairs. He swaggered through the open doors of the patio, jamming an unlit cigarette into his mouth as he sat down.

"Mornin'," Hanna chirped, buzzing on caffeine and sugar.

Richard grunted and lit his cigarette in reply.

"What *shall* we do today, dahling?" Hanna said in her best 1930's glamour girl accent.

Richard squinted at her through the smoke. "Don't know about you, *dahling*, but there's a revival showing of "A Streetcar Named Desire" at the art-house cinema down the street. I, for one, shan't miss *that*."

Hanna slumped back into her wire café chair. "Are you serious? We own that movie on video tape. You can watch it anytime!"

"Not in the Big Easy! And yes, I'm serious." Richard shrugged and snapped his fingers at the waiter. "It's something *I've* always wanted to do."

The waiter walked over, a forced smile on his otherwise pleasant face. "Sir—"

"Get me a black coffee," Richard interrupted. "Charge it to room 259."

"Sir," the waiter repeated. "I'll gladly get your coffee, but you need to know there's no smoking on the patio." The young man pointed to the sign positioned next to the door; a sign the size of a legal pad, so Richard couldn't say he hadn't seen it. Richard snorted and put the cigarette out on Hanna's plate, which she took as an act of war, as the smoldering coffin nail was right next to the last beignet. She pushed the plate away.

"Well, I'm going to walk around, explore the shops and what not around here. Talk to people, eat tasty vittles, buy unusual trinkets, see important landmarks. Have experiences." She threw her linen napkin down on the table as she rose.

"Knock yourself out, *dahling*," Richard smiled up at her. "See you back here around dinner time, I suppose."

"Or not," Hanna snipped as she walked away.

* * *

Truth be told, Hanna was relieved to be on her own. She loved the genteel decadence of this town: the beauty in the architectural curves and carvings all around, the way small tufts of grass grew between uneven brick pavers, the way layers of paint flaked and peeled on everything, revealing older, unexpected colors, the way humidity curled the hair of smooth skinned women into gentle tendrils. Sure, the air was sticky, especially in the afternoon, but the heat made Hanna feel pleasantly lazy and dreamy.

And so she daydreamed as she walked, completely wrapped in the contentment of the moment. Before she realized it, she was standing before the display window of Mr. Delacroix's. In old-fashioned gold leaf lettering, the name on the window announced: *Mr. Alphonse Delacroix / Curio Shop/ Special Orders, Pick-Up and Delivery / Satisfaction Guaranteed.* Hanna cupped her hands against the glass, to better see inside; a move that was unsuccessful, as the store was so crowded with merchandise, she really couldn't tell what she was looking at. So she went in, hoping Mr. Delacroix himself might be behind the counter. He wasn't.

A bell jangled overhead as she closed the door behind her.

A burly young man looked up at the sound of the bell. When he saw Hanna he smiled and

pulled himself up to his full height. "Yes, ma'am, may I help you?" He was at least six foot four, Hanna surmised, and with his high cheekbones and long braid the color of raw garnets, he looked like a throwback to the Scottish Highlands. Or, rather, Hollywood's version of a rugged, archaic Scot.

"Just browsing," Hanna said, as she examined the contents of the shelves against the wall: shrunken heads in velvet-lined display boxes, twists of dried sage bound with red yarn, bottles of exotic oils, sticks of incense, clusters of peacock feathers, candles of every imaginable scent and shade, bags of variously colored sand, small bottles of holy water, pouches of salt, roughly sewn cloth dolls. After meeting Mr. Delacroix last night, Hanna suspected his 'curio shop' would turn out to be a voodoo shop; this was a sort of voodoo shop, the sort for tourists, but probably not the real deal. Hanna's shoulders sagged in disappointment.

"Excuse me," she said as she turned her attention the towering Scot behind the counter. "I don't suppose Mr. Delacroix is in today?"

The clerk, who wore a bowling shirt with the name "Angus" (of course) embroidered in gold thread, cocked an eyebrow. "He'll be in shortly. You know him?"

"Met him last night, outside of the Club Gros Chien. He suggested I drop by—and so—here I am." Hanna smiled weakly. She couldn't tell how friendly Angus was; up close, his eyes were a cold gray-blue, and his skin was pale and taut across his face. His smile now seemed tight and false, more like a grimace. Angus looked older than Hanna had first thought. She tapped the glass-topped counter, to break the tension building between them.

"So, is this a real voodoo shop?" She asked, noticing the chandelier of bone overhead.

"As opposed to one for tourists?" Angus replied, tossing his braid behind his back. "Well, this one's frequented by locals, if that's what you're wondering. If you want souvenirs, *mon cher*, you'll have more luck down at Marie Laveau's. More expensive, but less spooky. And they'll do readings there, palm and tarot, if you're interested in that sort of thang."

The idea of readings appealed to Hanna, just for fun, for the experience. "Do you do readings here?"

Angus crossed his massive arms. "Mr. Delacroix does readings. By appointment only, and appointments made only with his approval." He

41

titled his head, like a bird of prey assessing its dinner. "I take it you're interested?"

"I'd like that, yes," Hanna decided as she spoke. "How do I get approved, so I can get an appointment?"

Now Angus smiled a genuine smile. "He gave you his card, yes? That means you've been pre-approved. As for an appointment, I'll pencil you in for 2:00 tomorrow afternoon. How's about that?"

"That's great; I'll get some more sight-seeing in. Thanks."

"*Mon plaisir*," Angus mumbled, not bothering to look up as she left the store.

* * *

With time to kill, Hanna grabbed an early lunch, a frosty beer and a po'boy over-flowing with fried oysters. As Richard was who-knows-where, she ate alone. She didn't mind, without him, it was a peaceful meal, one she could enjoy without listening to his criticisms of the restaurant, the food, the temperature of the beer, the busker playing the fiddle on the corner outside. With several hours stretching before her, Hanna felt free and giddy; she could do what she wanted, and what she wanted was something she couldn't get at home: something culturally enriching, something memorable. She opted for a visit to the St. Louis Cathedral, just off of Jackson Square.

The cathedral's interior was cool, gold-gilt, flag-draped, and well-lit. In the back of her mind, Hanna was hoping it would be dark and dank and not just a little bit spooky. The cathedral was still in use, with regularly scheduled masses, and with guided tours in between. Hanna decided to do the self-guided tour (for a charitable donation—she ponied up $5.00), so she might go where she pleased, and linger for as long as she liked. Her lingering included a long stop at the area to the right of the altar, by the baptismal font, where she lit a candle and intended to pray for her marriage. But Hanna's mind wandered, as it always did when she attempted to pray. She instead daydreamed about meeting Mr. Michaud in a Hollywood-scripted type of dramatic encounter: She'd be walking with souvenir packages through a crowded street, get rudely jostled, drop her bags, and the charming, handsome Mr. Michaud would appear out of nowhere to help her gather her things. Their eyes would meet, they'd end up having a drink, and the rest is a plot from a paperback romance.

The approaching voice of a tour guide shook Hanna from her fantasy. She scampered away before the tour group reached the baptismal font. It was time to be getting back to her hotel, anyway. On the cathedral steps, she looked at her watch. She'd spent hours in there! The sun was setting. How was that possible? She wondered if Richard would be worried. Likely not.

In Jackson Square, she stood puzzled, trying to remember which direction her hotel was from there. She longed to go back to their room and decompress by taking her shoes off and having a cold, cold drink. Preferably something alcoholic and strong. If Richard was there, he could join her, but she knew he'd be uninterested in her day; instead, he'd insist on telling her all about the movie. A movie they both knew by heart. And if he wasn't there—Hanna looked in her purse for the room key. She didn't have it. "Perfect," she groaned to herself, "I'll have that drink in the lobby."

As Hanna scanned the square before her, she thought—no, she knew—she'd spotted Alphonse Delacroix walking down the street to her left. His back was to her, but the clothes (that glaucous gray sharkskin suit), the hat, the walking stick—it had to be him! Hanna followed after him. Perhaps he could help her find her way.

Through the gathering dusk, and growing, noisy, crowds of drunken tourists, Hanna followed the man. No matter how fast she walked, he always seemed to walk just a bit faster, so she never caught up. Walking too fast tired her out; when did she get so out of shape? Hanna slowed down. So did this man who Hanna assumed, or at least hoped, was Mr. Delacroix. At one point, before he disappeared around a corner, he stopped and turned to look directly at Hanna. So it was Alphonse Delacroix! Hanna waved, and he smiled in return. And then he vanished around a corner.

Hanna panicked and hurried to that same corner, which led down a shadowed alleyway. She couldn't see to the end, but she was sure that's where Mr. Delacroix had gone, so she decided she'd go there too. She walked past piles of garbage overflowing their dumpsters, past walls tagged with obscene, incomprehensible graffiti, past back doors chained and padlocked, past rats snatching spoiled food back into their lairs. It was a side of the Big Easy she would have been happy not to have seen.

At last, she came to a dead end. A chain link fence prevented any further exploration; that is, until she saw the bottom of the fence was pulled up and away from the ground. And on that fence was a swatch of that sharkskin fabric—just like Mr. Delacroix's suit coat. Hanna took that as a sign to continue, so she crawled under the fence. She didn't notice that she got a deep scratch on her arm as she did so.

On the other side of the barrier, there was a street perpendicular to the alley, but she didn't see Mr. Delacroix when she looked in either direction. This was disheartening, as she was sure she was beyond lost, and she'd never find her way back to her hotel. And in her heart, she was certain Richard wouldn't care if she never came back. If she was honest with herself—and now she was, at last—she didn't care if she never saw Richard again. As she was tumbling down into the sucking mire of this depressive thinking, a sweet, deep, distant voice called her name. Hanna looked up and saw—yes! Mr. Delacroix, standing at the far end of the street to her left, holding out his hand to her. She tried to run to him, but her muscles felt like lead: heavy, soft, impractical for movement. It had been a long day and looked to be a longer night. Hanna struggled to move faster than a slow trot. She, at last, neared him.

"This way, child," Mr. Delacroix smiled. Hanna stopped to catch her breath. As she did, Mr. Delacroix raised his fist to her, and opening his palm, blew a handful of perfumed ash into her face.

"Hey—no!" Hanna gasped and choked. The dust made her eyes water, and as sweetly as it smelled, the ashes in her mouth tasted bitter. She tried to spit, to clean her mouth out, but it was so dry, she could hardly swallow.

Alphonse pulled the fresh honeysuckle blossom from his lapel and held it before her. As he pulled the stamen through the flower, he said to Hanna: "Open your mouth and allow me to ease your thirst. Just one drop makes everything all better." Hanna opened her mouth, and Alphonse tapped a drop of sweetness onto her parched tongue. A sweetness that took root in her mouth, her stomach, her lungs, her mind, and filled all those spaces with lush, limber, twining vines and tender green leaves. Occasional blossoms flashed like sparks within the cool depths of that newly planted jungle inside her.

"Don't you worry, pet, it's just a little something to help you on your way. Let it do its magic on you." His voice was soothing and rhythmic, like a lullaby. At once, Hanna felt peaceful, at ease, and connected to all things in the natural world.

"Mr. Delacroix," Hanna began, disturbed by the weakness in her own voice," will you show me the way back to my hotel? I'm so lost—" That's what she intended to say, but what came out of her mouth was more of a whispering sigh of vowels strung together like a newborn melody.

"Don't try to talk, my sweet, just follow. I'll take you where you need to be." And with that, he turned and walked out into the street. Like a puppy, Hanna followed close behind. He led her away from the crowds of tourists, down empty side streets, through shadowy short-cuts between historic buildings, to the Club Gros Chien.

Stopping across the street from the club, Mr. Delacroix maneuvered Hanna into the shadows and suggested she contemplate the moon, the beautiful honeysuckle moon. He explained he had business to attend to; he had to meet a young lady, who was unhappy with her life, and he'd been hired by a third party to see to her. A special order, as it were. Hanna nodded, almost imperceptibly, too absorbed with her moon-musings. The tendrils within her stretched down though the muscles and tendons in her arms and legs, tingling and warm. It was blissful.

Hanna knew Mr. Delacroix was meeting a young woman who'd just exited the club, a woman who'd stand around beneath the marquee, arms folded, people-watching. Hanna felt the woman's boredom and disappointment; she knew the woman wanted something else in life. In her mind's eye, she observed Mr. Delacroix approach the woman, chat her up, take a book of matches from her and light his pipe. This was all so familiar to Hanna. She knew he'd next hand the woman his business card, and he did. The woman slipped it into her jeans' pocket and went back inside. Hanna knew the woman would return to her seat in that stuffy, jazz-noisy club, and to her distant husband, who'd sit in the small booth across from her and close his eyes, pretending to dig all those crazy notes, but really he was just ignoring her. She'd drink too much and question her life. She'd promise herself to find Mr. Delacroix tomorrow. Hannah saw all this, without taking her eyes off the delicious honeysuckle moon.

"Time to move on," Mr. Delacroix said, jolting Hanna out of her musings. In unison, they turned and walked down the street, leaving the noise of the nightlife behind them. They walked and walked, with Hanna not caring where they were going, or how long it would take to get there.

Under the ivory moonlight, the world was a black and white movie. She was a character in a dream sequence, a sleepwalker led by a charming southern Svengali. Dreamy as she felt, she was aware of her surroundings, and for that she was thankful: the night air cool on her hot skin, the faint perfume of night-blooming jasmine, the buzzing of mosquitoes, but no bites. She was still lost in her thoughts when Mr. Delacroix gently announced, "Here we are."

They stopped before an ornate wrought-iron gate, covered on either side with thickly clustered vines of honeysuckle. With deft familiarity, Mr. Delacroix opened this stiff and creaking gate, and led Hanna onto Mr. Beauregard Michaud's property. On the sprawling front porch of the white manse with black shutters, a figure sat languidly rocking in a porch swing, watching the storm build in the distance. He spoke with Mr. Delacroix in such a low whisper, it was impossible to hear, though the details of their conversation didn't matter. The man handed Mr. Delacroix a small bag tied with string, and Mr. Delacroix placed Hanna's limp hand in Mr. Michaud's, as the thunder tolled in the distance, announcing the commencement of hurricane season.

Mr. Michaud patted Hanna's hand and leaning close to her, whispered, "I have a place for you round back. I think you'll like it here." He led her around the old manse, through the luxuriantly overgrown back garden. At the far end of the yard was a simple arbor, riotously covered with various flowering vines. Here he laced Hanna's thin fingers into the lattice work, and tenderly smoothed her hair as the vines within her began emerging, finding a hold all their own.

MOMUS
By D.J. Tyrer

New Orleans in July was hot. Too hot. Perhaps that was why David had
drifted off to sleep on the streetcar. He was a big fan of the streetcars; even
now, with the city changed forever, there was something about them that
was real, genteel. He loved to ride those that were left. They really made his
visit.

David Sosa was in the Crescent City getting in touch with his ancestors
who had sought sanctuary in the New World from the intolerance of the
Old, but had found he enjoyed exploring the city even more than he did
exploring his roots.

Which made dozing off odd. He woke with a start. It was, he realized,
cooler. And dark. He sat up and looked about in confusion. He was still on
the streetcar, but it was empty, shadowy and stationary. There was a hint of
silvery moonlight flowing in through the windows.

What was going on?

"Hey, anybody there?" His voice was a little shaky. The effect of just
having woken, he told himself; the confusion of processing where he was.
Not fear. Definitely not fear.

David was afraid. There was no way the car could empty and be parked
up for the night without anyone noticing him slumped there, surely?

What was going on? That was the question he kept repeating over and
over to himself, one to which he had no answer.

Okay, something wasn't right. What was the last thing he remembered?
He could recall climbing aboard the streetcar, riding it for a while. The heat.
Everything had been normal; all the usual characters, the diverse tide of
human life, had climbed aboard. It had been just like every other trip he had
ever made. But, something had been different. What?

David tried to picture his journey: every person who got on or off, those
who acknowledged him, those who didn't, what he looked at, every little
detail. There had to be something that would tell him why this had
happened.

Then, he remembered… something by his foot. He recalled his foot brushing against it. He looked down, but couldn't see it properly, and had reached down for it. His hand had brushed against it, and…and that was as much as he could recall. There was nothing but a blank until he woke.

He was, he realized, clutching something in his left hand. He hadn't noticed it before, but now, suddenly, it felt as if it were jabbing awkwardly into his hand. Almost painful. He was confused.

David lifted his hand and unclenched it. The thing he held—the thing, presumably, that he picked up off the floor of the streetcar—was a crudely-intertwined cat's cradle of twigs in the approximate shape of a Magen David, with a couple of feathers and a sprig of some greenery tied to it.

"Strange…"

"It's a gris-gris." The sudden voice made him jump. It had the New Orleans accent, but was somehow…drier than the usual rich mellifluence.

David looked around in confusion. There was a figure standing on the steps of the streetcar, peering in at him. He couldn't quite see him—the interior of the car was dark and the weak moonlight was behind the figure—but he could make out a vague silhouette: a thin figure, tall, with a top hat and some sort of frock coat. It was the very image of a Voodoo horror straight from Hollywood central casting. Was it someone playing a prank? A dream?

David laughed. "A dream! Or, a nightmare."

He felt a sudden surge of relief. This wasn't real. Any moment now, he'd wake up, back to the heat and the bright sun and the people, and all would be well.

The figure stepped into the car and began to walk towards him. Its movements, slow and exaggerated, reminded David of a long-legged wading bird. Yet, there was also something of the scuttling of a spider to it, and that unnerved him: It might only be a dream, but it was possible to be scared in a dream, even if you knew there was nothing to be scared of.

It neared him and, now, he could see the moonlight reflecting off pale bone beneath the brim of its tall hat. The figure seemed so solid, horribly real. He felt as if a scream were about to rise up out of him.

It was all just a dream—wasn't it?

"A dream?" said the figure. "Oh, no. This is real, I assure you. Not the real you are used to, but real nonetheless."

David screamed; he couldn't help himself.

"That's it." The figure chuckled and pressed its leering skull-face closer to him. David cowered away from it. "Get it out your system. I need you focused if you're to join my krewe."

"Your crew?" David tried to work that out: from a streetcar to a riverboat, perhaps? A skeleton crew?

"My krewe," it spelled the word, "You understand? For Mardi Gras. It's

Mardi Gras, tonight."

Confusion seemed to be a good cure for fear. "Mardi Gras? But, that's February, isn't it?"

"Here in the Twilight City, every night is Mardi Gras."

David shook his head. "I don't want to join your Mardi Gras. I want to go home."

The figure laughed. "You touched the gris-gris. You made the bargain. You made your choice."

"By accident. I didn't agree to anything."

"Look at it. It's in the shape of your soul. You made it that shape."

David looked down at it. There was some truth in what the figure said, but he didn't remember twisting the sticks into that shape. Why would he?

"My name is Momus, by the way," the figure said, reaching out with a bony hand to grasp David's shoulder. He pulled him to his feet. "Welcome to the Twilight City. Time to go."

"I don't want to go."

Momus chuckled. "You have an appointment…"

David tried to resist, but Momus propelled him firmly from the streetcar and along dark, narrow streets, down which echoed sounds of laughter and music. The further they walked, the less able he seemed to be to struggle against Momus. David felt as if his legs seemed to march along of their own accord, moving in time to the beat that was slowly growing louder. In some sense, he felt as if he were being absorbed by the music, being drawn into this twilight celebration.

"Nearly there," murmured Momus, pulling him along. David no longer resisted. He barely registered the gris-gris slipping from his fingers. The rhythm of the music seemed to fill his soul.

"Here we are," said Momus as they stepped into a street crowded with dancers; ghostly masks leered at him and faces that, he noticed with a sickening lurch, weren't masks at all. "I've got a float on which you'll take pride of place. Climb up."

Bony hands reached down to help David clamber aboard. The float, decorated in black and yellow crepe, was filled with corpse-faced figures in moldy suits and gowns.

David looked down at himself. He appeared to be wearing a tattered and dirt-stained suit, rather than the casual outfit he'd had on earlier.

"I love your mask," one of the others said.

"I wear no mask." It was true, yet there was something portentous about the words and he shivered as he understood the implications of the question and answer. It couldn't be…

"You are the Stranger." Momus chuckled.

"Stranger?"

"The *piece de resistance* of my tableau. You wear the pallid mask of death and, thanks to you, I shall be crowned the King of Mardi Gras."

"I wear no mask." David was beginning to feel hysterical, yet, at the same time, oddly detached.

"That's the spirit! Excellent, excellent. Right, let's go!"

The float gave a lurch, and the procession began to move. Bands playing instruments of bone and skin led them on their way, and David found himself waving at the frenzied crowds of horrors that surged about the float, tossing handfuls of gore and offal at them as if the strings of flesh were beads.

"Glorious! Glorious!" cried Momus. "I shall be King!"

"I wear no mask!" David screamed the words, but no longer quite understood what they betokened.

This was madness! A crazed harlequinade! He had to be dreaming, yet it seemed more real than the waking world, seemed to contain more truth: or, was it but a fleeting phantom of truth? His mind was swirling, and his ears were filled with the noise of the procession which echoed within his head so he couldn't think.

"This isn't real—it isn't true—it's a dream."

Momus laughed at him. David turned to see the grave-clad figure was now resplendent in tattered yellow robes, the new-crowned King of Mardi Gras. With a sudden jolt of horror, David saw that he, too, was clad in yellow. He stared at Momus, and Momus stared back at him in horror, his skull-face a pallid mask of bone that was no mask. He was, in some sense he couldn't understand, Momus, and Momus was him, absorbing him, just as the frenzy of the procession and its music had seemed to absorb him into itself.

He now knew he had mere moments before David ceased to exist.

Desperately, he groped for the gris-gris, thinking to break it and end the nightmare, but he no longer held it. It was gone, lost down some side-street or trampled beneath the feet of the celebrants.

He tried to recall words he hadn't uttered since he was a child, a prayer or a charm his uncle had taught him, but the words wouldn't come.

It was too late.

Too late: that was his final thought as he became Momus, and Momus became Rex, and the entire celebration swirled in upon itself in a peculiar pattern to become a hurricane of overwhelming yellow that consumed everything and everyone in that twilight world.

Yellow.

Then, nothing.

THE NIGHT OF THE THIRTEEN
By Brian Malachy Quinn

It was Thursday, August 18, 2016, with a full moon filling the clear night sky. The conditions were perfect. Rocco stood in the garden next to the Beauregard-Keyes House, looking across Chartres Street at the old convent. The wall around the property prevented him from seeing anything on the ground level, but that was not where he was interested. Even though he had been at Tulane University for three years, he still had not gotten used to the heat and humidity. It had reached ninety-four degrees in the afternoon, and sweat still beaded up on his forehead despite it being just before midnight. The humidity—unless you been around here at this time of the year you would have no appreciation for the humidity. He looked forward to taking another shower and changing his clothes when he got back to his apartment.

He looked through the FLIR thermal camera at the dormers on the roof—no unusual heat signatures. He glanced over at TC who was looking at his phone again. "You disrespect the dead and bad things happen," Joe always said. Joe was the founder of the Red Bayou Ghost Hunters, and all the expensive electronics were his. A carpenter by day, Joe had been paranormal investigating for the last fifteen years, long before ghost hunting had taken over the cable channels.

The other members of the group had been watching the Ursuline Convent all month. There was a good chance that the anniversary for "La Nuit des Treize" or "The Night of the Thirteen" was close. Supernatural activities seemed to occur on anniversaries of significant events. He didn't know how he had gotten stuck with TC; the guy really disturbed everyone. He often said inappropriate things, especially around women, making everyone uncomfortable. Actually, he did know why he was here: Joe did not want to pair him with Crystal. She was everyone's kid sister, and he did not trust TC not to try something. A sound caught his attention—he

50

looked back over at the convent—scanning for movement. He picked up the full spectrum camera, ranged through. Nothing.

The first Ursuline Convent in New Orleans, a French Colonial three story, housed the Ursuline nuns, who arrived from France in August of 1727. The mission of the twelve sisters was to care for the sick and poor of the city and to educate the young girls in their care. Their convent at 301 Chartres, finally completed in 1734, became renowned for its curving cypress staircase that seemed to float on air without supports. Legend goes that the man who built it, known as "L'Homme du Soir"—"The Evening Man"—only worked in the fading light of twilight, using the magic of the masons who built Solomon's temple and later the great cathedrals of Europe.

Less than ten years later, the building as it was, built on ever-settling swampland, resulting in shifting walls and sinking floors, was unlivable. Construction began in 1748 on a new convent, a lime plaster stucco covered Louis XV style building, with arched openings and dormers on a soaring roof, with casement windows, and with the jewel—the floating staircase from the first convent, saved from demolition and installed in the new structure. The legend of "L'Homme du Soir" continued, as stories circulated that he just appeared at the appropriate time, removed the staircase from the old convent and reinstalled it in the new one, working alone. The few people that saw him claimed that he had not only not aged a day in twenty years, but seemed younger. The Ursuline Convent is the oldest building in New Orleans having survived two fires that destroyed most of the city, several hurricanes, many floods, and a war.

The new convent became an orphanage and a school for young girls. It became a priority for the King of France to populate the Louisiana territory, as he planned an expansion of the French Empire into the new world to combat the threat of the British and the Spanish in the region. Soldiers, prostitutes, farmers, slaves, exiled French criminals, and Choctaw Indians populated the area in the beginning. Poor women from the streets and prisons of Paris, gathered by the French government, arrived in New Orleans to lure more men to settle the city. After limited success, they reached out to the French convents to bring orphaned young ladies to New Orleans.

Each girl arrived from France with a trunk shaped in the form of a small casket, with the girl's belongings and gifts from the French government. The girls, first known as "fille à la cassette" (girl with a casket), later became simply known as a "casket girl." These casket girls from the convents arrived in New Orleans, where they lived and were educated at Ursuline Convent and then introduced into New Orleans society, where they would meet their future husbands.

As more and more men of wealth, even of aristocratic lineage, began populating New Orleans and the area, wealthy loyal French families were encouraged to send their daughters to Ursuline Convent to eventually marry these colonists. As a symbol of their dedication to the wishes of the church and France, each girl received a beautiful chest, a cassette that put the earlier ones of the orphans to shame, crafted by religious artisans and intended as dowries. On the first ship, twenty-eight young women arrived with their wedding trousseaux in cassettes that were stored in the attic until finding proper suitors and resulting in marriages. In the meantime, the girls learned the elements of an education from the sisters that would serve them well in their new lives, eventually as wives, mothers, and heads of prosperous households, and even large plantations.

However, the Church in France suffered by losing most of its wealth to the French Government in the late 18th Century and early 19th Century, beginning with the Revolution and continuing into the reign of Napoleon. The Ursuline Convent was near ruin with the lack of funding. That is until a moonless night, "La Nuit des Treize"—"The Night of the Thirteen."

Crystal's research in the city's historic society library had turned up an entry in a diary attributed to Sister Constance Marie Madeleine, who had been at the convent during this period. For this entry, water stains had obscured the month and day of the date but the year was clearly 1804.

"An unexpected ship arrived in the dark of the night, flying no flag, late in the summer. Thirteen young girls, pale as death, disembarked, saying that they came to live at the convent. To the surprise of the men who unloaded their belongings, their caskets were the size of a man, elaborately carved, extremely heavy, and locked tight. They placed the caskets on the third floor of the convent as instructed. But what was unusual was that the previous girls would retrieve items from their caskets upon arrival—these girls did not.

During the day, the shutters on the attic windows remained closed, but at night they fluttered open as if some unseen hand had unlatched them. When the storm-driven winds howled, as they often do in these parts, the shutters would strike the sides of the dormers, making a deafening sound, causing those in the convent to jump nervously in their beds, worriedly fingering rosary beads. All except the thirteen, who slept soundly with wide beatific smiles upon their faces, like angels. Complaints by the sisters to the Mother Superior went unheeded. "It is forbidden," she ordered, "no one goes up there."

Eighteen-year-old Sister Mari Roseline, who had taken final vows six months earlier, could not resist the strength of her curiosity. She had argued with me, hoping to gain an accomplice, for we were close, as we had lived in the same village in France before taking the habit, but I, afraid of the possible consequences, refused.

On a night filled with storms, Mari "borrowed" the skeleton key from Mother Superior as she slept undisturbed in her bed despite the elemental nature of the night. I stopped her in the hallway, begging her not to continue. She smiled at me and told me to return to my bed. I went back to my room, but stayed by the doorway apprehensively.

The following is the account I recorded after the events, from Mari, in a brief moment of lucidity:

Upon unlocking and opening the door and stepping onto the stairway, I faltered as the musty, coppery smell engulfed me. Breathing in short gasps from my mouth, I carried the lantern in my left hand and used the right to steady myself as I climbed the stairs. The light cast out from the lantern on the stairs, walls, and floor ebbed and flowed with the shadows like a wave on a beach as the lantern swung from my hand. I stopped several times and listened, my mouth becoming dry, sounds like whispers echoing off the walls. I thought they said, "Sang, besoin de sang." ("Blood, need blood.") I stopped and blessed myself, then proceeded. When I had gained the top of the stairs, the room lay before me in deep shadows except where my lantern shone. The caskets were open, their lids on the floor. I took small steps, each one a test of my courage, to the caskets. Looking inside one, I saw the carapaces of insects layering the bottom, crushed as if something heavy had rested on them. Suddenly I smelt a stifling rancid odor behind me, like rotting meat, and sensed a presence. A voice, something between a laugh and growl, called my name. Turning, red glowing eyes towered over me, and the smell enwrapped me in a blanket of decay. I ran, and...

This is all she said. This is all she ever said again.

I was one of the first ones to reach her, as I was vigilant, knowing what she was doing. I heard her scream. I found her standing in the doorway at the bottom of the staircase, shaking. The scream was a high-pitched unnatural wail that could have shattered fine crystal. When the other sisters and the Mother Superior reached her all she could say, over and over, was, "Le travail du diable—les morts-vivants, ils sont ici!" "The work of the devil—the undead, they are here!" Many of the sisters responded by praying out loud with hurried, desperate words.

The Mother Superior grabbed the hands of Mari, shaking her, saying "La demence! Tout cela est folie!" "Madness! This is all madness!" She then quickly, too quickly, closed the door, looking up fearfully, and locked it with the key she took from Mari. She ordered the sisters back to bed and for me and another to stay with Mari. "I will show you tomorrow that this is all nonsense," the Mother Superior said, shaking her head angrily. When Mari was back in her bed, I was able to calm her enough for her to recount what had occurred, of which precedes this. She then became inconsolable, making an unending whining sound throughout the night, her eyes unfocused and devoid of reason, unnerving me. The next day Mother Superior gathered the sisters and the girls in our care, unlocked and opened the door leading to the attic and led us up, though Mari would not move, but lay with eyes open, always with eyes open. The caskets lay with their lids closed and the shutters latched from the inside. "You see, this is all madness!" she said, though she seemed more relieved than us.

Mari stopped eating, never regaining any sense of her former self, never speaking another word, and died several weeks later. She resembled a corpse when she took her last breath, cheekbones pronounced, eyes sunken in, skin stretched tautly over her skeleton. The rumors of vampires began as the sisters feared that the thirteen girls had brought the undead with them over from Europe. The convent, after "The Night of the Thirteen," never seemed in need of funding ever again.

The stories spread to outside of the convent walls as violent deaths seemed to occur at alarming numbers in the city, horrid deaths with throats torn out and bodies drained of all blood, as if by savage beasts. Because the Mother Superior feared the wrath of people of the city, she decided to take steps to quiet them. She had eight-thousand screws blessed and then used them to seal the windows shut on the third floor. This act, done during the night when the caskets were empty, was to prevent the vampires, if they truly existed, who were at this time out of their caskets, from being able to reenter the convent before daylight to sleep in the caskets. With the blessed screws sealing the attic windows, the thirteen girls became agitated and restless in their sleep. Later that evening a most terrible howl sounded outside the convent, and the windows that had been sealed shut with the blessed screws blew open. The windows were sealed shut again the following night using more blessed screws. Over the remainder of my years there, each time the windows blew open, they sealed them again with blessed screws. The sisters were terrified and none ever ventured into the attic despite what they heard. I hope God will have mercy on us and keep us safe, for I fear something horrible has been allowed to continue to exist in our place of refuge."

And so ended the entry.

The legend that developed was that the thirteen girls, whose aristocratic families had protected and cared for the vampires over the centuries, had come from France with the vampires in their caskets in the hold of the ship to the New World, as the Old World had become too dangerous for their kind. The vampires had fed enough on the girls in the ship for both to survive—thus the girls were strikingly pale when they reached New Orleans. On the night they arrived in the city, they left their caskets to feed on the new blood of the people of New Orleans, returning afterward to sleep through the day in the attic of the convent. Another theory was that the French Church and the vampires had made a pact—money for survival.

Stories of vampires had been with the city since its founding, for the people of New Orleans are a superstitious lot. They flourished as explanations for the high murder rates, unexplained disappearances, and mysterious deaths. In 1931, Archbishop John William Shaw, the eighth archbishop of the city, tried putting a stop to the stories as connected with the convent by taking further steps to close and seal the heavy shutters on the eleven dormers on the convent. He also forbade anyone but high-ranking members of the church to go in the attic.

In 1933, on two separate nights, bodies were found on Royal Street with their throats torn out and a complete absence of blood at the scene, confounding the police investigating. A witness on the second night had seen a figure bent over one of the bodies. When the witness began to scream for the police, the figure looked up, laughed at the man, wiped his mouth, and then slowly, calmly went to the end of the alley and *walked up* a twelve-foot wall, disappearing as if not beholden to the force of gravity. A shutter at the convent, found open during these two nights, stoked the fears of the city.

A story in the 1970s had a group of curious teens attempting to photograph the vampires after an open shutter piqued their interest. The story goes that the next day their bodies lay on the ground drained of all blood. Crystal had found no police reports or newspaper accounts of this, but documentation from this period was not complete, as much of it had been destroyed during Hurricane Katrina.

In 1984, over a four-month period in the French Quarter, nine bodies found with throats torn out resulted in the police to state in their official report that 'something or someone had removed all traces of blood'. Reports of unusual activity at night at the convent occurred in high numbers during this period, with open shutters and dim lights in the attic.

During Hurricane Katrina and its aftermath, there were many reports of open shutters and bodies found throughout the city, not consistent with drowning but of brutally violent deaths. Nine days after the hurricane, a special priest came from Rome to bless the convent in a secret ceremony. And, oh yes, the convent made it through the disaster virtually untouched!

The Red Bayou Ghost Hunters had asked the Archdiocese for permission to go inside and of course, they were denied entry. They weren't the first and would not be the last to try to get in. Consequently, they were across the street. Larry, one of the other members, suggested breaking in, but Joe threatened to kick him out of the group. Joe believed in respecting other people, alive or dead. He said they were likely to reciprocate in kind.

Rocco had brought a supply of batteries to keep everything powered up through the night. Every two hours or so a patrol car drove down the street, and TC and Rocco ducked down behind the shrubs making sure that any lights from handheld devices did not show. No need getting the law involved. Prepared for a long night of surveillance, they had folding chairs and bottles of water. The sweet scent of confederate jasmine surrounded them as the hours crawled by, with several occasions where noises grabbed their attention, but nothing showed itself except an old tomcat. Becoming agitated when his phone battery died and no longer having anything to occupy his time, TC began grumbling, "This is whack, man!" over and over again. At about 5:15 in the morning, twilight, Rocco was about ready to tell him to shut up and leave when the shutters on the central dormer on the right side of the convent flew open. Rocco jumped up, raised the FLIR and saw a red-yellowish profile, roughly in the shape of a man's upper body, in a purple background in the dormer on the screen.

"Oh man!" TC said, jumping to his feet and knocking his chair over, making a good deal of noise.

"Quiet!" Rocco said angrily.

"Is it for real?"

"Someone's there," Rocco said in hushed tones.

Then another dormer to the left of the first, facing Chartres Street, blew open. TC picked up the Full Spectrum camera and briefly saw something in one of the other dormers. It was there and then gone.

"Oh Shit!" he exclaimed.

"You recording?" Rocco asked excitedly.

A dim light went on inside the attic, and a soft glow filled the dormers. Then there was a squeaking noise, and a bright light shown from over the top of the street wall in the center of the convent.

"I think the front door just opened!"

TC started moving towards it.

"Wait you can't…" Rocco began

"I ain't passing this up. What, you scared?" Giving a derisive laugh, he jogged across the street and was up and over the wall and gone.

"Crap!" mouthed Rocco in frustration. He left the FLIR and full spectrum camera on the ground, grabbed his backpack with some gear, put it on, and ran across the street. He thought, *If any of that equipment gets stolen, I know it's coming out of my tuition money!* He jumped up and placed both hands on the top of the wall and pulled himself over, landing in some hedges on the other side, scraping his arms. "I'm going to kill you!" he exclaimed as he saw TC's back disappear through the open front double doors under the arched canopy.

Rocco entered the convent. The light was not strong, but he had taken the public tour of the convent, now a museum (at least the two bottom floors), so he knew how everything was situated. He found the impressive dark cypress floating staircase that wrapped around the walls and ascended, carefully straining his eyesight and hearing—hoping, but not hoping at the same time, to hear or see something. His heart pounded in his chest. The second floor was where the Archdiocese's archives were housed. He did not stop there. He could vaguely hear TC's footfalls up above him as he went to the attic. His legs burned, and he was winded from the climb.

Upon reaching the third floor, he at first could not discern what he saw in the dim light. Long rectangular boxes lay in the center of the room, and off to the side a dark mass floated in the air. He then recognized the blue t-shirt and jeans. Near the caskets was TC, suspended in the air, feet off the ground by several feet. Facing away, his head forced back and his arms hung down as if he was a coat on a hanger. Then two red lights began to glow above and behind TC's head. Eyes. The figure resolved itself. It was a man of undetermined age and of at least six-and-a-half feet in height. Was he a man? He had long dark hair swept back over his pale face. The hair flowed over his shoulders onto a purple velvet jacket. Wearing tight fitting tan trousers and a white ruffled shirt, he held up TC with one hand.

"Bonsoir. How good of you to come, mon ami!" he said in heavily French-accented English. He then threw TC to the ground, and Rocco could see a deep gash in his throat and his lifeless eyes, unfocused and glassy.

"We thought we would invite you over," said a deep sonorous voice behind him, and Rocco, startled, stumbled forward, turning around in fear. Another figure dressed similarly to the first, but blond with lighter features, chewed absentmindedly on the long curled nail of a finger, his mouth twisted in a sneer.

"Yes, we smelt you in the gardens," the second one said.

"Smells like…" The darker one was suddenly behind Rocco, though he had heard no motion. He arched his head down and sniffed deeply closing his eyes in ecstasy, "Petit cochon—Little piggy!" The two laughed together. The smell of rotting meat made Rocco gag.

"That one," and he pointed to TC's lifeless body, "sang goûte mauvais—his blood tastes terrible— like wine from grapes that grew in dirt that a goat urinated in," and they both laughed again.

"You can always tell how healthy someone is by the taste of their blood."

"You been taking care of yourself little piggy?" he said as he poked Rocco in the chest with his right index finger.

"Who are you?" The words tumbled out of Rocco's mouth.

"Ah, some banalities before the main course," the dark one said. He bowed his head and replied, "I am Malthus."

The blond said bowing, "And I am Neavus."

"Are you the original ones?" Rocco asked, his whole body shaking.

"What year is it little piggy?"

"2016."

"Mon Dieu, over two hundred years this very night!"

"Weren't there more of you?" Rocco said, curious to the end.

"Why yes. But c'est la vie."

"Yes, two were killed by you humans, several died from disease, two died during the great storm several years back, and others…Well, we killed the others ourselves."

"Quentin was an accident, Neavus," Malthus asserted.

"You keep saying that—maybe one day you will believe it yourself," Neavus said with eyes closed.

Malthus began to object, but Neavus stopped him. "No matter. It is done, his ashes lay in the swamps."

"Does the church know you are here?" Rocco asked.

"The Church. You would think we would be adversaries? No? Us and them. Funny how things work out," Malthus said with an index finger on his chin as if deep in thought.

"You humans and your money. For a little gold, you would sell your own mothers," the other said, laughing.

The light from the dormers began getting brighter.

"The night is fading, little piggy. Time to say goodbye."

The two figures came closer.

Rocco had been recording everything on his wristband EVP recorder, which resembled a watch. When what was left of his body ended up in the morgue, it would still be on his wrist. John Benoit, a pathology tech, would find it. The last sounds on it were Rocco's screams. The evidence was enough to start a movement that would begin the battle for the soul of New Orleans.

THE FAREWELL QUARTER
By Nathan Pettigrew

The psychic gypsy queen on Royal Street unnerves me when reading my palm, sliding her purple and spear tipped fingernail along my fate line, and revealing her vision.

The dead will come for me, she predicts, and I think she's full of it, until she refers to the dead guy from the bathroom.

He can see everything now, knows everything about me, she says.

At the bottom of my spine, the chill freezes, and forces me to swallow the lump that goes down hard like a block of ice. Colder is the sweat that smothers me in the South's inhospitable humidity.

How could this gypsy have known about the dead guy? Coincidence? Not a chance in hell. Not with that kind of detail.

"Tristan? Tristan, are you okay?" Felicia asks. My poor sister.

She thinks I've come home to offer moral support.

"Yeah. I'm fine, sis. Just—think I need to eat is all."

We step outside to a dark blue and blackening sky above the lantern street lights, the rare coin and Civil War gun shops, and the stench is no less potent than before we sought our indoor sanctuary. Twenty-four seven, streets in the French Quarter smell of fresh urine and vomit.

"Well that was weird," Felicia says. "I thought it would be fun. Sorry."

I shrug her off. "No worries."

"She didn't even make sense," my sister says.

Not saying much else, we make our way to Café Du Monde on Decatur Street for coffee and beignets. The best in the country. Flat, square shaped, and served freshly made with powdered sugar piled on top, the "French" donuts are far different from your typical donut, the fried dough hollow inside and nowhere near as sweet or artificial tasting.

Served in threes, we enjoy two orders at a couple's table outside, beneath the green and white striped awning.

"So, Tee. You agree with my decision?" Felicia asks.

While chomping a mouthful of hot dough and powder, I use a crumpled napkin to sweep the white from my lips.

"Doesn't matter if I agree. Doesn't matter what anyone thinks. It's your body."

"She'll never be able to have one on her own," she says.

"Then you're giving her a miracle. Question is, are you the one doubting your decision?"

"I had the ultrasound on Tuesday," she tells me, "but when the sonographer asked if I wanted to know the sex, I—I couldn't. I couldn't because it was the first time I realized this might be harder for me than I thought."

"Seriously? You don't know the sex?"

"It's easier that way," she says.

"Tracy's your best friend, Felicia. Talk to her."

"I'm afraid of losing her, too. After, I mean. I think it's only fair to keep a healthy distance. So the child's never confused, you know?"

She speaks of the unborn, but my eyes float to the undead—here in plain sight—sitting at a corner table and watching a three-piece band perform in the street, their brass and jazz so lively and exclusive to the eyes of the Quarter, the sound living on beyond its expiration date.

Confusion and panic unravel my mind. I do a double-take, getting the same result, seeing a face belonging to the deceased. It's definitely him—the dead boy from the bathroom. He doesn't make or allow eye contact, and he certainly doesn't appear dead. He appears normal, alive, quite visible, and fully fleshed.

My heart racing, I can hear the rhythm of its beat above the music and those around us, the conversations at surrounding tables failing to calm me or convince me that I'm amongst normal folks in a normal setting.

Because there he sits, the gypsy woman's prediction coming true. What in the hell did she do to me? Has to be a mind job. Can't be real.

"You're sweating again," Felicia says. "Are you sure you're okay?"

"I will be," I say, standing. "I gotta get to a commode."

Never stopping to look back, I pass three waiters sitting on chairs in front the French doors, and then the line of mirrored windows built into the wall inside.

The door to the bathroom is unlocked. I can't bring myself to push it open, despite the intensifying burn between my legs, now spreading to my gut. Don't know what I'll find in there. My hand shakes, and the dead can see it, apparently. The dead can see my every move, can see what I truly am, but I didn't see myself as a monster until watching my hand shake when going for the ice pick not twenty-four hours ago.

I'd popped open a can, draining the inside with one fierce gulp. I emptied three more, celebrating with peers who'd passed the LSAT. Between my legs, an iron-sharp sting intruded, pinching and pricking my bladder. I hurried to the bathroom down the hall finding the door unlocked and allowing a glimpse of more than one person around the toilet before someone shut the door in my face.

"Are you fucking for real?" one of them said. "You didn't lock the door?"

"Whatever, man. It's locked now," another said.

Yeah, whatever. I could piss outside in a bush. I started for the sliding glass door in the kitchen, but I stopped, unable to block the flashbacks of more than one person around the toilet. Two guys and a girl, and pleasure did not factor into the dried tears on her cheeks, or the fear possessing her eyes, both shaking, so wide and so green.

In the kitchen, I watched my hand move frantically through an everything-drawer housing a barrage of metal kitchenware, a meat tenderizer, scissors, a thermometer...

I swiped an icepick. My heart pounding, I shot a glance at the party around me, the others playing drinking games, laughing and carrying on—oblivious.

Returning to the bathroom, I slid my credit card into the crack between the lock and door frame. The knob turned, and I barged in on the males with their jeans around their ankles—both stunned at the sight of me and my weapon.

I brought the pick to the neck of the one standing closest. The kid tried to back up and tripped. The one still standing moved in, but wasn't fast enough; I stopped him cold, bringing the metal point to less than an inch from his eye.

"Shit, man," he said.

I smiled. Applying just the right amount of pressure, I pushed the sharp tip into the kid's cheek without breaking skin.

"I'll fuck you up right here and now if your friend even tries to get up. Comprende, motherfucker? I won't hesitate the way you're doing now."

"Yeah, man. Okay."

"Girl," I said, "get on up and get out of here. Lock the door behind you. Tell no one we're in here. Got it? Go."

She started to, but tripped and caught herself.

"Whoa there," I said, keeping my dead stare on the motherfucker in front of me. "You gonna make it, sweetheart?"

Staring at the floor, the girl wiped her mouth and her eyes. Leaving the bathroom, she locked the door behind her as I had instructed.

My peripheral vision caught the kid on the floor pulling his jeans up.

"Turn around," I said to the one in front of me.

"What?"

"Turn the fuck around."

He did, and I grabbed a handful of his brushy black hair while lightly pressing the pick into the back of his neck.

"Now turn back around. Slowly. Very slowly."

Turning with him from behind, I kept the pick against his flesh until we faced the kid on the floor. A marble soap dish next to the sink held a thin pink bar that I flicked off. My hostage peeked in the mirror above the sink to see what had happened, and I slammed the marble piece into the fucker's head.

He went down. I knelt on top of him, driving both knees into his back, and something inside refused to let me believe that I was in control. The marble soap dish in my grip, I struck another blow to his head while his friend watched in eye-wide terror.

"He'll live," I said, feeling the kid's neck, "but I'm telling you right now, he won't want to if you don't take your pants back down."

"What?"

"You heard me."

"What—what are you gonna do?" he asked.

"I'm gonna watch you do as I say." I checked the time on my cell. After a minute, I nodded. "Get up."

He grabbed his jeans to pull up.

"No," I said. "I told you to take those down for a reason."

To slow him down. To prevent any sudden moves.

"Now leave 'em down, go out there, and take your sorry fuckin' ass back to whatever shithole you call home."

"I'm not the one who drove," he said. "I don't have the keys."

"Fucking walk then, asshole. Think I'm playing here?"

He got to his feet with his jeans around his ankles and made his way to the door in quick shuffling half-steps.

Laughter in the seconds following his exit should've come sooner, and the laughter I did hear wasn't hysterical, but tame—far too tame.

I stuck my head out finding that the party had relocated to the living room where bodies were crowded around a coffee table, two couches, and a single flight of stairs. I looked to the left toward the kitchen, seeing the sliding glass door wide open.

First locking the bathroom door, I returned to the kid I'd put down, trying to feel for a pulse, trying to feel anything, panicking and sweating profusely.

A shoulder tap brings me back to the now, back to Café Du Monde, my mind having strayed too far.

"Excuse me. Are you in the line to use the bathroom?"

"Right. Sorry. I'll make it quick."

Gotta get a grip. There's no way a dead guy is sitting in the café. That's impossible. I won't entertain that. Won't look in his direction again. I have to stay in the moment. For Felicia. For Sanity's sake.

My sister's concentration on the band is broken when I find my way back.

She smiles. "Everything come out okay?"

"Aye okay. Wanna hit the bars?"

"Watching you drink all night? Can't think anything more fun."

"Hey, it's quality time, sis." I push my chair in against the table. "It's all about the quality time."

We cut through Jackson Square—the pigeon shit capital of the world.

Unsettled inside, I'm still able to smile. The square does that for me, producing a memory of a tale my grandma used to tell about a man in the square on a Sunday afternoon. Must've been a tourist. Fascinated, he couldn't get over how many of the stout little birds there were, bobbing and concealing the concrete in a mass flock. A burst of movement sent them flying while the man watched in awe, staring overhead, his mouth wide open, and a pigeon shat right in.

I break out laughing, can't help it and love it. Funny stories related to the city are refreshing to recall in this post-Katrina world.

Our mother and father divorced shortly after, and I was all too willing to leave a devastated city that resembled nothing like the home I'd known, when Dad found work up north, while Felicia had decided to stay near our mother in St. Charles. The law became my focus, and though I'd yet to pass the LSAT, I found myself determined to fight the ineptitudes and corruption that consumed FEMA, the Bush II administration, and local politicians during the aftermath, the devastation—watching New Orleans fall to her knees, assaulted—and doing shit about it, as if they wanted to close the door on her, but the world had already stepped in and seen.

And then the world was no longer mine to own when I sold out. Say it ain't so, Felicia. Your brother's a monster.

Muscles in my shoulders tense up, a haunting presence having occupied my peripheral vision on the left side.

Yards away on the sidewalk, the dead boy from the bathroom is heading in the same direction as us, still avoiding eye contact. Too real. Can't be a figment of my imagination, or any kind of hallucination. Best case scenario? A doppelganger.

A heavy chest and breathing tell me differently. I know better. Adrenaline and fear make the walk seem a lot longer than it should be.

Hundreds of people around us every day—what if he's not the only one? What if dead faces look no different from ours? How on Earth would we know? Has anyone ever actually seen a ghost?

Or do only killers see them? And how many murderers are among us on the streets, blending in and doing everyday things at all too familiar places?

Only the dead know for sure.

I reach for my sister's hand. She squeezes mine, and lets go.

Forget ghosts. Felicia wants me focused on vampires. Wannabes. We stand with them on the balcony of Felicia's favorite club on Bourbon Street, watching while the gang of posers expose their surgically implanted fangs, all dressed in black and body nets, all too skinny and strung out to be taken seriously. They couldn't draw blood if they tried, and they never have.

They're part of the façade, this entire city obsessed with mystery and magic, keeping it going while I keep my own façade alive in a pit stop for partiers who travel from all over for hand grenade drinks and debauchery.

Down below, I see my dead stalker, his face just another of many crowding the street, but unlike everyone else, he doesn't look up at us. He looks at the people around him. Maybe he isn't anything to be afraid of: a façade like me.

Two white girls lift their tops for beads, and it isn't even Mardi Gras.

I always despised the sexism in this city. Then again, these young ladies tonight are willful participants in a degradation performance, unlike those who are stripped against their will.

"Damn," Felicia says, wiping the slime from her forehead.

It's got her wrapped—NOLA's heat blanket.

We go inside and watch people dance from the mezzanine.

It's hotter in the club than outside, and my clothes stick to my skin like blood, all caked and causing discomfort.

The dancers below don't care, their heads and faces shining off and on at different moving points like sparkling glitter.

Tables and booths to the side of the dance floor are equally bombarded with bodies, their hands and mouths all moving, but failing to compete with the music's blaring volume.

Until the screams. High pitched. At first, I think a moment of hysteria and unchecked excitement has split the air, but like the pigeons of Jackson Square, a burst of movement sends the people packing. The crashing wave of panic sends a ripple effect through the club, and the bodies all flee from just one—a knife wielder throwing jabs and drawing blood.

Dressed in camo and hooded, the maniac moves quickly and calmly, slicing and spilling more screams out from faces.

The music stops. The screams soar.

In one hand, he holds a pistol, but doesn't shoot it, simply uses it to keep any would-be heroes at bay while chasing and tearing flesh.

"Jesus Christ," Felicia says.

My sister's at my side, at a safe distance from the massacre—thank God.

A second thought brings me shame for feeling relief in the face of those getting stabbed.

"Come on," Felicia says.

I don't. I can't. I'm stuck in my head.

How does a man go this far? Is that me down there? I'd lost my way, too, had known what if felt like, and still I'm unsure about the answers to my questions.

Or maybe deep down, I'm not. Maybe the killer was always there, waiting for release, waiting for me to drop the façade so the killer could flourish like the streets of the Quarter at night.

"Tristan!" Felicia slaps my arm and takes my hand. "Let's go."

She leads the charge, knows the club.

Others are clearing the mezzanine. A line at the stairwell clogs, then moves again—too slow for comfort—but we're moving. Still, people behind us are pushing and polluting our breathing space with the acidic stink of armpits.

Ahead, the crowd pushes back, coming the wrong way.

Screams have entered the stairwell.

A motherfucker crashes into me and knocks me down. Felicia's quick to pull me back up. Another slams into me, and then too many, breaking me apart from my sister.

I retreat to the mezzanine's railing, letting everyone pass, and achieving a visual on Felicia.

She approaches me, while someone watches us.

With two calm brown eyes, frighteningly normal in appearance, the maniac holds his gun on us. Shakes his head, making it clear. Don't even think about running.

No way in hell is this fucker getting the chance to cut into my sister's pregnant belly. He'll have to cut through my bones first, and any other part of me I'm called on to give.

Bracing myself, I make two fists and use my forearm for my only shield.

Another couple runs out in front of us, not realizing the situation until it's too late. He cuts the guy down. Goes for the girl. She screams behind both hands stuck out.

Her guy manages to regain his footing and strikes her assailant. He goes for the knife, and the struggle pushes them both against the railing.

The opening is there, a perfect opportunity to run past.

I take it, but don't get far. I freeze at the sight of the dead blocking the stairwell.

That kid. My stalker. He looks like anyone else in the club—minus fear. Nothing here is for him to be afraid of. He's dead, after all. Gone to Hell. Having come back for me.

He may appear solid, but can I walk right through him?

"Tristan!" Felicia yells.

Something changes. My dead stalker steps closer, staring right into my wide eyes.

I see it. He isn't here to haunt me, but to help me.

To remind me. I am a murderer, but a savior, too. I prayed for his forgiveness, and he gives me strength. I send my sister into his arms.

Another scream. Facing the horror, I'm just in time.

The maniac has prevailed, getting the drop on his male victim. His knife goes down. Blade comes up.

We dance: I catch his arm and yank him off; I crack my fist into his nose.

Bleeding too, now, like his victims, he maintains a strong hold on his hunting knife. Reaching for the .45 that he's holstered since shredding into the mezzanine couple, I move in to keep him from drawing, but there's not enough time to dodge the blow from his blade into my back.

We fall to the ground, my weight not enough to hold him down. He rips the blade from my back, and I scream, the excruciating burn and pain like none I've known, making me nauseous and weak, like the strength in my arms has abandoned my body.

He comes in for the kill. No. I shove my boot into his shin.

He drops. His knife on the floor, I'm slow to retrieve it. I can barely stand.

So I let myself fall. On top of him now, I thrust his weapon of mass destruction into the camouflage that covers his shoulder, his upper chest area. I don't stop.

I've been here before, and I take it out on him. I've wasted too much of my life repressing rage, and I'd taken it out on that kid in the bathroom during his deplorable act against another.

I can run from this, or face myself.

I'm just another nobody who made no difference in the world. I couldn't keep the city that raised me from falling apart, adding insult to injury when I jumped ship from flooded streets in need. I couldn't keep my mother and father together. Couldn't tell my sister how proud I was of her for always being the strong one—strong enough for others, strong enough to stay home and confront the tides—and strong enough to carry and give life instead of carrying rage and causing death like me.

I couldn't keep myself whole when it came to anger. I let it tear me in two.

I'm no different from the monster I cut into. My body going numb, I'm losing more strength, but feel enough to deliver a final blow to his neck if I choose.

I relent, and when I feel for a pulse, I find one.

Coming up from behind, Felicia places her hand on my shoulder.

"He's still breathing," I say.

"Doesn't matter now," she says. "The police are coming for him."

"And for me too, sis. I'm giving myself up."

"What are you talking about?" she asks.

I take her hand. Tonight's voyage through the Quarter was my last with her—my farewell ride.

"It's time I told you the real reason I came home. And it's not good. But I have to own it."

Felicia squeezes my knuckles, clutching hard before easing her grip, but she doesn't let go.

DANSE MACABRE
By P.L. McMillan

Clementine Dupart was walking down the street when she was reminded of the murders. Two gentlemen were talking, heads tilted close together, and their moustaches practically entwined.

"Ghastly!"

"The newspapers reported that there were no bones, just the muscles and organs!"

"Neat little piles, I heard!"

"Who could do such a thing?"

Clementine couldn't help but turn a bit to look at the newspaper they held as she passed. The headline was unforgettable.

ANOTHER GRISLY MURDER! EIGHT SO FAR! POLICE STUMPED!

It was nothing new to her. These piles of organs, muscles, and skin had been turning up in the French Quarter since last August, and it was now February of the following year. The murders had started shortly after the 155th anniversary of the French rebellion of 1768, which had been quashed by the Spanish. A recent article had connected the details between the murders and the rebellion more than a hundred years before. It had been a bloodless revolt but that didn't stop the Spanish governor at the time from catching the five rebellion leaders and having them hanged. Even in 1923, there were tense undercurrents of resentment between the French and Spanish, and now locals of French heritage were falling victim to a serial killer of some kind.

She looked up at the angry, gray sky. It would rain soon, a late winter tempest that would drown the streets in a dark flood, so Clementine strode past the men and many others, on the way to the café. Overhead the storm clouds were like a black roiling ocean. A block away from her destination, the storm began. The rain poured down, ricocheting off the cobblestone streets and creating a thick haze in the air. It poured down the walls of the buildings, playing like waterfalls over the second-floor balconies, and running like rivers over the roofs.

Clementine hurried down the side of the slippery street, avoiding the major puddles and charging through the minor ones. All around her, people huddled under the awnings of their second story balconies or in the deep doorways of the restaurants and cafés that lined the street.

She turned the corner and ducked into the entryway to the Café du Monde. She opened the door and dashed in. Inside, it was deafening with the sounds of laughter, conversation, dishes, and the constant drumming of rain on the windows. The place was packed, but her friend had managed to secure a table near one of the steamy windows. Marlena Albinus was simply beautiful, with long curling blonde hair done up stylishly in a braided bun and captured by pearl-head pins. From time to time, the men in the café would stop and turn to glance at her, their expressions making it clear they hoped she would glance back.

Clementine pushed her way past a dowdy woman who stunk of tobacco and magnolias,who was gesticulating wildly and yelling at a table where three young men sat. She snaked through the rest of the tables, dripping a path of rainwater the whole way. Marlena looked up, caught her eye, and smiled. Clementine sat with an exaggerated sigh.

"I don't know why you decided we needed to go out in this mess," she gestured at the window, where nothing could be seen through the condensation that fogged it.

"I have news," her friend replied, pulling out a silk fan and hiding her face behind it.

Clementine envied Marlena's impeccable fashion taste. She was always the best dressed, no matter where they were or who they were with. Of course, it helped that Marlena's family was rather wealthy. Clementine eyed her friend's crimson dress and necklace of tiny rubies.

"And what is your news, my dear Marlena? Another man after your heart, perhaps?"

Marlena blushed suitably but couldn't help her smirk.

"No, no. Still only three."

"Then what, pray tell? Speak before I die from hunger waiting for some service!"

The waiter, a tall dark-skinned man who stood well over six feet tall, appeared at her elbow.

"A plate of your beignets, thank you. A café au lait for me, and a black coffee for my dear friend," Marlena said, snapping her fan closed.

The man nodded and wove back through the crowds as easily as a ghost might.

"There. Satisfied, my hungry beast?" Marlena tapped Clementine's wrist sharply with her fan.

Clementine had been peering over to the table next to them where a man, sitting by himself, was reading today's newspaper, so when her friend slapped her wrist, she jumped in her seat.

"Where is your mind at, Clementine?" Marlena snapped.

"Sorry, Marlena. I've been a little distracted lately."

"You're not still concerned over those murders, are you? My father has said that the victims have all been –" Marlena lowered her voice, despite the clamour. "Members of families known to have been Spanish sympathizers in the past."

Clementine shivered.

"So that means neither you nor I have anything to worry about, so let's talk about the important things," Marlena smiled.

The waiter appeared at Clementine's elbow again, holding a tray of steaming drinks and a plate of pastries. Marlena snapped open her fan and looked up at the waiter coyly from behind it while he placed their order in front of them.

Clementine wrapped her hands around the steaming cup of coffee, breathing in the clean and heavy scent of chicory. Marlena dipped a small silver spoon into the foam on the top of her café au lait and licked it off as delicately as a cat, waiting for the waiter to leave before resuming the conversation. Clementine found her eyes drawn back to the man sitting at the table next to them. He was still nose deep in his newspaper, the pages quivering in his hands.

She couldn't read the small text from so far nor did she need to. Everyone knew about the murders in the French Quarter. They'd been going on for months. Every full moon, there would be another pile of offal, organs, and muscles found put neatly to the side of a road. The bones of the victims were never recovered.

Marlena was right about one thing, though; the victims had all been citizens that had ancestors known for being sympathetic to the Spanish rule of New Orleans. Clementine shivered again. She thought of Ferdinand.

"Now, where was I?" Marlena asked, picking at one of the beignets on the plate between them.

"Your good news," Clementine replied, wishing she'd thought to have brought her own fan.

Despite the heavy rain, the air was thick and heavy in the café. There were no breezes to clear away the mugginess.

"Ah yes. Monsieur Louis has asked for my hand in marriage," she said.

"Really, Marlena? That's just wonderful!" Clementine said, genuinely happy. "You said yes, didn't you?"

"Well, of course not. It doesn't do to agree right away," Marlena said and laughed at her friend's expression. "I must admit that I am hoping Monsieur Gabrielle and Monsieur Phillip will hear the news and come rushing to make their own bids for my heart!"

"Oh Marlena, that's just cruel," Clementine said, thinking of her own love who she'd never marry.

"Foolish Clementine. You can never agree to a man's first proposal. Love isn't meant to be easy, and a little tension to the heart goes a long way to strengthen a man's devotion," Marlena said and took a tiny sip of her drink.

Clementine just shook her head and tucked a piece of beignet in her mouth, wiping the sugar from her fingers onto the napkin by her cup. She hated the taste of the plantains inside, but knew Marlena would be insulted if she didn't eat any. She washed down the sickly sweet taste of the pastry with more bitter coffee. In the pocket of her dress, the note she had seemed to burn. She felt that at any moment, Marlena would spot some tell-tale bulge and ask what it was. Everything was so easy for Marlena. She didn't have to hide the men in her life. She had nothing to be ashamed of.

"And of course, you know that Monsieur Louis is my first choice, so I will say yes in a week or so," Marlena finished.

"I am so happy for you, Marlena. He's a perfect match," Clementine said, choking back her envious thoughts.

"I agree completely," she smiled, showing off her white teeth and pointed incisors.

* * *

The rain had ended by the time the two women had sipped the last of their drinks. After their bill had been settled, they walked out arm in arm. Overhead, the sky was clearing, revealing a pale washed-out blue between the dark gray clouds. The air was still like lukewarm soup, but a small breeze had picked up, casting small moments of relief over the people that walked the wet streets of New Orleans.

Clementine escorted Marlena home, as was their custom. The whole way, Marlena chattered on about her wedding plans and the three sons she planned on having. She'd even picked out the names and sports they would excel at. Clementine slipped her right hand into her dress pocket and ran her fingers over the edge of the little note, thinking of the carefully written words on it, and did not listen to a single word her friend said.

They walked beneath the thick branches of the Southern live oak trees that lined the streets. Each tree had its own shawl of heavy Spanish Moss. One particularly long tendril of the ethereal plant brushed Marlena's perfectly curled hair, and she looked up in disgust, knocking it away with her fan.

"How I hate it!" she spat. "How appropriate that such a bothersome plant be named after such a troublesome people!"

Clementine looked up. The strands of moss swayed in the weak wind, swinging into the beams of sunlight and out again. When it was in the light, the moss glowed briefly like pale green fire. In the shade, it looked like expensive green lace, as intricate and delicate as anything you could ever find in the shops. To Clementine, Spanish Moss was beautiful.

"After me, it will be your turn to finally meet someone, I should think," Marlena said as they approached the walkway to her family's house.

"I suppose so," Clementine said, reaching into her pocket to make sure the note was still safe and sound.

"As a married woman, I won't be able to selfishly keep all the men to myself anymore. I suppose, in their broken-hearted despair at knowing Marlena Albinus is now Madame Louis de la Poer, these bachelors will flock to you for comfort!"

"Of course," Clementine said, too antsy to think of a wittier reply.

They kissed each other on both cheeks and hugged briefly.

"Now, get home safely, dear one," Marlena called, flapping her fan at her friend as she retreated down the walkway to her front door.

Clementine waved and began to make her way back to the French Quarter. As she walked down the streets, weaving through the shoppers with their bags and the mothers with their strollers and the men smoking foul cigars, Clementine took out her note several times. Each time, she would hold it with the fingertips of both hands while she examined the writing that made up her name on the front of the envelope. She would then turn it and lift the envelope's flap, looking at the creamy white edge of the page within. But she could never find the courage to take the note out to reread it. She felt sure that all eyes were on her as she walked. That, should she take the note out, someone would step up to her and demand to know what was written upon it.

This fear, this paranoia, was so strong that she would hurriedly close the flap and hide the note away again, looking here and there around the street to make sure no one was watching her. No one ever was. The shoppers busied themselves with their new possessions, the mothers crooned over their babies, and the men chewed on their soggy cigars and talked about the murders.

The streets were growing busier as the sun began its descent and the afternoon grew deeper and cooler. Clementine watched young couples parading down the streets with their heads bent together as they whispered to each other. She felt the sweet tang of jealousy and reached into her pocket to touch the note once more. She turned down Port Avenue into the narrower back streets, away from the main hustle of the shops and cafés. Here, the sounds of the crowds were muted by the tall houses that lined the streets. The streets were too narrow for carriages or trees, the buildings too crowded to allow even a breath of a breeze to find its way in. Clementine felt sweat dripping down the back of her neck, between her breasts, and dotting her forehead.

The area was also poorer than that of Marlena's. The houses may all have had second stories and tiny balconies guarded by wrought iron railings, but they were old and failing. Many had peeling paint and cracked windows; others seemed to tilt forward as though on the verge of collapse onto the cobblestones. The streets were dirtier as well. There was refuse in the gutters and dirt that had turned to sticky mud from the rain. Clementine did her best to avoid stepping in these swamps and kept her face down, away from any prying eyes that might be spying on her from the second-floor windows. Checking her pocket watch, she saw that she was running late.

Her heart picked up its tempo, and she picked up her feet in response. As she made her way through the winding streets, Clementine reached up and captured any locks of her chestnut brown hair that were straying, pinning them back into place beneath her hat. She pinched her cheeks hard and bit her lips to add a little color to her face. Finally, she pulled her scented handkerchief from her other dress pocket and pressed it to her damp neck and around her hairline, trying to absorb as much sweat as possible while, hopefully, leaving behind a few traces of rose and lilac.

Ferdinand was waiting for her when she knocked softly on the door to the narrow house at the very end of Dryades Street. He smiled when he saw her, taking her little hands in his very large ones. Despite the anxiety, despite the fear, and despite the stress of hiding their love from everyone, Clementine couldn't help but smile back. She allowed herself to become lost in his dark eyes, ringed with the thickest lashes she'd ever seen. Still holding her hand, Ferdinand led her up the stairs, deeper into the house, and to the bedroom.

* * *

Clementine hadn't meant to fall sleep in Ferdinand's arms. So when she finally awoke to find the sun already gone and the full moon risen above the buildings, she was in a whirlwind of panic as she dressed and dashed down the stairs and out the front door.

As she hurried through the dark and shadowy streets away from her lover's house and towards her own, on the opposite end of the French Quarter, Clementine rehearsed a few excuses to use when she finally got home and had to deal with her parents' questions. Her mother, she knew, would be the worst. She had been suspicious for weeks now, only allowing

Clementine out with chaperones until today. Now, Clementine knew, she'd be in a world of trouble.

Lost in her thoughts, Clementine didn't notice how empty and quiet the streets were until she heard the music. It was lively and loud, echoing through the silent streets. Clementine slowed, straining to hear it. The song sounded familiar but also, so very strange. It was a slow melody that sounded like so many of the new songs played in the cafés around town. It was also coming from the way she needed to go if she wanted to get home.

Clutching her skirt, Clementine made her way out onto the main shopping streets, where all the windows were black and lifeless. She jogged a little, wanting to get home as soon as possible. Farther and farther down the street she went, and the music grew louder and louder. Now she could hear men singing along. She felt a bit relieved to know that she wasn't alone out on the streets.

From Canal Street, Clementine went left on River Avenue. She was only ten minutes from home now and began to worry solely how her mother was going to react once she finally arrived.

A block down, Clementine saw a group of shadowy figures. The music was all around her now. Her very bones seemed to resonant with the beat. She had finally found the source of the music. Five of the figures were playing the instruments and the others stood about them in a loose circle, not moving but merely listening to the band play.

She moved closer, intrigued by the light-hearted and jaunty notes and the hearty singing that accompanied it. A few houses away, she still could not make out the people who were playing the music but she began to hear some of the song more clearly.

> "Say, I've got a feelin',
> That you've got a secret,
> A dirty little secret you've been hiding!
> It's a weighin' heavy,
> That much I can see!"

Clementine shivered, though the band and its audience were still a few houses away, the voice sounded like it was coming from right beside her. She remembered the French Quarter murders right then, and she felt the cold wave of panic wash over her. The five band members jigged and swayed to their own music as they played their instruments. Clementine shook her head. It felt like the music was filling her up completely, pushing out every other thought and feeling. Her feet carried her forward.

> "Take a little turn, sweet mama,
> Take a little turn and join our dance!

The dance, the New Orleans dance!
Lighten up, dear,
And take a little ole turn for us!"

Now she was only a house away. The moon broke through the thinning clouds and she could finally see the group. Her heart froze.

Ahead of her, gleaming very whitely in the moonlight were seven or eight perfectly clean skeletons. They were standing in a loose ring around five mummified corpses. These corpses held instruments—guitar, flute, trumpet, upright bass, and a rough drum set—made of bones and sinew. The bones could have only come from the skeleton spectators as many were missing femurs, ribs, fingers, and even a skull or two.

Clementine wanted to scream. She saw the dead musicians turn and smile at her. They were all dressed in their Sunday finest suits, albeit each and every suit bore the stain of dirt and grass and rain. Their faces were a mass of wrinkles, dry skin that was porridge white with undertones of a sickly green. The bass player was missing an eye; the flutist's left cheek hung down in a dry flap. All five of them bore a dirty noose around their necks. The tallest one, the one with the guitar and freshest looking face, beckoned.

"Say, I've got a feelin',
That you've been a seein',
Someone you ain't supposed to see,
It weighs heavy, don't it, sweet mama?
That heavy 'o heavy o',
Secret o' yours!"

The skeletons had moved aside for her as her feet led her onward. They watched with hollow holes and said not a thing to her as she passed them. The band pounded out the rhythm and the music filled her up again. The tempo went faster and faster until she felt herself carried away. Her feet tapped out a matching pattern to the beat as she raised her arms to the full, bloated moon above. She swung about in a wide arc, kicking up her heels and flipping her skirts to and fro. The skeletons stood and watched; something about them made her feel like she was being pitied.

The musicians went faster and faster. She couldn't keep up. Clementine knew it was of the utmost importance that she kept up with their music. She struggled and stumbled. The singer shook his head with a wry grin that revealed his mossy teeth.

"Say, don't you know it?
Don't you know it, dear?
Someone will teach you,

Come on and do that dance,
They call the skeleton dance,
Yes, ma'am!
We've got the music for you,
Lighten up, dear,
And take a little turn for us!"

Clementine grinned and nodded a "thank you" to the singer. With her left hand, she reached over and, oh so easily, ripped the skin and muscle from her right arm. She tossed the bloody chunks into the air. The skeletons reached up and caught the bits, blood pitter-pattering down against their white bones. Clementine felt lighter now but it wasn't enough. She reached with her right hand and tore the skin and muscle from her left arm. The ripping sound as the muscles pulled away from her bones harmonized with the music perfectly.

Clementine laughed, her anxieties forgotten. She forgot about her mother, waiting angrily at home; her father, with his disapproving looks; Marlena; with her perfect life; and Ferdinand, with his vague promises. She forgot everything and danced. It felt so wonderful to finally be free.

"Say, come on now and do that dance
They call the danse macabre,
O, sweet mama!
You've got to take a little turn,
Sweet mama, lighten up, dear!
And take a little ole turn for us!"

They were right, so right. The music was getting faster but she was still too heavy. Clementine tossed her head back and reached up with both hands. She took hold of the skin at her neck and pulled; down the flesh came like a heavy blanket. She pulled and ripped, tearing the breasts from her ribs and the muscles off her shoulders. She tossed these up in the air to be caught by the watching skeletons. Her dress was hanging down in tatters, cinched only at her waist now. Clementine spun around, ripping the skirts away to reveal her smooth, white legs. She paused a moment in her dance, reached down and yanking the flesh from her ankles, calves, and thighs. She relished the thick, wet sound the flesh made as she freed her bones from it.

The musicians played faster and faster, the guitarist threw his head back, casting the torn and desiccated skin on his neck into sharp illumination as he laughed. She laughed too, whirling around. Free of her heavy skirts and skin, Clementine kicked up her legs, splattering the silent skeletons with blood. She laughed to see their pristine bones marked with the crimson stains. The flutist, the bass player, and the drummer stomped on the pavement to the beat and hollered along with the music.

She whirled and twirled. The skeletons watched on in silent pity, holding the scarlet chunks of Clementine. She looked down. She saw her bloody bones; she saw the strings of tendon and vein hanging down from her ribs. The horror began to creep in past the music.

"What have I done?" she moaned, her feet still skipping to the music.

Clementine looked up at the skeletons, her mouth a deep dark cave of fear. She looked over at the musicians, reaching out her hands to them in supplication. The five corpses laughed and played faster and faster as the guitarist sang out to her:

> *"Lighten up, lighten up,*
> *And take a little turn, sweet mama!*
> *Take a little ole turn and join our dance,*
> *The dance, the New Orleans dance,*
> *Lighten up, dear,*
> *And take a little ole turn for us!"*

Now all the corpses had joined in the song. Clementine drowned in the music once more as it pounded into her skull. She threw her hands up toward the full moon, in despair, and in ecstasy.

> *"Say, come on now and do that dance,*
> *They call it the danse macabre!*
> *Sweet mama, oh sweet mama!*
> *You've got to take a little turn,*
> *Sweet mama, listen here,*
> *Lighten up, dear,*
> *And take a little turn for us!"*

Clementine dug her fingernails into her cheeks and pulled. Clawing her cheeks away, she hurled them into the waiting audience and began to scratch the rest of her skin away from her skull with her nails. She ripped the hat from her head, tossing it to the street and began to yank out handfuls of her hair and scalp. She ripped and scratched and dug until her skull was bare and free and bloody. Clementine kicked off her shoes and savagely tore the flesh from her feet.

Now all that was left were her hands. Clementine tried to stop. She tried to throw herself down, to stop this mad dance from finishing. But the guitarist picked up the lyrics once more and for the very last time.

> *"Woo, sweet mama, love to see you dance,*
> *Doesn't it feel good to let that secret go?*

I've got a feelin',
You are feelin' lighter,
All because of this dance!
So, come on now and finish the danse macabre!
Come on, sweet mama,
Come on, come on!
I've got a feeling,
You want to finish this dark o' darkest o' dances,
So, one more little turn, sweet mama,
One 'o one last little ole turn!"

Kicking up her feet in a wild flourish, Clementine reached up and plucked her eyes right out of her skull. She pirouetted and Clementine tossed these to the right and to the left. Her fellow skeletons caught them easily.

The dance was done. The musicians rested their instruments on the ground. The skeletons turned and gathered at one point by the side of the road. They carefully put Clementine's organs, muscles, flesh, and offal into a neat little pyramid on the cobblestones. They folded the tatters of her clothes next to it. The musicians were silent. They picked up their instruments and began walking down the street, their nooses swinging in time with their steps. The skeletons turned and began to follow. The skeleton that was Clementine was the last to turn and go.

DEAD WEIGHT
Erin Crocker

"The *only* reason I'm helping you is because I was a horrible friend." Alice looks at me with those furious blue eyes, and I shake my head and hand her a silver flask filled with gin.

"How were you a bad friend? Take another drink, you'll feel better," I suggest as she pulls the metal container from my hand and empties the bitter drink in her mouth. We shouldn't be driving, but the bayou doesn't seem to be heavily populated. Not like the city.

"If I never left you alone…"

* * *

Her words fade into a kaleidoscope of Skittled floats lining Bourbon Street, the lights folding into metallic trumpets that wail loudly— and him. He touches my shoulder, and I turn, ready to shove the tip of my heeled boot up his perverted ass, but I look in his grass green eyes as they dance to the brassy music.

I've known him forever, screams the three straight shots of tequila I'd taken an hour before.

I'm in love, coaxes the twenty-ounce concoction of cranberry and vodka I'm holding in my shaky hand as he stares long and hard into my soul.

I melt into his soft voice as he takes my hand. "Bourbon Street is for tourists," he smirks with the arrogance of the super-star quarterback I went out with senior year. "The party's over here." He grabs my hand with a strong, sex-grip, and I'm hypnotized.

My drunk-ass follows him around a corner, down an alley, around another corner, until I'm dizzy from the alcohol, until he rips the button off my dark-wash denim, until I scream 'no', and until he refuses to stop.

* * *

"Not your fault," I reassure Alice as the Range Rover eases over mud that's sloshed over the road. The screech of skinny tree branches wail, warning us we shouldn't be there.

"How's this?" she pulls off the street and somehow maneuvers behind a group of rain-soaked shrubs.

I shrug and survey the marshy ground, as we both open our doors and make our way to the back of the vehicle. We pop the hatch open. I smirk at his near-lifeless body: hands bound by white rope I was fortunate to buy on clearance, eyes half-open and shut, drugged by some herbal tincture I purchased at a voodoo shop people had whispered about.

* * *

"In cases like these, we rarely find the guy," detective Anderson lifts his eyebrows and glances at the clock. I sit, alone, on an unforgiving examination table and wait for the SARS nurse to come back to the room. "Is there anything about him you remember?"

"No," I answer, honestly. "I was…"

"You were drunk," he finishes and shakes his head.

"Yes, but there have to be other instances. I can't be his first victim," I argue, in hopes that something will jog him, and he'll try to make a connection.

He jots a few notes in a book and walks out of the room. From the hall, I hear him speak to an officer. "C'mon Joe."

Joe replies, "What about the girl?"

"She was drunk. Who knows? If we listened to every case of drunk sex down here in New Orleans, our DA would have cases backed up for years. Relax, let's get some lunch." He's whispering, but my senses are on edge. I can make out every small indention in the wall; I smell the metallic hint of saline from the room next to mine.

* * *

"Earth to Jen." Alice waves a hand in front of me and pulls me back to the unconscious perpetrator.

"Crap, sorry!" I unfold my arms and help her drag the body out the back. We quietly pull the hatch back down.

Half his weight is on me, the rest, she's carrying. He moans.

"Hey dick-face, can you carry some of your own weight?" Alice complains.

I shush her, worrying someone could be out in the bayou. Getting caught isn't what bothers me, it's getting discovered before we can exact revenge.

* * *

Alice looks at me as I work on zipping a leather mini-skirt and lace up a pair of black boots. "How do you know you'll find him?"

"I'll remember his voice. Plus, if I go back to Bourbon Street, I'm sure he'll be there. I'll pretend to be drinking, ask him if he wants one, then I'll put this in." I hold up a mixture of herbs Madame Jeanette hesitantly sold me earlier that day.

"O-kay," comes her uneager reply.

I shush her. "You just wait in the corner, and we'll escort him out together."

She nods, and we both make our way out of the hotel room.

* * *

"Can you grab it for me?" she pants as we both struggle to set his body straight.

"Huh?" My head's light from the alcohol.

"The rope!" She points at a spool of polypropylene. "Grab it up," she pants.

I pick it up and sling it around my right shoulder. The monster is in between us, both of us holding his weight and tramping through the mud while dodging stray limbs reaching for loose strands of hair and catching our jackets. When we near the water and a sturdy looking tree with a thick branch, we come to an unspoken agreement that we'd walked far enough.

We drop his body in the sludge, and Alice looks at me. "Do you know what you're doing?"

"No," I reply, wondering how we are going to get his body roped and hanging from a thick limb that hovered over us.

"Here," she reaches for the rope. "I'll make a swing hitch." She gulps as though she's second guessing being out here at all, and before she throws the end of the rope around the branch the first time, I fear she's going to back out.

"Start tying the other end to his body," Alice instructs, "Like, maybe around his shoulders or arms."

Hanging the bastard upright isn't good enough; instead, I knot the rope around his feet. I'd turn him upside down like he'd turned my life upside down.

* * *

I walk into Madame Jeanette's on Dumaine Street, searching for anything I can find to knock him out. I never believed in magic, like I never believed I'd be raped. I still don't believe in woo-woo witchy type stuff, but the Madame emerges from a beaded curtain.

"Dear girl, in so much pain. How might Madame Jeanette help you this afternoon?" She comes closer to me, her long fingernails wrapping around my hair and pulling it from my face.

I take a deep breath. "Alaine Rousseau was my SARS nurse at the hospital. She sent me here, said you could help."

I wait for a reply, as she turns for some time. She doesn't speak, but finally says, "I was once a girl in your shoes. I'm not one to use my magic for dark purposes, but I consider situations such as yours darker than the darkest of arts."

She reaches into a deep pocket sewn into her wildly colored smock and pulls out two tiny bags. "The pink bag is a mixture of herbs. It will knock him out, but be quick in what you do, he will awaken to full consciousness," she explained and then pulled a dark bag. "Use this sparingly, for we are not all predators such as this monster of yours. Burn this like you would camphor, as it burns it will cloud your head. You won't see him as a person, you'll see him for the monster he is, and it will numb your senses. It will help you bar off your humanity and compassion."

The wrinkled lady holds the bags out, and I take them from her, my eyes wide with trepidation. She nods her head. "You're doing this for you and every other girl he's attacked. You are doing good," she reassures with a nod.

I sigh and thank her. The bells elicit an understanding ding as I exit the shop.

* * *

"Are you gonna burn that shit or what?" Alice hands the black bag and a lighter to me.

"Oh, yeah," I reply in a nervous stutter.

We'd hoisted him up, well, upside-down, that is.

I place a bowl on the ground and set the brown rectangle inside. I flick the lighter once, twice. It lights, and I touch it to the brick until the flame takes.

"What the hell?" comes a frantic voice from behind us.

I turn to see blue, panicked, wide eyes, his black hair blowing from the light breeze.

"You're awake." I walk toward him and bend until I'm nearly eye-to-eye. "Remember me?" I ask, blandly.

It's him, *it has to be him*; I know the voice, the arrogance.

* * *

Alice and I walk down Bourbon Street and into a small bar. He's sitting on a stool, hitting on some red-head. He says, "You know, Bourbon Street is really just for tourists." She giggles.

* * *

"No, I'm sorry. I don't," he pleads.

He's good, a great actor.

Alice rolls her eyes, "What if we got the wrong guy?"

"We didn't. Soon you'll see. That crap's gonna burn, and we'll see the truth," I contend.

"Whatever," Alice crosses her arms.

"What's going on? What'd I do to you?" the monster bellows.

"You fucking raped me!" I scream at the jerk. "Just admit it already!"

"Rape? No way…not me. I teach tenth-grade math at De La Salle High School," he tries to explain. "I'd never think of doing something that vile to anybody. Let me down, and we'll discuss what happened."

Alice and I inhale-the smoke, and all of a sudden any regret or feelings of backtracking waft out our nostrils into the misty air. I can't hear his pleas as Alice pulls a hacksaw from a bag she's been carrying.

Our brains are the haze suspended over the murky swamp. We don't hear his screams as I saw his limbs piece after piece, and we don't notice the blood as it spews and spills, soaking into the soft ground.

All is finished, and we dispose of soiled clothes, weapons, body-and-all into the dark waters. We stand next to the green Range Rover.

"Umm, did we drink too much?" Alice rubs her forehead, her eyes bloodshot.

I look to her. "I don't know. One minute we're in a bar, and the next I hallucinated, I think…" I shake my head.

She puts her arm around me. "You've had a rough couple days. How are you feeling?"

"Surprisingly, the hole is gone. I don't feel so bad, now," I answer, the entire incident with the blue-eyed predator feeling more like a mirage than something we did.

"Do you remember last night?" I blink and put my hair up in a messy-bun.

"No, not at all," her eyes still blank.

We don't stick around. We don't go back out into the now sun-filled swamp. And we don't see next week's paper.

RAVEN'S CALL

By Pamela Q. Fernandes

Jimmy's life changed the day they buried his father. At seven years old, he only registered that he'd never see his father again. He didn't understand why his mother howled and stayed in bed with a mountain of used tissues. But he did understand that he was on an extended holiday from school. No more homework or waking up early.

The house help was on holiday too. So when he woke up, he took out a chocolate milk from the fridge and searched for the cookies. If he wasn't swinging on the tire, he spent hours playing in the garden and often times close to the Pearl River, where his grandma met him occasionally. Sometimes she had a word, a joke, sometimes she'd even play a game of catch. But she tired quickly. She was like his mother said, lazy to the bones.

The four-bedroom home in the Pearl River suburb was grand, with all the trappings of Southern lifestyle in the St. Tammany Parish. The large acreage spread to thick trees before spanning toward the river. Jimmy loved this place. The purple vetch and buttercups all splashed across the garden. The music of the birds, the music of the hasty river, the music of the leaves, and the music of the trees: it was different from the constant beating he heard in the French Quarter where his father liked to visit on weekends. An occasional buzzard flew above, and no matter how high he sat in his treehouse, it still looked out of reach. He loved chasing the squirrels, pretending he was a horse, rolling in the grass, and playing hide and seek with his father. He missed him. Terribly. When lonely, he'd go up to the treehouse his father built him and wait with a book, hoping he'd come around and read it to him.

He'd been in an accident, he'd heard people say at the funeral, a nasty one. He didn't make it to the hospital in time. That's not what his mother said, though, she said the doctors were all 'retards'. That was a new word for him. But he liked the sound of it, repeating it, "Re-tard," and giggling. The air was a bit chilly, he'd worn his big boy pants and a cardigan. He didn't like all the extra clothing though, it made climbing trees and playing in the river very difficult. He couldn't even chase the squirrels well in it or throw rocks.

Today he colored the treehouse with his crayons. His father told him this was one space that he could do anything, and his mother wouldn't complain. Scratch, paint, make figures anywhere on the wood floor or the walls.

His grandmother called. She was downstairs, wearing the same clothes she always wore: a rose-colored dress, slightly tatty and out of style. His mother would never wear something like that. She had those thick glasses that made her eyes look big and scary, and when she took them off, he could see the crisscross of lines on her face. Millions of them.

"Jimmy, have you been paying attention?"

"To what?"

His grandma helped him down the rope ladder. "To the birds! If I were you I'd keep an eye on them. It's said that sometimes the people who die come and visit us in the form of ravens."

Jimmy held that thought. *Ravens?* He'd been too busy watching the squirrels. "So Dad could come visit me like a bird?" he asked, craning his neck to the sky, to see if there were any birds.

"How would I know it's him?"

"You will just know. Now come on, there's rain coming, and your mother won't want you catching a cold."

"Mum doesn't want me anyway," he informed her.

"Why do you say that? Your mother loves you very much." His grandma made that funny noise in her throat when she disapproved of something.

"But she hasn't been to see me. She doesn't read me stories or make me pancakes. All she does is sleep."

"Aww, you poor thing, let me make you some pancakes instead."

"Have you used the camera I gave you for your last birthday, Jimmy?"

"No, Mum said I shouldn't be using it at my age. I might spoil it."

His grandmother poured the batter into a sizzling pan. "That's true, you might not have the manual dexterity for it yet. Maybe in another year. You know when I was your age I was already snapping people. That's where I learned to be a photojournalist. From snaps of Mardi Gras to soldiers weeping, I've captured it all."

When his grandmother let him eat his pancakes smothered in maple syrup, he ate with gusto, not one, but five. And soon he fell asleep. When he woke up, the rain had gone, but the clouds were dark. There was no sign of his grandma, so he ventured outside, finding a long branch that had fallen from the trees. Tapping it on the ground rat-a-tat, he was oblivious to the gathering storm. The grass was wet and mushy. The air smelled delicious; somewhere someone was making a pie. All the trees glistened and looked greener than usual. He stared up at the dark sky. No birds at all. So he walked to the river, helping centipedes on the route, picking up some fancy looking rocks, and talking to himself. When he reached the river, he tested the water with his hand to wash his rocks. The blue water was ice cold and rushing downstream. He picked up small stones and threw them into the water, hoping to empty the bank of its pebbles. There were no squirrels here to chase.

Without warning, a large black bird swooped down on him, before settling on an open branch. Jimmy's eyes went round with wonder, his jaw dropping and his hands glued to his face.

Walking on tippy toes around the branch, Jimmy asked, "Dad, is that you?"

The beady-eyed raven tilted his neck one way, then another, before cawing.

"Where have you been all this time? I've been missing you."

The raven cawed and took to flight, perching itself on top of a barrel, away from the river. It was the blackest black he'd ever seen, with smooth scalloped wings, his beak shiny and long.

Jimmy followed the black bird, slightly tentative, and his eyes widened when he saw the barrel filled with pebbles all painted. "It says, 'Daddy loves you'. Wow, Dad! These are so cool, I'm going to take them to school and show all my friends."

Jimmy stuffed his pockets with as many pebbles as he possibly could, some in his shirt pockets, pressing the Velcro to shut them tight, waddling a little with the additional weight. He even shoved some in his pants zippers near his shins.

Soon the pitter-patter of rain on the river beckoned. Jimmy wanted to see it. He ran towards the water, but the raven flew in front of him, swooping down, aiming its talons at Jimmy.

"Dad, I need to go the river," he protested, but the raven wouldn't allow him, constantly flying into him, making Jimmy fearful. Why was his dad not letting him go to the river? Then the raven made a quick swoop towards his face, and Jimmy turned around and fled to the house, the raven close on his heels. He stumbled and fell on the jagged rocks, slicing open his soft knee, causing some of his precious 'Dad loves you' pebbles to scatter. The sharp twinge of pain made Jimmy hobble as he dashed to the house. He stopped for a moment to catch his breath, but the raven was relentless, picking on his shirt, flying behind him, forcing him to run towards the large home.

Just then a huge explosion boomed, causing Jimmy to fall forwards. He couldn't see, but a quick rumbling followed the rushing sound.

His mother darted downstairs. "Jimmy, where have you been? I've been worried about you. Did you go out with someone?"

"No, I was out by the river."

His mother gasped as she looked out the window. The telephone started ringing and Jimmy, atop a stool, nose to the nets, saw the scene outside. Water, lots of it, had swamped their garden and was skirting their home, creeping a little at a time.

He heard his mother. "No, he's right here, just in time. How did the levee give way? No, I heard the sound."

"I'm alright, we'll just stay put. Probably go upstairs with Jimmy."

His mother took two steps towards the window, stretching the telephone wire to its fullest, "It's just an inch of water, but I'll go upstairs and see."

Forcing Jimmy's hand into her own, she dragged him down from the stool into the kitchen, to get a plastic bag.

"Did you do all this?" she asked, still harried and dumping food from the pantry, chips and biscuits, into the plastic bag. Granola bars, cereal, milk, and fruits followed.

"Grandma made them," Jimmy said. "She made me pancakes when I told her that you weren't making them for me," he said, wiping his runny nose to his shirt collar.

"Jimmy, don't be silly."

"No, Mom, she made me pancakes and even gave me a candy from her tatty rose dress, you know, her favorite one."

For a moment, his mother stopped what she was doing and looked at him, and then at the countertop, the griddle, and the leftover bowl with batter. Without thinking, she dumped the maple syrup and the remaining pancakes in a tin and lifted the boy, balancing him on her hip.

"What else did she say?"

"She told me that maybe in another year, I would have *man-ual dex-terity* to operate the camera she gave me for my birthday"

When they reached upstairs, she set the boy down, peering outside the window, and then turned to him.

"Jimmy, stop fooling around. Grandma's dead. So is your father. Didn't I explain all this to you?"

"But Mom, they're not."

Her mobile rang, and she picked up, "Yes, Reverend, all is well. I understand, yes…so the service is canceled. No, I didn't forget, it's just that we just had the month's mind, so I wasn't going to come to mass for All Soul's day."

"Yes, we should pray for their souls. I know my mother used to say that too, that my father's soul would come to visit for prayers. Made us listen to three masses for him. I just forgot today was the day, besides Jimmy's giving me a hard time. Yes, we're safe. Thank you. Goodnight."

After putting down the phone, she yanked Jimmy's hand and sat down on the bed, pulling him in front of her.

"Now are you saying, you saw Grandma, and she made you pancakes? Is that what you're telling me?"

Jimmy nodded, his whole head and neck bobbing, chin touching his chest. "Grandma told me that Dad would come as a raven to see me, and he did."

"Goodness Jimmy, I told you there is no such thing as ghosts. Who has filled your head with this nonsense?"

"It's not nonsense, Mum, I promise. Dad came to me at the river. I asked him, and he showed me these cool rocks he made me. See?" Jimmy fumbled with his pockets, first from his shirt and then from his zipped pants. He laid out a few of them on the bed.

His mother seemed interested enough. She turned them over, then gently ran her fingers over them. "After that, he was a bit cross with me, didn't want me to play near the river. He almost took out my eyes. I fell over, look at my boo-boo."

His mother was still fixated on the rocks, ignoring his knee. She went to the window in haste, eyes scanning the scenery. The thick of trees, a murder of crows perched on their branches, and the growing pool of water in her garden.

She hugged and pulled Jimmy close.

Pulling the tin, she took a bite of the syrup-drenched pancakes. Banana and pecan pancakes. Just the way her mother had made them. Jimmy could be right. No one else would teach him to say things like 'manual dexterity.' What about her husband? Again, she stared at the black birds all together. One flew near the window, perched on the sill.

Immediately, she lit a candle. Today was All Soul's day. While other families had pumpkins and decorated front yards, she had departed souls protecting her son. The least she could do was offer a prayer in return.

Lighting a candle, she and Jimmy began, "Our Father…"

By the end of the evening, all the birds departed, but the one on the sill remained. All she could mouth was, "Thank you," before he finally flew away, until next year.

THE SLIMY UNDERBELLY

By Laurie Moran

Bourbon Street is alive with revelry and debauchery. Glorious and opulent costumes, glittering with sequins, shimmering in poured-on metallic spandex, floating in gossamer layers of tulle, brush past bare skin and exposed breasts, pendulous with piles of colorful plastic beads swinging between them. Some dance, some stumble, clutching giant tubes filled with beer and colossal travel cups emblazoned with the purple logo of a "world-famous" daiquiri bar chain. A cacophony of music pours from the doors along the street: bold, brassy jazz, the twang of country guitar, and the pulsing beat of house club music. The people mix and mash like the sound, forming a colonial organism, becoming a single creature moving as one, like a millipede writhing its plethora of legs, squirming along the street.

The colors of Mardi Gras, purple, green, and gold, though each vibrant in their combination, mixed together like watercolor paints, form a greasy gray palette. In the gutters along Bourbon Street, a slop of that same gray tone collects: a combination of rainwater, spilled Hurricanes, piss, and vomit. It is punctuated with a floating raft of detritus: flattened aluminum cans, clear plastic cups with their straws poking up like snorkels, lime green yard-long drinking vessels, a pair of hot pink thong underwear, and a scattering of brightly colored feathers and strings of beads. The flotsam and jetsam clog the storm drains, and the sludge grows, sloshing up over the curb and onto the sidewalk, wafting its putrid, clinging scent into the air.

In the morning, on the first day of Lent, the city sanitation crews will beset the street, raking and collecting the refuse and freeing the drains. The street sweepers will rumble by, throwing the last droplets of ooze in a gray mist onto the sidewalk, where shopkeepers, armed with garden hoses, will wash the remnants away. But for now, the sludge grows, marinating and macerating, becoming more viscous and vile.

As the crowd ebbs and flows, unwary revelers shuffle or stumble into it, submerged past their ankles, the rancidness settling between their toes, climbing their legs, and stealing a measure of joy from their hearts. The sludge will dry and crack on their skin, crusting and sticking to them like they were dipped in cement. The showers of New Orleans' hotels will run long and hot in the wee hours of the morning, as the victims scrub and swear and scrub.

A drunken man, young, blond, and shirtless, breaks from the march of the crowd, standing in the middle of the street as people push around him. Someone's shoulder collides with his, and he grabs the offending collarbone by the shirt with his left hand, throwing his right fist in a wobbly haymaker. Cops suddenly appear on all sides. He swings wildly at them. One of the officers forces his arms behind his back and pushes him to his knees. The shirtless man slides forward, off-balance with no hands to break his fall, and lands face-first in the gray gutter sludge.

The slime washes up over the curb and crashes in a wave onto the sidewalk. Passersby jump into the doorway of a Voodoo shop to avoid the cadaverous spray. The shirtless man kicks and sputters as the arresting officer applies handcuffs with practiced skill.

The glop coats his torso and climbs into his nose. He screams a string of obscenities as the slime crawls into his mouth. He strains his wrists against the handcuffs, twisting and pulling at them, throwing his strong shoulder muscles forward to test the will of the steel. The muck slides up his naval cavities and fills his eye sockets, drops of squalid ooze dripping from the corners of his eyes. The slime follows his optic nerves and feels its way into the frontal lobe of his brain. It wraps around the prefrontal nerves, dissolving them like acid, a mass of bubbling, foaming mire, and severs the connection to the rest of his brain. The shirtless man stops thrashing and lies still in the pond of nebulous liquid.

The police officer, grasping the drunken man's bound hands and one bare shoulder, pulls him up to his knees. The half-dressed man, his belly coated in a gooey gray frosting, smiles beatifically, his lips drawn back too far in a grimace. He stares at the cop with calm, vacant eyes. His mouth drops open, oozing a combination of drool and foamy gray slime, and along with it, his hopes, his thoughts, and pieces of his brain. The leaden mire dribbles from his chin and collects back into the gutter. In the morning, it will all be washed away.

LES MORTS OF THE BIG EASY

By Joshua James Jordan

When she went out of town and someone asked her what she did for a living, Lulu Pelletier told them she smells the future. It was almost true.

Lulu wore a white dress with a red band tied around her waist and a white turban draped around her head. She had long fingernails, and a python as thick as her arm rested on her shoulders and looped around her neck. She wore a costume, or maybe better thought of as a uniform.

She crossed Bourbon Street on her way to work. The city had already power washed the asphalt, but the sidewalk still clung to congealing remnants of the previous night's sin. New Orleans: The American Southeast's Disneyland of vice.

Miss Pelletier couldn't judge them. These white folks came in from all over, and she fed on them the same way all the other tourist fleas did: jumping on, sucking down all the money she could, and jumping off before they went home. She entered her shop in the French Quarter, the sign reading "Miss Pelletier's Voodoo Tarot."

Inside the small lobby, Troy lay sprawled out on a couch, his dark skin contrasting with his white collared shirt.

"Long night, Troy?" Lulu asked.

Troy groaned and sat up slowly, rubbing a hand on his forehead. "Oh yeah. Gonna need coffee today. LSU's on spring break. College girls looking for a taste of the Big Easy." He smiled. Some fleas want more than money. He stood up and strode to the break room in the back, while Lulu set up linens for about a day's worth of customers in the changing room.

She washed the clothes every day. The business couldn't work if the particles from the customers' attire interfered, and the white linens added to the whole voodoo vibe.

"You ready?" she asked down the hall.

"Nah, I need the day off," Troy yelled back.

"Shut up, boy. You know this don't work without you," Lulu said.

Troy stumbled into the tech room with a mug in hand. "Doing this coffee Irish style, if that's alright with you, Miss Pelletier."

"Just do what you," Lulu said. She plugged the dark flesh-colored earpiece into place.

The first customers entered, a portly white man in his fifties and his slightly younger, much thinner wife. They changed in the dressing room into their white robes, cracking jokes. Lulu had heard them all before. *Nice cult gown, when do we drink the Kool-Aid?*

The mister came in first. They had to be separated otherwise their distinct *futures* would interfere with the reading. Lulu made small talk, not because she wanted to, but because she was good at it, and Troy needed some time to get the reading straightened out. *Where you from? What you do? Cha ya blah. Most folks is talkers and not listeners. Love to recite they memoir when they can.*

Some folks will start asking about voodoo but the city has tour guides for that. When they start asking questions it's time to move on to the main act.

Lulu shuffled the deck while Troy briefed her. "Pretty weak correlation on this one," Troy began, "he either just started or just got off some blood pressure medication."

A barrier of glass sits between her and the customer. On the customer's side, small micro-particle detectors suck air in and instantly diagnose the DNA of the bacteria floating off of the customer's skin, hair, and breath. Each person's combination of bacteria looks different and is affected by medical conditions.

Lulu knew what to do about this blood pressure medication. She would lead the interpretation of the tarot cards into the right direction. Lulu placed down three cards and flipped them over. The arbitrariness of the amount of cards made her smile sometimes. They charged more money for more cards, but usually for the desperate and repeat customers.

Gran Ibo: A wise woman sitting on a porch, overlooking a swamp.

Deluge: A storm washing away a tower and a house, a bolt of lightning splitting the card in half.

Les Barons: The wild card. Three skeletons dressed in purple, walking up a flight of stairs. One gets the feeling they were large in life and in death.

Lulu explained each card to the customer. She described their individual meanings and followed with the creative interpretation of their synergies.

"I see Ibo with Deluge often, usually meaning to guard your property, but the Barons are here to guard your life itself. Perhaps…" Lulu paused for effect here, summoning the spirits within the customer's mind,

"...perhaps your heart has too much life. Too many worries in the here and now. It taxes itself, flooded with your thickening blood."

"Jesus, I stopped taking Zestril lately. Could that be it?" he asked.

"Most certainly I think that could be it," she said.

"God lady, maybe you even saved my life."

The mister left and in came his missus. She had enough real life problems that even if Troy didn't pick up anything, Lulu would be able to work something out. The missus talked about her first husband's new financial successes since they divorced. The jealousy didn't even need to be put in words.

"Weird. She's either on maternity hormones or some weird birth control. Work with it if you can," Troy said in Lulu's ear.

Miss Pelletier avoided it and went the traditional route. It didn't end well.

"I knew this was bullshit but Roger just had to try. Thanks anyway," the missus said, getting up to leave.

Can't win 'em all. Besides, ol' Roger will be out drinking on Bourbon Street, telling strangers, but friends for a night, how Miss Pelletier saved his life. Many would give her a try, and Troy would be able to get some good ones. The smokers scared the easiest and the particle detectors picked them out too. Why didn't more folks smoke?

It went like that until the Mob walked in. Martin wore a suit more expensive than he could ever afford. His milky skin wouldn't let you know of his quadroon heritage, but nobody really cared about that anymore.

"Can we talk?" Martin asked. He flipped the 'CLOSED' part of the sign to face the window and locked the door.

"Guess you ain't giving us a choice," Lulu said, sitting down in the lobby. Troy came in but stayed in the hallway, leaning against the wall.

Martin sat down opposite her, rubbing the upholstered leather awkwardly for a moment. "Two days ago, some guy took gold bars from us. Two of our guys went missing."

"Mississippi catfish bait by now," Troy said.

"Most likely," Martin said.

"What's this got to do with us?" Lulu asked.

Martin sat up straight, interlaced his fingers in his lap, and crossed a leg. Business pose. "He wore a mask. Had an answer for all of our security systems. Except one," Martin looked deliberately up at Troy.

Troy chuckled then said, "Micro-particle detectors?"

Martin nodded. "Installed it not long ago. Just for laughs at first, but the cops put one of our guys away with it, so we figured we'd give it a shot. Got a clean read on him in one of the rooms."

"Again, Martin. What's this got to do with us?" Lulu asked, responding with a business pose of her own. Whenever Martin came by it was usually to demand money. "We do tarot fortunes. We don't track down gold thieves."

Martin smirked, looking down at a ring on his hand and twisting it around like he was checking the tightness of a bolt. "Miss Pelletier. Your business partner brags a bit too much when he's on his second glass of absinthe."

Lulu turned to Troy and gave her best angry face, but Troy just shrugged. *You know me.*

"Besides, you ain't the only game in town. Mama Berdine down the street got herself a white girl that do the same as Troy here. Dropped out of Tulane."

Lulu fidgeted in her chair and almost repeated herself a third time before Martin stopped her with an outstretched hand.

"We just want you to tell us if he comes in here. That's all. I'll send Troy the file. You just call me right away if he comes in here."

"What do we get?" Lulu asked.

Martin smirked again. "Isn't my eternal gratitude enough?"

"No," Lulu said, emphasizing her business pose with I *could slap you* eyebrows.

Martin laughed. "So serious, Miss Lulu. What happened to ol' fun Lulu that we all used to know?"

"She got knocked up and had to grow the fuck up, Martin," Lulu said. "No more payments." She jumped right into the negotiations.

Martin's face turned to stone. "Okay. Deal. If you get 'em."

"And you close down Mama Berdine," Lulu said.

"Now that hardly seems fair," Martin said.

"Stopping payments means none or less. Ya'll will end up short on cash and back in here with loaded gun and loaded words in no time. Or ya'll get shot up and go swimming in the river. Next ones ain't going to respect your deal. Putting down Mama Berdine gives me more of mine until then."

Martin spun the ring on his finger again, thinking it over. "Deal," he said.

Two weeks passed and this man with a bounty on his head hadn't shown up. An unlikely event anyhow, wasn't in the cards.

In walked a sailor with that strange white outfit on, that if a person didn't know better they would ask him to bus away their dishes at a restaurant.

Lulu worked on him with small talk, "So why'd you join the Navy?"

"Sometimes, I don't know, you just feel like you want to make a difference, you know?"

Lulu nodded.

"Now, I don't always feel like I'm changing the world or protecting my country. Not at night when I sleep with my nose pressed against the ceiling, but every now and then…"

"Every now and then you do," Lulu said.

"Yeah, it feels great. Seems to come with the wind just when I need it the most," he said, a smile on his face.

"Lulu," Troy said loud enough the earpiece rang in Lulu's ear. "Get in here."

She grimaced and stood up. "I'll be right back," she told the customer.

"I'll be here," the sailor said.

Lulu left the room and walked into the tech area, where Troy had brought up two charts on the monitor.

"Troy, what?"

"Look at this. This is the readout of the guy Martin's looking for." Troy pointed to the graph on the left. "Here's our guy." Finger to the right.

"So? They're close but not the same," Lulu said.

"The reading they got he was wearing different clothes. There's enough variety here, it could be him."

Lulu stared at the screen. "Are you sure?"

"Hell no, but it's close enough. Let's let Martin bag this guy."

"Troy, I can't turn someone over unless we're positive, and I don't think it's him."

"Listen. We can't afford to pay off these crooks anymore. And puttin' Mama Berdine out will send more business our way. You'll be able to send Jean-Luc to private school."

"Jean-Luc," Lulu whispered.

"Besides, you know they offered the same deal to Mama Berdine. She'd turn us in just as soon as she could. You don't wanna' end up back on Jackson Square next to the fucking magicians do you?" Troy asked.

"No," Lulu said.

"Then I'm calling Martin. You make sure that guy stays here," Troy said.

Lulu walked back into the tarot room. She had lost any mood to fake a reading. "Hey, great news. You just won a free trip around the city."

"Really?" he asked. His face beamed. "What about the cards?"

"Oh, we can do that later. Why don't you go back and get changed and wait? Someone's coming to get you," Lulu said.

Lulu waited with the sailor in the lobby. He talked about his family back home in Carolina. How he had a girl he was sweet on back there. How he couldn't wait to go back and wished she could go sightseeing with him.

Martin walked through the door.

"Oh there you are," Lulu said. "Treat our guest well and show him a good time."

Martin had a moment of confusion on his face, but he caught on quickly. "Oh for sure, for sure." He looked over at a the sailor. "You ever been on a steamboat?"

"No, but I've been on plenty of regular boats," the sailor said. They both laughed. The sailor stood up.

"Well, you're gonna love it. Did you know that just there is the deepest and fastest part of the Mississippi?" Martin opened the door and the sailor went out.

"No, I didn't know that," the sailor said.

"Yeah, you can drop anything out there and nobody'll ever find it," Martin said.

He closed the door.

Bon voyage.

* * *

A month later, "Miss Pelletier's Voodoo Tarot" experienced an unusually slow day. Business had picked up since Mama Berdine moved her readings to Jackson Square, but the cold weather that day kept folks inside.

Bored, Lulu had drawn three cards for herself. As she shuffled, she felt a strange chill run from her toes through her fingers. An overwhelming sense of everything filled her, like those rare times in church when everyone felt as if God actually dwelled in the room.

She didn't like the first three cards. Lulu shuffled again and got the same cards. An incredible coincidence.

It happened one more time.

Legba: An old man with a cane tells a story to three children around a campfire. A black sun hovers behind him with its dark tendrils reaching out. His fiction fills the minds of the children with the seeds of darkness.

Ancestors: Two sages bestow treasures to a crowd. To the good go the rewards. For the sinful? Well, there is always…

Les Morts: The purple and rotting bodies of the dead writhe in the flames of hell. Holy hands reach down from the heavens, eternally out of reach.

Lulu entered the tech room. "Troy," she said. Troy sat in front of the computer, headphones forming a shell over each ear. He played some game where he ran around and shot people.

"Troy," she said again, snatching the headphones off.

"What?" Troy asked, annoyed. He spun around. His computer-self died. The screen filled with crimson.

"I just gave myself a reading. I got the same three cards." She held up fingers for emphasis. "I got the same cards three times."

"So?" Troy asked.

"The cards were terrible. If I got those cards for a customer I would tell them to say goodbye to their family."

"Listen, Lulu. You don't believe in this shit, do you? Just relax. So you got some cards in a row. Here, let's go do it again."

They walked back into the reading room. Lulu shuffled the cards but there was no chill. No overwhelming sense of…anything.

Dance. The Market. Hounsis.

"Are those the same ones?" Troy asked.

Lulu shook her head.

"See. And those don't seem so bad. Whatever they mean," Troy said. "Alright, imma go then pray for some business."

"Sure," Lulu said. "Sure."

* * *

Troy hadn't been to work in three days. Sure, a year earlier he had gone on a bender, but that was during Mardi Gras.

Lulu struggled between the tech room and the reading room. She'd make up an excuse to leave and then wait for the results.

She wasn't an expert. She didn't know all the nuances that Troy did. She guessed to the point that it became as reliable as just reading the cards. Besides, lately she could almost summon that strange feeling she first had a while back, with the tingle in her fingers as she shuffled the deck. Sometimes she wouldn't even use the micro-particle detectors at all. Lulu loved relying on this newfound power, spirits, or whatever it was.

A man came in, and she didn't really like the look of him. She wasn't comfortable running the business alone just for safety. She should probably hire somebody, especially of Troy kept running off on these trips.

The man had dark skin and a gold front tooth that glimmered from between his lips even when he wasn't smiling. He wore a black suit and refused to put on the linens.

In the reading room, Lulu began to make small talk but he just said, "No. Do the cards." He smiled. Gold tooth.

Lulu shuffled with an ominous aura filling the room. She felt short of breath. Nauseated. She put down three cards.

Les Morts. Les Morts. Les Morts.

There was only one in the deck.

Lulu glared at the cards and then at the man. It seemed as if his face shifted.

"Let me tell you somethin' you don't know. Troy went swimming for catfish. I think he'll be doing that for a while," the man said. "There's a price for working with Martin's gang."

She darted out of the room and into the tech room. She bolted the door.

Lulu grabbed a stun gun from inside a drawer, hid it behind her back, and then sat on the floor next to some cabinets. She pulled out her cell phone but it read "NO SERVICE" at the top.

Footsteps approached the door. "I'm going to break this down," the man said, his voice growing deeper with every word. "And you're gonna be a good girl once I'm in there. Understand?"

"Fuck you," Lulu screamed.

He laughed.

The computer monitor flashed. It read, "Exact match." It must have been a program Troy had made to link up with the man Martin was looking for.

The door crumbled at the handle and flung open. He entered.

He picked her up at the wrist and lifted Lulu into the air. She jammed the stun gun into his side and turned it on.

His head jerked for a moment before he looked down in a wrenching motion and twisted her other arm until it nearly broke. She dropped the stun gun.

"Now," he said. "You're going to call Martin and have him come here. His life for yours. You understand the deal."

"But my phone, it doesn't..." he set her down and she looked at it.

Six bars.

What the...

"Go on. Call Martin."

Lulu started dialing 911. She thought that maybe she could call them and pretend to be on the phone with him. *Come on down to Lulu Pelletier's Voodoo Tarot for a party.* She figured they would catch on.

Before she could press the last number, the man said, "On speaker."

She obeyed, calling Martin instead and inviting him over. "I've got to show you an interesting reading," she said. Her voice shook as if she nervously gave a presentation.

Martin didn't seem to pick up on it. "Be right there," he said.

While she waited, she couldn't figure out what this man could be. He could only be semi-human or infused with a demon. She hadn't encountered anything like it.

Eventually, the front door opened, Lulu could hear the door chime. "I'm here," said Martin.

The man glared at Lulu with his head slightly bowed and an evil grin on his face.

"In the back," Lulu said.

The man held up three fingers. He had long fingernails that curved at the ends. She didn't know what that meant. He blew on them and then made his hand into a fist.

A woman she'd never seen before turned the corner, holding a sawed-off shotgun. The evil man slapped it out of her hands and the gun went flying, landing next to Lulu, who lay on the ground in the corner.

The evil man clawed her face and threw her down. He put a pistol to her head when Martin turned the corner, a shotgun in his hands. He unloaded a shell into the man's torso. Before Martin could pump the shotgun for the next round, the man had fired three bullets into Martin's face. He landed somewhere in the hallway where Lulu couldn't see.

The man held a giant hole in his chest with one hand while holding the gun to the other woman's head.

"Don't," said Lulu, now holding the shotgun pointed at his direction.

"Or what? You ain't ever shot a gun. You wouldn't kill nobody," he said.

"Les Morts," she said. She fired. "Les Morts." She fired again.

He fell to the ground, pistol falling out of his hand.

Lulu stood up and grabbed his firearm. *Three cards. Three fingers. Three lives.*

"Les Morts," she said a third time and fired the rest of the bullets into his head.

* * *

Lulu sat at her new table in Jackson Square. Mama Berdine gave a reading nearby. A magician summoned a half-circle of tourists. *Watch this rope do something ropes don't normally do...*

An artist held a lens above a piece of lumber, using the sun to burn images into the wood. Other pieces with famous cartoon characters hung against the black metal fence with varying prices depending on the size.

A young college aged girl sat down at her table. "How much does this cost anyway?" she asked.

Miss Pelletier shuffled the deck. A chill started from her feet and filled her body. A soft wind blew and the hairs on her arms stood. With each flick of a card, the spirits hopped between them, putting them into just the right place. When she grabbed three from the top of the deck, energy nipped at her fingers.

"For you dear? This time. It's free."

SIBYLLINE GREEN

By Jonathan Shipley

Heavy wings flapping at dusk. A man in formal evening dress running through a hazy tangle of trees. A shadow descends, like a stone plunging from the twilit sky. The man falls, arms flailing to ward off the dark wings. "L'ange vengeur!" he screams, blood flowing from his mouth.

Sebastian came awake with a jerk, staring at the unfamiliar room cloaked in soft grays by the gaslights outside. Where was he? The hotel, he realized a moment later. The room he had taken at the shabby Saint-Louis Hotel in the Creole Quarter. Against all odds, he was back in the city. The dreams had dragged him back.

He pulled himself from the tangle of sheets and stepped to the window. Across Saint-Louis Street, lacy ironwork galleries fronted the old buildings, and the scent of wisteria floated on the air. Yes, he was back. The death dreams had started again—therefore the rituals had started again. His nine years of safety in Chicago were as nothing.

Sebastian could barely remember who he was nine years ago: a very young man at Tulane University who had been much too free, much too trusting of a classmate who offered escape from the dullness of life.

He was older now and perhaps wiser. Less stupid, at least. Now he questioned even that. He had assumed New Orleans would be safer after the Ban of 1912 descended, but he didn't feel safe at all. He feared his old haunts too much, feared the absinthe even with the force of Law against it. But still, he had to come. For the rituals to start, they had to trap some other fool to be their green sibyl. At the very least, he could deliver the warning, fool to fool, that he himself never got.

Crossing to the sink in the corner of the room, Sebastian doused his head under the faucet. The porcelain bowl bled black as the cold water saturated his hair, washing all the color out. This, too, he had learned in the intervening years—to black his hair as fops did to mask their gray. It enabled him to live and work in Chicago without the stares. But here the disguise was to no avail. He was what he was, and the city knew him. He would face the day in all his pale glory, such as it was, and suffer the stares of the ignorant and the attention of the knowing.

It was still very early as Sebastian stepped out on to Saint-Louis Street to wander, to let himself be seen, to announce his return. He held a secret terror that he was not strong enough, that these self-styled magi would suck him into the old pattern as easily as last time. Except he was less naive now. They may have created him sibyl and aroused the dark visions with their drink, but they no longer controlled him.

A wave of déjà vu rolled over him as his feet followed the old paths. How old he felt. The thought followed him down Saint-Louis and onto Bourbon Street. In Chicago he could pass as a young man; here he was old and jaded. He was surprised that anyone could look him in the eye and perceive him as young. He had seen too much, both of this world and the next. But few people looked him in the eye, he noted of his early morning street companions. Heads turned toward him at his approach, and then turned quickly away. He heard one old Creole mutter l'ange vengeur— avenging angel—and heard an echo from his dream. But he had heard that all through childhood growing up on the far side of Lake Pontchartrain. The bayou people held albinos in special awe, though with no special affection. They were supposed to be vessels of the Spirits. Once he had thought it mere superstition, but that was before Monsieur Philippe and his family had blooded him to make him prophesy.

Bourbon Street eventually led him to The Opaline. The grandeur of the bar was so fixed in his brain that the locked doors and boarded-over windows did not at first register as the place he sought. But the Ban would have settled on this bar above all places, with its famous fountain that perpetually dripped water and cognac and a variety of white and red wines over sugar cubes, catering to every customer taste. Here at the fountain, the city's magi had met.

Sebastian wasn't sure what he had expected from The Opaline now. His feet had taken him there out of habit. The next step was less clear. He could picture the moonlit facade of Monsieur Philippe's elegant mansion, but he had never gone there by day. Surely it was in the Garden District, but he didn't actually know. Always it had been a first drink at The Opaline, then a ride in a sent carriage to the mansion.

What a child he had been, that youth fresh from the countryside with the wild dreams. He had wanted to shed the backwater superstitions of the bayous and conquer the world. He had known nothing and less than nothing.

The Garden District. Sebastian turned from the boarded-over bar, wondering if eyes were watching him even now, recognizing his return. Once he would have known. A single glass of absinthe would have heightened his senses where intention and action mingled like drips from the fountain to form the currents of the future. But no more. He had broken the spell of La Fee Verte, or so he hoped.

These days a horseless streetcar ran between the Quarter and the Garden District. All his mental images of Monsieur Philippe's mansion were shrouded in evening shadows, but he didn't trust himself in that place at night. He would take the streetcar now, this morning, and hope that daylight did not play foul with his recognition.

The streetcar came, taking him westward along Saint-Charles Avenue. The route was the same as by carriage, and he eyed the passing buildings with growing anxiety, waiting for one of them to trigger recognition. Turn here, he hoped to hear from one of the galleried mansions, but the call never came.

Finally, he exited the streetcar on the far edge of the Garden District to wander on his own. The streets were less clear in his memory. Some houses had the lacy wrought-iron galleries of the Quarter, while others boasted wooden porticoes and steep mansard roofs with dormer windows. Attic rooms for servants, one would think, or storerooms. At Monsieur Philippe's, the little rooms had been used by special guests with private needs. One had been reserved for him.

Up one street and down another—there was an almost hypnotic rhythm to his meandering. He stopped looking for conscious landmarks and began navigating by feel, letting his feet be drawn whither they would. In time, he found himself staring up at a narrow, arched dormer window lit by a flickering oil lamp, despite the daylight, and thought he saw himself peering down. A pale youth certainly. His eyes traveled down to the house itself, an Italianate mansion of cut stone and iron galleries nestled among the oaks and palms of a manicured yard. Near the iron gate was a great, waxy banana tree whose shape he remembered. This was the place.

He looked up to the attic window again, letting old, fuzzed memories surface and circle in his brain.

* * *

Years ago in that room, he lay on the cot unmoving, not knowing, not caring if the pounding was at the door or in his head. If only it would stop. Finally, it did. He drew a deep breath and slowly exhaled. Even without opening his eyes, he could sense that the day had come and gone without him.

The pounding came again, sending shards of pain into his brain.

"Get up, Sebastian!" someone yelled from the corridor. "Monsieur wants you. Get up!"

Sebastian's mind sluggishly supplied the identity—Arturo, Monsieur's mulatto steward. "Later!" he managed to yell back, though the effort split his head in two. "Leave me alone!"

The pounding stopped, and the steward moved off, muttering down the corridor. Sebastian gave a long sigh of relief. But the respite wouldn't last. With monumental effort, Sebastian cracked open an eye and stared blearily at the little attic room with its water-stained ceiling and dingy walls. It had never been intended as anything other than a storeroom, but that cold, leaky attic room with its bolt on the door bought him a little privacy.

The flapping of wings in the twilight.

Sebastian winced as fragments of an image surfaced. The dream again. Would he never be able to sleep without the visions? He pushed the memories away and resolved to get up.

Trying to open the other eye, he found it stuck shut. He hadn't cleaned off the kohl and rouge last night when he dragged himself up to his room. Amazing that he had remembered to bolt the door before he collapsed. Using the back of his green silk sleeve, he rubbed his cheeks and eyelids until the stickiness was gone. The shirt sleeve was ruined, of course, but that was Monsieur Philippe's problem, not his. When entertaining guests, the merchant routinely dressed him in green silk to enhance the drama of the absinthe and kohled his eyes to accentuate his exotic paleness.

Taking a deep breath, Sebastian pulled himself up off the cot and waited for the walls to stop spinning before trying to stand. At least he had reached his room this time. Half the time he never made it up the stairs.

His thoughts wandered back to the night before—what he could remember of it. Just a small ceremony of foreseeing for the family. Nothing to trigger the gut-wrenching sickness that followed the darker, more intense rituals of the assembled magi. Even so, the memories were ugly.

Crossing the room with sluggish steps, he pushed open the shutter to let the breeze dissipate the heavy air of the room. It was already evening again, and a smoky, fishy smell wafted in from the river. He peered over the rooftops at the early evening silhouetting the chimneys of the Garden District mansions and cursed all that he saw. He would die in this city of decadence, and maybe that was best for everybody.

He took a deep breath and forced the thoughts aside. He didn't want to think about his life. He didn't want to think, period. If he could move through his days numb and uncaring, it made things easier.

He considered putting aside the crumpled silk from last night's revelry for a more mundane coat and trousers of worsted wool. He could return to town, to his meager room at the university, and pretend that he was never coming back to this place. But the pretense never lasted. They always found him—how could they not? The white of his hair marked him. They found him and fed him the dark drink that forced the visions. They would never let him go.

The pounding came again at the door, this time accompanied by a sharp, "Sebastian! Our guests are arriving!" Monsieur Philippe himself.

Sebastian sighed and shuffled over to unbolt the door. He was used to obeying that voice. In the narrow corridor outside, Monsieur Philippe stood waiting in tie and tails, as though this evening were nothing more than a dinner party. His gray-tinged hair was slightly curled, his mustache, waxed and shiny. "Tonight is important, Sebastian," he said, his voice turning gentle as he drew Sebastian out into the corridor by the hand. "We've discussed how important this evening is."

There was always a measure of helplessness whenever he faced Monsieur Philippe. The man could make anything and everything sound reasonable. It was all a trick of the mind, of course, but Sebastian had no defense against the current of his voice as it rolled over him, drawing him down the stairs and into the evening's ceremony.

There were different degrees of visions, brought on by different combinations of the drink. The small ceremonies induced by dripping cognac over the sugar were almost tolerable. As Sebastian walked into the dining room, he saw that tonight was not to be a small ceremony.

The long table was bare except for a quilted pad in the center of the expanse of glossy mahogany. At each end stood a flickering silver candelabrum—the only light within the room. Half a dozen men waited around the table, their eyes assessing his colorless hair hungrily as he entered behind Monsieur Philippe. Also at the table was the older son Jean-Paul, Sebastian's erstwhile classmate at Tulane who had brought him into this circle. The rest of the family, Monsieur Philippe's wife and younger son, would be hovering somewhere close, perhaps the pantry. They, too, would be hungering for prophecy, even though the dining room circle was not a place for women and children this evening.

Monsieur Philippe moved to the sideboard to pour the absinthe into a heavy snifter and place the slotted spoon in position. Then he took up the engraved dagger that lay beside the snifter and slashed at his palm. Blood glittered darkly as it dropped onto the sugar and through the spoon. Then he wrapped a napkin around his hand to contain the bleeding and brought the drink to the table. "Come, Sebastian," he coaxed, swirling the snifter with its milky green-red contents. "It is time."

"Not blood," Sebastian cried, staring at the glass in horror. He had drunk many mixtures on these occasions, some exceedingly vile, but blood was the worst. He took a step backward.

Hands gripped him, dragging him up onto the quilted pad and pressing him down against the table holding him for the inevitable spasms to come. His mouth was forced open, and Monsieur Philippe tipped the glass against his unwilling lips.

The taste burned his mouth and turned his stomach.

"Prophesy, O Sibyl," Monsieur Philippe intoned. "By the blooded wormwood, show us the future . . ."

There was more, but Sebastian's head was already swimming. "Death and more death," he cried suddenly, though the vision was not yet upon him. These were his words only, brought to his lips by his own fears and frustrations. How he wanted to be quit of Monsieur Philippe and his circle, but it would never happen in any natural course of events.

"Dark wings descending in the twilight," Sebastian babbled, drawing the images from his own troubled dreams. "Dark wings bringing death for defiling a sibyl for your own base purposes. Even now I hear them coming, flapping in the darkness . . ."

He lost his focus as the images went wild behind his eyes. He could no longer understand his own words, though he knew he could hear himself babbling. His voice crescendoed to a scream and fell back, only to crescendo once more. Come, oblivion, he entreated silently. He wanted this night to be over.

Suddenly there was commotion around him. A gurgling shriek emerged from the throat of one man as he sank to the floor, frothy blood spraying from his mouth. He kept shrieking until he was dead in a pool of his own making. The hands holding Sebastian tight fell away as men scrambled away from the table. But still, he kept screaming prophecy at them.

He never knew how he had gotten home, but the next morning he had awakened, sick and shaking, to find himself back in his own rented room. He had spewed up bloody vomit all day, and when he was strong enough to run, he had taken the first train north.

* * *

When Sebastian came out of memories, he was leaning against the streetlight opposite the mansion. Time had passed, but it was still day and the same day. But his joints were still so he must have been standing there for hours. He gave a great sigh and forced himself to cross the street, seeing a curtain in the parlor twitch as he did so. Now they knew he was coming. Fine. Let them. Passing through the iron gate with practiced ease, he slowly climbed the steps to the portico.

On the stoop, all he could do was stare at the oaken door panels carved with leaves and roses. He was a fool to come here. There was nothing to gain by coming back to this place except pain.

The door creaked open. A lanky, terrified youth in green silk peeped out and beckoned Sebastian inside. Sebastian looked more closely. The hair wasn't white but very pale blond. Monsieur Philippe and his circle had made themselves another green sibyl, but they hadn't found a true albino this time. "What's your name, son?" he asked.

"Paddy, if you please, sir." With even those few words, the boy's Irish Channel accent came through. This one was drinking the blooded wormwood for money, no doubt.

"Paddy," Sebastian repeated. "Whatever they promised you, it isn't worth the cost to your soul. Have the dreams come yet—dark wings descending in the dusk?"

The boy started to tremble. "In the front parlor," he squeaked and hurried away.

Sebastian stared after him. Paddy was having the dreams. But would the warning have any impact? He shook his head and headed for the parlor. He walked a long hallway and turned to the right through a silken-hung doorway. Ashen faces stared back at him—the lady of the household, a younger son standing stiffly behind his mother's chair, the elder son who had seduced Sebastian into this darkness. Only Monsieur Philippe himself was missing.

The elder son, the treacherous Jean-Paul, stepped forward and suddenly went down on his knees. "Sibyl—Sebastian—spare us," he murmured. "We were foolish." His mother and younger brother nodded mutely.

Sebastian backed up unsteadily. "Monsieur Philippe?" he demanded. "Where is he?" The words fell harshly into the silence, their intensity surprising even Sebastian.

No one answered, but the lady gave a ragged groan and looked toward the next room, separated from the parlor by only a tapestry curtain.

Trembling, Sebastian stepped to the curtain and drew it back. Monsieur Philippe lay sprawled on the floor next to a toppled table, a cup in his hand, green foam on his lips. A decanter of green liquid lay overturned next to him, its pungent contents seeping into the carpet. Pure oil of wormwood, Sebastian noted numbly. So potent it was toxic. It was turning Monsieur Philippe's lips dark in death.

Sebastian stared at him, feeling nothing. No sweetness of vengeance, no release from old burdens. Nothing. In the man's other hand was clutched a folded note. He stooped, pried the paper from the clenched fingers, and unfolded it. The message was penned in Monsieur Philippe's precise hand: 'Let your wrath die with me, ange vengeur. Take whatever you will, but spare this household. Do not bring the rest to pass, I beg of you.'

The rest of what? Sebastian wondered. What all had he foretold that final, bloody night? And had he ever felt wrath? Or merely shame? He let the note flutter to the floor and returned to the parlor. Jean-Paul was still on his knees.

"Take this as a token of our penance," Jean-Paul cried, offering up a heavy box of gold twenty-dollar pieces. "And this." He held out a casket of jewelry.

There was more, but Sebastian didn't wait. He had to get out of that absinthe-scented shrine of death. He stumbled down the hall and out the door. The whole encounter had been ghoulish—the pasty-faced family sitting quietly while the master of the house drank poison in the next room. The offerings of gold and jewels. They truly feared the monster they had made of him.

What had he prophesied that last night nine years ago to terrify them so? The sibyl rising up to cleanse the city of his abusers? So he had said, but it had been a lie. The blood had made him desperate.

Sebastian increased his pace, unable to abide the deadly charade this had become. Then he turned abruptly. There was one bit of cleansing he actually could do, what he had intended to do since the beginning. He walked back to Monsieur Philippe's house, slipped inside, and went directly up the back stairs to the attic. In his old dingy cell, he found Paddy huddled in a corner.

"Please don't kill me, sir," Paddy murmured as Sebastian approached. Just a touch of bittersweet licorice on his breath. "Or else do it quickly."

Sebastian saw himself huddled on the floor, kohled and fogged. He grabbed Paddy by the arm and hauled him to his feet. "It's ended. Leave now and you have a chance at life. Stay and you shall die." Another forced prophecy, but Paddy needed to hear it in those terms.

Paddy's eyes grew huge. "But the debts—"

"There's gold in the front parlor. It should cover your debts. Now get ready."

He waited while Paddy changed into street clothes, and then walked him through the house to collect the box of gold coins. The ashen family stared up at him unspeaking as he took the casket. "This ends here," he told them. He prayed that was true.

At the street, Sebastian handed the gold to Paddy. "You've got one chance," he said. "Never come back, never look back. In time the dreams will fade." Paddy still looked confused, but nodded and ran off down the block.

Sebastian turned down Saint-Charles, not minding the distance on foot back to the Creole Quarter. He needed to think. The green sibyls had all fled and perhaps no one remained with the skill to make another. No more blooded wormwood and no more deaths—that much, at least, he hoped for.

But he had lied to Paddy. The dreams would never completely fade.

ONE HUNDRED AND ONE

By Corrine Phillips

I awoke in a cold sweat. My bed sheets twisted and wound tight around me as though I was some giant caterpillar waiting to break free from my chrysalis and emerge a butterfly. I didn't feel like a butterfly, I was far too heavy to take flight. I was a bag of bricks, leaving a thick imprint of perspiration on my bed. The ceiling fan spun slowly, menacingly, from the steady musty breeze that blew in through the open window from the street. I heard voices outside and the piercing tones of car horns and Dixieland bands playing on corners for crumpled dollars. The shadows beginning to form on the walls danced a slow waltz to welcome the day's twilight hour. What time was it? 6:30? 7:00? Had I slept the entire day away? My vision was blurred; spotty and wavy, like when you rub your eyes too hard in the middle of a long, tiring day and see blasts of Technicolor fireworks and dots. My heart was pounding so loudly that I could hear it in my head, and the damp stench that covered my pillow was matted onto my dirty hair.

My god. What a hangover. How did this happen?

I remembered having one beer while sitting on some driftwood watching the bullfrogs out in the swamp. I watched their bloated little bodies comically jockey for position on lily pads, and scour the weeds for insects. I remembered feeling hypnotized and relieved by the sounds; the hums and buzzes, the moss swaying from the gnarled cypresses in the breeze. The months leading up to my moment of clarity weren't great. I drank a lot and was caught in a cloud of oppressive anxiety. The death of my grandmother hit like a ton of bricks, sending me into a sad spiral of monotony and complete depression. I was emerging slowly from that dark pit, though. I had stopped drinking all day and felt healthier, and the vulnerable sadness was slowly leaving. I was instead intoxicated by the quiet and solitude the swamp gave. It became the perfect place of solace to decompress before work and whatever other miserable things the following day might throw at me.

Work.

I fumbled with the covers, trying to desperately untangle myself in a panic while staring at the blinking red light on the answering machine across the room. My body seemed fused to the damp sheets, sticky from sweat and heavy. I crawled to the light.

My boss's voice spoke on the tape. "Where are you? It's 10 am. Get here now."

The ticking clock on the wall read 7:12 pm. I picked up the phone, my thumb feebly pressing the glowing buttons, but before my finger pressed the fourth number, my body was flooded with a wave of terrible nausea. Heaving chest, watery mouth. I tried to stand, to make my way to the bathroom, but my legs wouldn't support the seemingly dead weight that was my body. Instead, I grabbed anything nearby to be sick in; the large decorative vase adorned with silk foxgloves my mother had given me to help "spruce up the place." I hurriedly pulled out the fake flowers and used it for its new purpose.

The surroundings of my tiny dim apartment were bleak; curtains drawn, dishes piled in the sink that I had meant to do days ago. The television was on local news. For a moment I envied the sharp dressed weather man blabbering on about the stifling New Orleans humidity. He was tan and smiling, standing in an air conditioned studio in front of a green screen adorned with cartoon suns wearing sunglasses, sipping cartoon lemonade. He was happy and doing his job. I, on the other hand, sat in the middle of the floor, pathetic, sweating profusely, and desecrating a fancy gift my mother was kind enough to give me.

There was no point in trying to speak to my boss now. The day was over; he was home in his comfortable cavern of solitude, cursing the idiot who failed to show up on a busy Friday. When I was able to finally contain the sickness, I crawled to the bathroom; the cold shock of tile on my scraped knees felt like a million tiny ice picks, all gouging away at my legs. As I hoisted myself up slowly with the aid of the sink, I stared at my reflection in the mirror. Whatever illness was plaguing my battered body presented itself explicitly on my haggard face. I was pale, practically transparent, and for a moment I became entranced with the thought of counting the maze of uneven lines of teal that pulsed beneath my skin. Tiny legions of burst blood vessels speckled the dark blue hollows around my eyes, and a trail of yellow bruises adorned my jaw. Thankfully, I hadn't shaved in a few days so some of it was at least semi-hidden.

Clusters of blood-filled blisters, or boils, covered my chin and made their way down the tender skin of my neck. Faint lines around my throat, were they fingerprints or nail marks? I must have gotten into a fight. I hadn't fought for years, never felt it necessary, and I was no longer a pompous school boy, but a decent adult. Regardless, no fight had ever left me this bruised and mangled. I definitely lost. I looked like absolute hell: some wretched animal that crawled out of the deepest depth of some devil swamp or dark abyss that knows not the light of day.

I stood staring at the thing staring back at me for what seemed like ages. The eyes seemed to not belong to me; the usual bluish green irises were now two dark and morbid pools of tar, vacant and chilling me to the bone. My apartment grew darker, the sun was setting, and my nausea began to subside. I walked around slowly and decided I was starting to feel better, that this would not be one of those debilitating two-day hangovers where I'd curse the thought of ever touching another glass of alcohol. I decided to dress and head to the pharmacy for some pain pills before closing time. I washed my face, grabbed a shirt hanging on the bathroom doorknob and put it over my head. As I pulled it down my torso, I winced in pain. My back was on fire. I slowly lifted up the fabric and stretched my neck to look in the mirror. My skin was red and raw, bloodied and torn, covered in long thick gashes. My heart pounded.

"My God…I'm never drinking again." The color was starting to come back in my cheeks. I sighed in relief, threw on a hat and sunglasses, sprayed a cloud of cologne in a quick attempt to mask the horrid stench that was exuding from my pores, and headed out the door, hoping I didn't draw attention to my unfavorable countenance. I was in no state to be anywhere near people, especially people I knew.

The air outside was dense, thick with the scents of sweet olive and the festering musty sewer; the good with the bad, always. I felt a strange exhilaration the longer I walked, taking notice of the sleepy sunset. The sky was shimmering gold and speckled with purple and pink cotton candy clouds. A storm was coming. My heart was beating wildly, lively, excitedly. The French Quarter was full of tourists and citizens alike, all meandering on the crowded sidewalks, stopping to throw a dollar in hats that belonged to street performers. The sound of upbeat jazz in full swing, men spitting into their brass mouthpieces and sending shrill baritone and trumpet notes into the atmosphere. Everything was alive around me, completely bloated with energy and sweat, upset stomachs, and sunburned shoulders. People laughed and screamed, spilling beer-filled cups down chins and stained white t-shirts. I was a member of that summer night, swimming in the belly of the beast, afloat in the middle of a sea of excess that is New Orleans.

I arrived at the store and opted for a bottle of little red and white capsules to take care of the remains of my headache. The walk did me a world of good, and I felt thankful to be up and about. I decided an even longer walk would do more good, and instead of going the same direction home, I kept to the path I was on. I counted my steps, and I thought of the night before. It was still so incredibly fuzzy, and only slight unimportant details flooded my mind: a mosquito I slapped from my arm that still managed to drink a few drops of blood, the mud on my shoelaces, the single beer I carried in my cooler with a few sodas and a sandwich, the ripples on the water, and the sense of serenity it gave me.

As I walked, I thought about missing work and wondered if I even still had a job. I didn't know. I didn't know how I ended up bloodied and bruised in my bed. I didn't know if someone attacked me, or if I fell. I didn't know why my back was covered in deep scratches and scrapes, or if I should have gone to a hospital, or whose eyes I was staring at in the bathroom mirror. There was no recollection, and I was almost terrified at the thought of not really caring. I thought of Grandmother, who at the ripe old age of one-hundred and one had decided it was her time to die. I felt selfish for missing her so much. She would have hated seeing me bruised, broken, and sad over the inevitable. I wondered how she managed to live so long, how she remained so optimistic and carefree even when life got tough. I owed it to her to be a good person, and to enjoy the life I was given.

The walk seemed to be having an effect on me. The farther I went, the happier I became, euphoric even. My vision was crisp and clear, and every smell from the surrounding streets permeated my senses. I was alive. The tiny hairs on my arms and the back of my neck exuded electricity, and with each passing moment of the setting sun, I felt it. I felt the rush.

I finally stopped at the corner of Basin Street and found myself staring at the gloomy white wall that guarded the City of Ghosts, St. Louis Cemetery Number One. I hadn't ventured in since I was a young kid, usually with friends who looked forward to the possibility of seeing a ghost, or sometimes my grandmother. She enjoyed visiting the tomb of Marie Laveau, bringing with her tiny crystals and old lipstick containers, or a sample sized bottle of whiskey to place at its door as an offering for the Voodoo Queen. I didn't believe in Voodoo, or ghosts, or any otherworldly beings that are said to prowl the city at night, but I always enjoyed the stories. They're important, I suppose; that fear of monsters keeps you semi-honest and good, and the sense of the unknown keeps you humble. I realized that perhaps we needed the superstitions and cautionary tales of supernatural creatures living under our beds, otherwise, we'd have no good stories to tell. I decided to walk in, spend some time with the dead, and revel in the quiet.

The last bit of color faded from the sky, and the moon loomed large, bright and shimmering, as though it were a giant spotlight illuminating the gray roofs of century-old mausoleums. The air quieted as soon as I passed through the gates. The cemetery at night does that; it turns off the outside world, muffles the sound of car horns and sidewalk talk, creating a veil of emptiness where all that is to be heard are the inhales of the living, and the exhales of the dead. My damp shoes trudged on through the paths of muddied puddles and broken shells from The Mississippi and Ponchartrain. Through the rows of dead and iron fences, each little gray sanctuary housing the bodies of people that, at one time, could only imagine what death was like. I wondered if they finally understood the meaning of it all: life, pain, love, and death. I selfishly wished they would let me know.

I almost understood, then, why the living felt the need to ask the Voodoo Queen questions, and I couldn't help but wonder if she ever answered any of them. Did Marie know the answers? Was there really magic? Was there an alternate world where things we couldn't comprehend lurked in the shadows? I began thinking of my grandmother and all of her superstitions; how she burned her hair trimmings instead of simply throwing them away, so birds wouldn't use them for nests and cause her to go mad, or when she refused to leave a house by a different door from which she entered because it would cause bad luck. I'd listen to her at night, telling me stories about the lonely ghosts staring out to sea from lighthouse towers, or the vampires roaming the French Quarter searching for unsuspecting victims. There were monsters in the forests and bayous, great shape-shifting man-eating creatures, secluded back roads where deformed villages of people lived in the deep shadows and only ventured out at night to feed on the blood of cows and goats. There were witches and chupacabras, lake monsters, demons, all cavorting and clamoring in some netherworld between the living and the dead, waiting to frighten whoever was unfortunate enough to cross their paths, or who didn't believe in them to begin with. She had a story to tell about everything, each one stranger than the last, and sometimes I wondered why she believed in such things.

The dim streetlights outside the walls guided me through the maze of graves, my shadow passing in and out of corners, through narrow walkways, tripping over bricks from deteriorated tombs. A candle was glowing ahead, flickering in the wind, reflecting Mardi Gras beads and dew on wilted flower petals. An entire wasteland of dirty costume jewelry and objects glistened in the light: the offerings to Laveau. I marveled at the damp folded papers, wishes written to her ghost. There were empty mint containers, soda cans, half-full whiskey bottles, articles of clothing, hair barrettes, squished candy bars and rotten fruit, painted shells and stones. A graveyard of treasures and junk. I stared at the X's marked on the walls, some etched lightly, painted with markers or red and pink lipstick; others forcefully carved and jagged, rife with desperation and a small glimmer of hope. I had never left a token there, but I reached into my pocket and tossed the tiny bottle of pain pills onto the muddy earth: my offering, my curiosity and hope to understand that other world that is supposedly invisible to the naked eye. I stood for a moment, and then decided it was time to head home.

I made my way back slowly, content and rather tired. The lazy southern wind suddenly presented an odd chill, and I felt the need to put my hands in my pockets. The glow of the moon began to dim, clouds moving in slowly, creating a foreboding gloom. My head began to throb, first a slow nagging pressure then a pounding so great that I could hear my heartbeat in my ears. My eyes twitched; I felt the nerves pulsing and jumping wildly, as though they were desperately attempting to burst through my skull and out of my eye sockets. A wave of terror flooded my mind, and sheer panic became the only emotion I knew. I stopped dead in my tracks, put my hands on my knees and bent down gasping for air; cowering, and unable to catch my breath. I forgot the cemetery. I forgot the moonlight. My ears rang, like an endless siren blaring inside my head. There was no more quiet and calm. All I knew was fear.

I remembered the previous night in flashes: the swamp, the scent of moss, the cypress trees. I watched the sunset, gold and beautiful. It was dark when I stood to leave. I was tired, looking forward to my comfortable bed. I killed another mosquito and cursed myself for forgetting bug spray. I tripped over my shoe lace, sighed and bent to tie it, mud collecting under my fingernails with each loop. I recalled the blood rushing to my head while squinting in the dark as I tied my shoe, making me dizzy. The tree frogs chirped, while bullfrogs jumped into the murky water, the sound of their slimy bodies breaking the surface. Something rustled behind me, but I ignored it. Suddenly everything went quiet, no buzz nor hum of insects, no breeze or movement, just dead silence. I stood up straight.

Something wasn't right. Something was watching me. I felt its stare crawl up my neck. My face grew hot. I checked my pocket for my flashlight. I must have left it in the car. Darkness pervaded my senses, the dim light of the moon beckoned with a sense of urgency, a forceful and nagging warning to follow its light, to start walking away, to run.

My mind was between the past and present simultaneously, kneeling in cemetery mud with my head in my hands, and the night before, in the swamp and in fear. My stomach churned, twitching, attempting to expel the great mass of horror that was growing inside it. My back began to burn, the broken skin searing in pain. I fell to my knees in agony. I remembered running from something in the swamp, and it chasing me down, its heavy growling breath and heaving lungs swiftly trailing behind me. I wasn't fast enough.

As I lay twisting and convulsing on the hallowed ground, I thought of my grandmother again. I was young, a boy of maybe ten or eleven, tucked in bed with a sore throat and a mug of tea steaming on the bedside table. I was bored from the flu, and the only thing I looked forward to every day that week was for the sun to finally set and make the room dark, so I could grab my flashlight and create shadow shows on the wall. I would act out the *Three Little Pigs*, contorting my fingers to create the shape of that big bad wolf, and she would laugh at my theatrics while she rocked in her chair.

That night I wanted to hear a story, preferably a scary one; something about ghosts haunting houses, or the undead lurking in the shadows on Halloween night. She urged me to close my eyes, said that a child shouldn't listen to tales of horror before drifting off to sleep. I kept begging. I was brave and unafraid of anything because my mother always told me that monsters weren't real. Grandma just loved telling scary stories because she had a vivid imagination. The poem she recited didn't matter then, and I at the time I had thought, disappointingly, that the story about the three pigs and the wolf was scarier, but the words suddenly echoed between the current fear and desperation in my mind:

> *"When the moon hangs low,*
> *and the dark sky turns blue*
> *stay away from the swamp,*
> *don't even pass through,*
> *It'll follow you closely,*
> *see all that you do,*
> *A one-hundred and one day curse,*
> *will be passed onto you,*
> *You can scream, you can cry,*
> *but whatever you do,*
> *Beware the red eyes,*
> *Beware the Rougarou.*
> *If your body is changed,*
> *the only solution for you,*
> *is to find an unbeliever,*
> *and make him a Rougarou, too."*

My neck pulsed, my tendons and joints stretched and buckled. My bones were breaking apart, crunching and twisting violently, and the pores of my skin felt like they were sprouting tiny sharp knives. I stood and screamed a horrible guttural sound that rose from the pit of my stomach. I heard my grandmother's voice repeating the words:

"Beware the Rougarou."

I remembered the eyes, glowing red in the darkness. I was transfixed as the thing held me by the throat, lifting my body by my neck, the flesh of my back tearing against the bark of a tree. I tried to close my eyes, but could only stare.

"Beware the Rougarou."

Somewhere beneath that-face of a wolf, the sharp pointed teeth and dirty black hair and the scent of blood and death on its breath, lived something hopeless and scared, urgent and sympathetic.

"Beware the Rougarou."

I screamed and cried, my heart raced, pumping frantically and faster than it ever had before. I couldn't move, and I thought it was going to crush my throat as it held me a few feet above the ground against the tree. Its claws dug and burned cuts into the delicate skin of my neck. I felt the heat from its body, like an oven turned on the highest setting, like the burning fires of Hell.

"Beware the Rougarou."

Then everything went dark.

I stood hunched over in pain, but towered over the tombs, my body gigantic and heaving, transforming, stretching, frantic, and feeling an insatiable thirst for blood or reprieve. Power coursed through my veins. My body was the myth, my brain the reality. My fingers long, fingernails replaced with thick, sharp claws, my clothes reduced to shards of dirty fabric lying in the mud. The cemetery candles flickered and the fireflies danced in the moonlight. The night grew darker, and I heard thunder rumbling in the distance. I collapsed there once again and dreamed of a great bird pulling out strands of my dirty hair.

* * *

I wait in the swamp now. I feed on whatever unlucky animal I find, silently stalking or waiting for them to cross my path, and slowly fall deeper and deeper into permanently becoming what I am: a beast with a thirst that is never quenched. I wait, feeling the nagging dread of my time running out with each sunset and moon rise. I have only thirty-one days left to find some unsuspecting eyes, a soul to curse with this horrendous affliction, otherwise, I am doomed to walk as this wretched thing forever. I'm growing accustomed to the darkness. It consumes more of my being with each passing moment. Memories are leaving me. I can no longer clearly remember the sound of smooth jazz on a summer night, or the feeling of peacefully drifting off to sleep in a comfortable bed. I am no longer among the lively sidewalks and celebrations, or life as I knew it to be.

Instead, I am a part of the undiscovered world that creeps in the shadows. Everything exists here, as my grandmother always said; the ghosts and magic, demons and vampires, the monsters hiding beneath beds and in closets, the sharp fangs, and claws, and any other ungodly thing the dark recesses of your mind can conjure up. It is best that you proceed with caution on dark nights, for we will always be watching, waiting for you.

Never scoff at the darkness.

Never disregard the warnings.

If you feel brave or refuse to believe me, I invite you to meet me in the swamp under the bright light of the moon. I will follow you while you remain unaware and brave. You will not hear me; I will never make my presence known until I decide it is the right time. I'll catch you off guard. I will be the slight snap of a twig that your own foot didn't break, or a strange whisper or hollow moan floating on the breeze. You'll feel the goose bumps begin to rise on the back of your neck. Your throat will choke back the slightest whisper. You'll catch a glimpse of my dark shadow when you turn your head quickly and mistakenly believe your eyes are playing tricks on you. You'll see mine glowing red, and you will not be able to look away. I won't let you.

So please, I'd love to meet you, and hurry. I'm running out of time.

FIRES OF APRIL

By Jonathan D. Nichols

Her eyes shot open. She jolted up, sitting and staring. The stars twinkled in the black sky, the crescent moon barely a sliver. She gasped. Her dried throat felt like it cracked as she inhaled. She clutched at her neck, liquid slipping between her fingers, oozing, trickling. She held her hands in front of her face, saw the dark thick fluid, and she screamed; the sound came out hoarse and raspy. She searched her throat, stroking with her fingers, looking for the wound, finding nothing.

Placing her hands on the ground, the thin grass sticking out between her fingers, she pushed herself up. Slender green blades of zoysia clung to the sticky red glue covering her palms. Small stone houses stood around her, stretched in a long row. She looked between two and saw more going out in either direction. Names above the doors to each were worn and aged; dates, from birth to death—homes for the dead.

She tripped over something soft, lumpy on top of the grass and dirt, and plummeted. She rolled off, landed with her face staring back at it, and she gasped.

The body lay like a dismembered mannequin, bloody stumps from the missing limbs marking the grass and dirt in dark scarlet. She turned from the corpse—what remained of it, leaning between two of the mausoleums, and vomited. The stomach acid against her already raw throat was unbearable.

Walking amongst the burial chambers, she kept her back to the gory remains. The wind tossed her auburn hair; several strands hung straight, weighted by coagulating plasma clinging to it in gel-like clumps. Turning her head in either direction, looking amongst the graves, she saw an arm resting in the grass. She hurried, past another arm and a leg. Straight ahead, beckoning to her, open and waiting, stood the gated archway marking the exit. Something swung in the wind beneath it, centered and dangling. She approached slowly, cautiously. It was round, and she knew even before she knew. Blonde hair stretched up, tied to the twists of black metal above. Eyes stared wide, terrified and tortured. The mouth dropped open in a silent scream. She knew the face, although her memories did not come back completely. Everything was a blur, and then she realized. Andrea. Her name is Andrea. They were friends, but she couldn't recall any details beyond this—nothing. Just the name. And her own name…what was it? Amber? Ariel? No. It was April. *She* was April.

She ran through the gate, the words *Lafayette Cemetery No. 1* stretched across the wrought iron arch in large gray letters. Cars lined the street outside. She turned right, ran past a restaurant with darkened windows. Headlights approached the upcoming intersection. She ran toward them. Red and blue lights rested atop the vehicle. April screamed out.

"Help! Help me!"

He stopped, and for a moment she wondered if he'd continue on. The car turned toward her.

"Oh, thank Christ."

He got out of the car, looked her up and down, and un-holstered his gun. He pointed it at her, arms outstretched, ready to fire.

"Hands where I can see them." She held both up.

"Andrea…she's de…I just woke up in there. I don't know what happened, how I got there. But she's dead. She's…Oh God, she's in pieces. She's in fucking pieces."

He kept the barrel pointed at her.

"Show me."

"They hung her head from the…"

She froze. The gate stood in front of her. Nothing dangled beneath.

"It was just there." Her voice wasn't much louder than a whisper. She ran beneath the black iron. She kept straight. It lay just up ahead. She stopped. She'd gone too far. Turning around, she looked to see where it should have been. The officer stopped and stared at the ground.

"Where's the body?"

"It was here somewhere. Oh God, that means somebody—"

The officer screamed. A dismembered arm tore away at his chest, digging into his flesh. The fingers burrowed fast, blood spurting, seeping from his ribcage. The man's heart lay clutched in the fingers of the arm before April could fathom what had happened.

Something gripped her ankle and jerked her leg behind her. Her head cracked on the edge of a mausoleum, shooting pain through her skull. Soft dirt pressed against her cheek, her arm, her side, and she shut her eyes, only for a second.

When she opened them again, it was gone. The officer, the arm, the blood—nothing was there. A voice laughed, deep and harsh. A man stood on one of the roofs, not visible except for a silhouette against the starry sky behind him. The wind blew, and braided strands of dreadlocks moved with the breeze. He held a stick...no, a cane, in his right hand, his fingers wrapping around the middle and stretching it outwards. He jumped forward and landed on the ground in front of her. He smiled, teeth shining bright against his dark skin. He bent and grabbed her ankles, a hard and firm grip. She kicked at him. He pulled and dragged her. She struggled to sit up, but the moment she did, he slammed the end of his walking stick onto the top of her head.

When she awoke, she was on her back staring up at the night sky. Four walls of earth enclosed her. Something dropped onto her legs. Again. Then again. Particles trickled down her sides. Her hands were bound at the wrists, her feet at the ankles. She screamed. Dirt fell onto her head. It went down her throat. She coughed and choked; bile wanted to come up from her stomach. The dirt fell onto her eyes. Another shovelful. Her face was covered. She couldn't breathe. She couldn't move.

She flung the blanket off her head, her hands finally free. She coughed and bent over to vomit. Mucus came out. The dirt. She could still taste the dirt. What dirt? Why would she be tasting dirt? She sat up, her sudden terror of suffocating now a disconcerting thought. What was that dream? The details fled her memory the harder she tried to recall them.

She sat up on her bed—not her bed. It was her friend's. She hadn't visited Danielle in years. Now she was spending the night at her house. Why was she here? She got up and walked out of the bedroom. Danielle sat on the sofa watching television.

"Hey, sleepyhead," said Danielle. "How are you feeling?"

"Dani, this is going to sound weird, but how did I end up sleeping on your guest bed?"

"I told you I wasn't going to let you stay in a hotel."

"No, I mean, why am I here?"

"Um...are you talking about Andrea?"

A vague recollection formed in her head—a funeral. Andrea, one of her best friends since grade school, had...had died in a car accident? Memories didn't make any sense to her.

"I'm talking crazy. I'm sorry. Still somewhat asleep."

"Want some coffee?"

"Yeah, I need some."

April stood staring at the wall, at the photographs hanging there. Some showed Danielle's family—parents, her brother, her boyfriend—but the one she focused on showed three women, arms around one another, smiling. Andrea stood in the middle with shoulder-length dirty-blonde hair; her brown eyes and big smile always brought comfort. Dani stood to the left, long dark hair reaching the middle of her back. It had always been straight and shimmery, so beautiful. April's hair, auburn and wavy, hung past her shoulders. She smiled big at the camera, her deep green eyes almost a distraction amongst the group.

Inseparable since second grade, thirty-nine years old now. Their lives were intertwined for almost as long as she could remember. She'd moved away to Texas for a job while they remained in Louisiana, but they still spoke all the time, still shared every aspect of their lives, still remained like sisters. It felt wrong for one of the trio to be missing. It *was* wrong.

When had this happened? When had Andrea died? She would do anything for these two women, and they would have done the same for her. Just thinking about the loss, regardless of how confusing the thought became, caused an ache to form in her chest. The calendar on the wall had days marked off. Only one remained for this month—March 31. The funeral was tomorrow, on April Fool's Day.

She took her cup and stepped outside. Danielle had a patio swing with purple cushions facing the street. Down the road, walking with a limp and using a cane to assist him, a man with incredibly dark skin stepped slowly, steadily; she sat and found herself staring, watching him. Dreadlocked hair hung in his face, strands swaying with each step. He stopped in front of the house, turned to look at her, and waved. She nodded, and he walked toward her. Something about him creeped her out. He moved closer, his presence giving off an aura, a foreboding sense of unexplainable fear.

The man halted a few feet in front of her, bent forward, and stared into her sparkling jade eyes. She leaned away, preparing to throw hot coffee in his face. His warm breath stank like rotten eggs. Reaching into his gray jacket, stained with dirt, he pulled out a small object and dangled it in her face—a little rag doll with red hair. The eyes were green dots, and on the center of its nose was a light freckle, the same as her own.

"You know this isn't real, chère."

His voice was almost demonic. It bored into her mind, a verbal drill into her consciousness, pulling her from false reality. The daylight dimmed and disappeared. The air grew thick and heavy, the smells of death and rot surrounding her and filling her nose and lungs. She pulled her arms, stretched above her head, and found them bound with a cord which dug into her skin, strands of twine scratching her wrists and hands. The same was with her ankles.

"Don't pull too hard, girl. Wouldn't want to lose nothin'." The footsteps approached, accompanied by the clunk of the cane. The man stood over her, held up a fist, and released the pieces of a doll—arms, legs, head, and body. "Not like your friend did."

The light inside the dank room flickered; candles surrounded her and bordered the walls.

"What do you want?"

"Why, your life, chère. And I'm sorry to say this, but it's gonna hurt."

He held up a knife with a wooden handle, strange markings carved into the surface.

"Shit."

April pulled her arms with all her strength. The cord held tight, digging so far into her skin she thought she'd rip off her hand. She didn't stop, the pain racing down her arms, her hands so cold and numb, feeling dead, the skin probably a deep blue tint. It cut her. Blood seeped from between the cord and her wrist. The pain, the insurmountable pain, meant nothing if she were to die within seconds. Almost as though fate saw her plight and decided to offer assistance, the unexpected occurred—the cord snapped. She rolled and his blade grazed her side. Blood soaked her shirt, but she was alive. She fell, her weight knocking over the box on which she lay. The lid fell off and a skeleton in a gray suit stared out with the holes in its skull. The jawbone broke off.

The fall had broken the cord on her ankles. Her legs were free from the coffin but still secured together. He came after her, the knife in his hand moving fast. She crawled, and it stabbed her calf. She screamed. The blood oozed from the slit along her leg, the wound distracting her from the syringe he jabbed into her arm before depressing the plunger.

* * *

April entered the store with Danielle and Andrea. The small silver bell hanging from a rope jingled when they walked through. The store smelled of incense; the air was smoky and warm.

"I feel so weird coming in here."

"Come on. I've passed this place so many times and always wanted to check it out," said Andrea. "Now I have a reason to."

"I don't need a stupid voodoo love spell. I don't feel right messing with that stuff."

"Let's just browse what they have here."

"If you want to attract your soul mate, I got the binding love spell that would do the trick." A deep voice carried across the room, flowing with the smoke, mysterious and hidden. It came from everywhere and from nowhere. The girls looked around.

"If you had somebody in mind that broke your heart, I can give you a spell for that as well. I call it the 'get back your man' spell."

Danielle smiled. "I might need that."

"We're fine," said April. "You know it's kind of creepy that we can't see you."

"I'm not hiding," said the voice, this time from a definite location. The man stood there, a huge grin on his face, his bone white teeth flashing brilliantly in contrast with his almost black skin. "So why'd you come to a voodoo spell shop if you have no interest?"

"*She* wanted to come here," said April, gesturing to her blonde friend.

"This kind of stuff creeps you out, don't it?"

"I just don't have an interest."

"I get it," he said. "Probably raised Christian, probably see stuff like spells and potions as evil. We all got our beliefs. If I can't sell you something, at least let me offer some tea. It'll soothe your nerves, help you feel relaxed."

The girls looked at one another; April's face was cautious.

"At least try a cup. Herbal, that's all, Nothin' with voodoo or spells. It's good for stress relief."

He poured the hot water into three small teacups over the leaves. Before sipping, they looked at one another for approval. April shook her head.

"It's ok," the man said as he took all three cups from them and poured these back into the kettle. Steam hissed and billowed out from the top like a smoke bomb. A sensation of euphoria overtook their minds, and all three blacked out.

* * *

The unsteady light didn't help her blurry vision. She knew that last memory had to be a real one. The graveyard, Andrea's car accident, none of that happened, had it? She didn't know anymore. The coffin rested on a table. She was still inside a mausoleum, that much was true. Was Andrea dead? What had happened to Danielle?

Tied to a wall, this time with much thicker ropes, she stared into the dark, trying to see everything. A figure to her right stood still. The hair—the long straight hair. Danielle. Arms outstretched, bound the same as her own, the woman remained unconscious. To her left, ropes hung, but no body. No sign of Andrea. Markings painted on that wall dripped a pool onto the floor. She studied the ropes. They were stained red. Smears of crimson decorated the walls. Andrea was dead, of this she was certain.

The man stood and walked from the back corner of the room. A dark blanket lay spread out on the floor, several jars and vials set out in a row on it. He took a ceramic bowl from this arrangement and whispered something she didn't understand. Dipping his fingers into the bowl, he drew on her forehead with blood. He chanted, murmured, his voice so deep it sounded like thunder grumbling, eyes rolled up into his head so that only the whites shone.

"Fuck you and your ritual."

She spat into his face. His eyes snapped back, and he stared at her with the blackest irises she'd ever seen. Setting down the bowl, he wiped his fingers off and picked up the doll—her doll. He gripped the left hand and crushed it. A crack echoed in the room, and she screamed.

"I'm…" she groaned, barely audible. April took a deep breath, closed her eyes, and blocked out the pain. "I'm going to rip your eyes out." Her words came out in an explosion, a forced scream. She glared with fiery hatred that seemed to match her red hair. "Going to claw them out with my fingers."

He touched the dolls other hand, smiled his taunting grin, and squeezed. Her fingers compressed, her bones shattered in her hands, and she shrieked. His smile disappeared. His eyes went white again, and he continued his chant, turning toward the coffin on which the knife rested.

The torment in her hands, like lightning jolting through her arms, nearly blocked out all thoughts of anything else. He would turn around, he would carve her with the knife, she would bleed, and she would die. There was no escape. She'd never untie the ropes now, not without the use of her fingers. Her knees crumbled for just a second as she gave into her desperation. When her hands pressed against the ropes, they slipped, just partially, but the pain was horrendous.

She gritted her teeth, squeezed her eyes shut, and dropped her full weight against the ropes. The shock sent blinding agony across her body, but her broken hands slid through. The man didn't turn around. He continued his low volume repetition.

A candle burned to her right. She crept toward this, reaching out both arms, her hands a mangled mass of fingers. She pressed her forearms against the sides of the hot cylinder and brought this over to her feet. Melted black wax spilled from the concave puddle surrounding the wick. She held her legs over it. Without enough slack to coordinate her position, she touched her ankles to the fire. It blistered her skin, licking up the outer epidermis layers, tasting these and burning them away. The scent of her own flesh cooking and burning wafted to her nostrils. She cried out, and her captor turned, fuming. The fire touched her ropes, fibers transforming into glowing embers. She pulled and these snapped apart. He lunged at her, carrying his knife, and she kicked the candle at him. It knocked over one of the vials, and flames rapidly spread across the blanket.

He jumped out of the way and walked around the fire. He ran at her. She didn't flee. She watched the knife. He held it in his right hand. Heat radiated from the blanket. She kept to his left and lunged forward when he reached her, aiming for the fire. He fell over backward; she landed on top of him and rolled away fast. He screamed, his clothes, hair, and skin ablaze.

"Danielle." She ran to her friend, still not awake or aware. "Danielle. Dani. Wake up." She nudged her, shaking her as best as she could with her injuries. Danielle stirred.

"What? Where…Holy shit!"

"I've got to get you out of here."

April couldn't touch the ropes. Her hands, her distorted fingers, had no use in their condition. The knife. Where was the knife? She turned around as the man ran at her, a human fireball. She kicked him, her adrenaline level so high she didn't feel the burn on the bottom of her foot. He fell over and the knife dropped in front of her. Without hesitation, she knelt and gripped the handle in her teeth. Danielle took it from her, twisted her hand, and sliced through the ropes using a sawing motion. The fire spread. Time ran short.

"Try to hurry. I can't help you, but I won't leave you."

"I got it," her friend called out as she pulled her hand loose. April turned to look at the voodoo man once more. He lay motionless, his skin flaking away, revealing an ash-covered skeleton beneath.

"I'm free," said Danielle.

Both women stared at the door. It was a flaming trap. There was no way out.

"Now what?"

"Fuck this," said April. "If we were meant to die, we wouldn't have made it this far." She looked into Danielle's eyes. "Roll on the ground as soon as we're outside."

She pushed her friend forward, and both ran at the door. They burst through, catching the flames while escaping the tiny monument. The fire on Danielle's clothes extinguished almost immediately as she turned over frantically on the ground. April caught fire and screamed in panic when it didn't extinguish from her efforts. Danielle ran toward her, smothering the flames as well as she could. Before the fire caused damage beyond her clothing, the rain fell. It came down in a torrent, immediately dowsing all cause for injury.

Both women stood and stared at the fiery home for the dead. It stood isolated from the rest. Despite the rain, the sun peeked over the horizon as morning approached. The shower washed signs of death from the women's faces with the month's first April shower.

CHECKMATE

Richard Pastor

Finally, the convention was over. Sam had spent the last three painful days scouting the competition at the New Orleans Interior Design and Home Show. The Chinese had been flooding the market with cheap, elegant plumbing fixtures for years now, and it was having a devastating effect on the small Indianapolis-based company his father had started back when Nixon was still defending his honor. Now, judging by was what he was seeing at the show, the sleek European designs were bound to take off and leave his sturdy, well-built, but more expensive products in the dust. The writing was on the wall, and his company would not last the year.

He dreaded sharing his news with his family. His beautiful young wife had gotten used to a certain lifestyle and social position that was about to be drastically re-evaluated, and she surely would not stick around long after he had lost everything. His children would have to be taken out of their expensive private schools and enter into the under-funded and dangerous Indianapolis public school system, throwing their overindulgent and entitled futures into doubt. Fear and depression were taking hold and gripping his heart with the icy hand of a mortician. He needed a drink.

New Orleans provided an endless source of bars for drowning out one's sorrows. The bright, festive drinking establishments filled with music and laughter, that the tourists flocked to, was not what he had in mind. Sam needed a cool, dark smoke-filled dive bar where he could be anonymous and invisible. His plane did not leave until tomorrow afternoon, and he was planning on tying one on. The hangover would be brutal, but relief from the truth of his impending poverty was paramount.

He left his hotel on the riverfront and took the bright yellow, slow rolling trolley to Jackson Square. The crowds were still lined up at Café Du Monde anxiously awaiting their coffee and beignets. A sugary donut and a bitter chicory-laced coffee was not what Sam had in mind. A shot of house bourbon with a beer chaser and an attentive bartender was more of what he was looking for. He ignored the street artists and musicians as he cut through the square, and before he realized how far he had walked, he found himself deep in the French Quarter on Royal Street. A wedding party was coming up the street, and the revelers were marching to a Dixieland Band, waving their ruffled and brightly colored parasols, following the bride and groom on their march to the gallows of matrimony.

After the jubilant parade had passed, Sam spotted the Black Knight Bar and Social Club, with its faded sign depicting a single horse headed chess piece. The neon sign shone bright orange, even in the middle of the day, clearly inviting him to enter and order up the first of many rounds of memory fogging drinks.

Sam pushed open the door and had to wait for his eyes to adjust to the cool gloom before stepping forward. Perfect. Just what the doctor ordered. All heads turned to the light flooding in the open doorway, invading their private hells, bloodshot eyes squinting out the sun and reminding them of the fact that they were hiding from something beyond that door. As the door closed behind him, Sam spotted a few open spaces at the bar and chose a well-worn red vinyl stool repaired with a few strips of gray duct tape. His butt conformed to his new temporary home quite nicely and creaked a friendly welcome as he settled in. The AC rattled softly on the wall, and the sound was reassuring as he felt the cool breeze from it strike the back of his sweat covered neck. Glancing around the bar at his fellow escapees from life, most had tall sweating beers in front of them accompanied with shot glasses in various stages of emptiness. Sam's mouth began to water with both thirst and anticipation.

The bartender strolled over to Sam and placed a napkin in from of him. The same black knight chess piece was printed on it and already was doing its job of soaking up any residual memories that may have spilled onto the bar.

"What will it be?" he asked. He was a tall middle-aged man, whose obvious personal preference was not to shave and shower on a daily basis, instead choosing to combat the natural oils in his hair with massive amounts of gel and his body odor with an overabundance of Old Spice, a tactic which was not entirely successful. His wife-beater t-shirt showed off his body going to seed, and his unruly gray chest hair was slowly taking over as the main focal point of his overall presentation.

"Cold beer and a shot of bourbon, please," Sam said. "And the first few rounds are going to go fast so don't get too far away." He meant this as a friendly ice-breaker but instead, the bartender simply nodded in recognition of a common request.

The first round came and went as quickly as foretold, as did the second, and as round three settled in Sam was already feeling the edge being taken off of his disastrous life. Resignation was setting in on the end of his business as he knew it. Thank God his father did not live to see the day that his only son was trampled to death by foreign invaders. Sam remembered his father praising Nixon for visiting China, not knowing it signified the beginning of the end of his family's livelihood. Fuck Nixon, what an asshole. Sam gulped down his beer, and before he could put down the empty glass a fresh chilled mug and shot were placed in front of him. *Perfect, a good attentive bartender; a true professional,* he thought.

As time passed and the cheap bourbon worked its magic, Sam suddenly wondered how long he had been sitting in the dark bar. Then the door opened, and a few people entered from the street. He realized that no light streaming in from outside had announced the new arrivals. He had come in just after noon, and it was now completely dark; time to settle up and make his way back to the hotel. The true test of any long-term bar experience is stepping off the bar stool to determine how drunk you really are. Keeping both hands securely on the bar, Sam slid off the stool and planted both feet on the sawdust covered floor. Slowly, he let go, one hand at a time, until he was satisfied he would not stumble or fall. Sam paid his tab and left a generous tip. The man had done his duty well and deserved to be rewarded for his efforts.

Sam pushed open the door and stepped out onto Royal Street. He was sober enough to know that venturing the few blocks to Bourbon Street would not be in his best interest. He was drunk enough that he would not resist the temptations he might find down there. Instead, he headed back toward the trolley station at Jackson Square. Slowly, Sam made his way down Royal until he found himself on the backside of St. Louis Cathedral. The statue of Jesus was keeping a watchful eye on his flock from behind the safety of the iron gates and casting a massive shadow onto the back of the old church: an image that can be both awe-inspiring and foreboding depending on the level of sin one is currently perpetrating. In the Quarter, that level has the tendency to reach great heights.

Sam staggered on and turned left onto St. Peter Street, hoping to locate the trolley station down near the river without having to ask someone for directions. He was not quite sure how well he could communicate in his current condition.

Now he realized the sidewalk in front of him was blocked. As he approached the barrier, he could see it was an elderly black man seated on a battered plastic milk crate and leaning over a chessboard that was precariously balanced on a rusty five-gallon bucket. The man looked up as Sam stepped out of the shadows. The light that Jesus was so gloriously presenting a few steps away was barely filtering through this part of the darkened street, but it was enough to see the man's features. He had the look of homelessness about him, surrounded by a few meager possessions and black garbage bags filled with God knows what. His clothes were rumpled and ill-fitting, covered in multiple stains of unknown origin. When their eyes met, the man smiled the yellow grin of decades of dental neglect and nicotine. His eyes, too, were yellow with age and the jaundiced look of liver damage.

"Good evening, sir," the man said with genuine politeness. "Please forgive me if I am obstructing your passage." He spoke clearly and precisely, as though well-educated in the good social decorum of the South.

"Not at all," Sam slurred and began to swerve around the old gentleman. Unfortunately, in the process of stepping off the sidewalk, he misjudged the curb height and tumbled into the gutter, going down hard onto the street. The old man came to his rescue at once and helped Sam to his feet.

"Please sit and rest yourself for a moment," the old man said graciously, producing another milk crate for Sam to sit on. When Sam was once again steady, the old gentleman extended his hand and said, "Cain's the name. Abel Cain. My father had an interesting sense of humor." His yellow teeth seemed to glow fluorescent in the dim light as he smiled broadly.

Sam reached across the chessboard and shook the old man's filthy hand. "Sam," he said.

He glanced down at the pieces, set up and ready for play. Even in his half-drunken state and in the poor light he could see this was not a cheap set. The polished black onyx pieces were as dark as a starless night sky and seemed to absorb the light, and he was pretty sure the white pieces were antique ivory, perhaps carved from the tusk of some long extinct or endangered animal. He picked up a white bishop and examined it as closely as his inebriated eyes would allow him to focus. The detail was remarkable and so lifelike. The carver was indeed a master craftsman.

"Do you play?" Abel asked.

"Not for years. My father taught me as a young man, but after he died I never played again."

"Truly a shame," Abel said. "Chess is such a challenging game and keeps the mind sharp."

Sam returned the white bishop to the board and took great care not to disturb the other pieces as they were set up with such precision.

"Shall we?" Abel asked and waved a grimy hand over the board.

"Here? Now?" Sam said incredulously.

"Of course," Abel replied.

"I am sorry, but I am in no condition play chess," Sam said.

"Yes, I can see that you have been out celebrating. New Orleans has that effect on people, and there is much to this life worthy of celebration. Is that not so?" Abel said.

"I have nothing to celebrate," Sam admitted. "My life is in ruins."

"I see." After a short pause, Abel responded to the admission. "What would you say if I told you there was a way to right the wrongs done to your life, and you had the opportunity to restore things to their proper order? Would you be willing?"

"And just how would I do that?" Sam asked.

Abel spread his deeply lined hands over the chessboard palms up, presenting it as if the board itself was the solution to Sam's problems.

"Close your eyes," Abel said in such a way that Sam was compelled to do as he asked and close them.

Abel took a deep breath and slowly let it out into Sam's face. Abel's breath smelled of anise and alcohol. As the warm air ceased, Sam opened his eyes once again and realized he was now stone cold sober. The strangeness of the current situation came sharply into focus.

"This board represents your life, Sam. Each piece is a significant person that can affect the course of the game, and each move your life's direction. My black pieces are the negative forces out to do you harm, and your white pieces are there to protect you. If you can overcome the losses and obstacles put in front of you and prevail, then your life will be as you wish it to be."

"And if I lose?"

"If you lose, then you must give to me the only thing of value you have left: your everlasting soul."

Sam looked into to the man's eyes and saw that he was dead serious. Obviously, the old man was insane, or at the very least delusional.

"I can see that you are skeptical, as a wise man should always be. Please, let me prove it to you," Abel said.

He picked up a white pawn and placed it into Sam's hand.

"Look at the face of the pawn and tell me what you see."

Sam peered closely at the chess piece as a face came into view. It was Howard Applebaum, his largest customer! After fifteen years, Howard had given his account to a Chinese competitor, resulting in a twenty-five percent loss of business for Sam's company. He had to lay off eight production workers.

"Now make your first move with this pawn, and I will not take it from you."

The old man returned the chess piece to its original position, sat back, and waited for Sam to make his move.

Sam reached for the piece and slowly slid it forward two spaces.

"Now look at your phone and observe your messages," Abel instructed.

Again Sam did as Abel told him and scanned his email. There were multiple messages regarding delivery dates and paid invoices from Howard Applebaum, along with additional orders that would force him to hire and train more people to keep up with the added demand. How could this be? Just a few hours ago he was on the verge of bankruptcy, and now these orders would easily get him through the end of the year and then some.

Sam looked up from his smartphone and into the grinning face of Abel Cain.

"Shall we begin? White makes the first move," Abel said still smiling broadly.

San weighed his options. On the one hand: bankruptcy, divorce, and destitution. On the other: success, family, and prosperity. His father had taught him the game well, and he had even reached a skill level with which his father could no longer compete. It had been a while, but the moves were not forgotten. Sam reached for his first piece on the board and slid it forward.

"Ah! A classic opening!" Abel proclaimed and countered with his black pawn.

Sam responded with another pawn, and Abel did the same. Sam released his bishop, and a black knight appeared on the board. Another white pawn bravely stepped forward, and an ominous black bishop threatened from behind the protection of his guard. A white knight charged forward, and a black foot soldier took one step ahead for no apparent reason. The white queen bravely crossed her rook, and the black queen mirrored the move, then a pawn to a pawn. The white knight pressed on, forcing the black king to sidestep the danger.

"Marvelous! Your father instructed you well!" Abel was overjoyed with the competition.

Sam called out the backup cavalry, and another knight was in play. Abel did the same, and now all four horses were on the move. A white rook slid forward while a black bishop plotted his attack. Sam saw the beginning of an opening, and freed his rook from the crowd. Abel made a small adjustment with his pawn. There it was! Sam brought out his bishop well into black territory, catching Abel by surprise.

"Wonderful!" Abel said. "The classic Stonewall Attack! Now I recognize it!"

Abel was correct, and now Sam's strategy was out in the open. The black knight took the invading bishop, and first blood was spilled. A dreadful scream arose from where the white bishop had fallen, but the black knight showed no mercy, and the body was dragged from the board. Immediately, Sam went on the attack and launched his queen, who ignored all warnings of caution and defiantly took up a threatening posture in black territory. Abel made another small defensive move with his rook. The white queen stepped forward one space to face the black king personally.

"Check," Sam announced with smug satisfaction, and the dark king shyly withdrew from danger.

While his queen remained on high alert, Sam brought out reinforcements from his foot soldiers. Abel stepped forward as well. *Now!* Sam thought, and charged with his bravest knight.

"Check!" Sam proclaimed once again. He could taste the beginnings of victory! He would be wealthy and happy once again very soon.

The black king stepped forward under the protection of his personal guard, avoiding disaster. *So predictable.* Sam continued with his strategy and put his rook into play. Abel did the same. Sam again called in the cavalry, and Abel sent his into a strategic retreat. Once more the cavalry charged. Then out of nowhere, a black knight leaped over the line and crushed the white invader! Sam was caught completely unaware. His bravest knight was attacked from behind in the most cowardly fashion. Sam was suddenly down two pieces. Sam retaliated knight to knight, and the blood of both sides was spilled on the same square.

The black bishop once again plotted, but the white bishop sensed the conspiracy. Then the black queen made a big aggressive move into white territory, with a clear diagonal line to the back of the board, one space from the king himself, distracting Sam from his strategy and forcing him to take notice. Was it real danger or merely a distraction? He took no chances and slid in his rook to protect his king. An audible sigh of relief came from king's square as the rook arrived. The evil queen again looked for an opening and continued her threatening moves. In his aggressive moves with his queen, Abel had left his back door open, and Sam sent his only remaining knight in for the king.

"Check!" Sam announced once again.

"Impossible!" Abel screamed. The joy of the competition was now gone from his voice, replaced with indignation and denial. His king retreated to the protection of his rook. The white queen advanced to block the next retreat. Abel was now visibly shaken by the aggressive play and scrambled for a safe exit strategy. He took the last white knight that Sam had willingly sacrificed, leaving him horseless. The white queen haughtily stepped in to decapitate an insignificant pawn. The black king was in jeopardy yet again.

"Check!" Sam yelled. His excitement barely contained. Since Abel could not purposely place his king in danger, he could not take the white queen while the white rook backed her up, so he slunk cowardly away. Now was the time to destroy the black defenses, and Sam moved his rook into black territory. Abel continued his royal withdraw in desperation. Sweat had formed on his face, and his yellow eyes bulged in concentration. His teeth were now showing, not in a grin, but gnashing together, making the sound of a dog crushing bones between his powerful jaws. Sam watched him as he contemplated his next move. The fear in Abel's face was itself fearful to witness, as it contorted his former friendly features into a hideous mask.

Sam's rook slid left, slaughtering the defenseless black bishop who was crushed under the weight of the stone castle. Death, however, was not swift, and the painful cries rose from the board as the bishop bled out in agony. Again, it was a short, weak move from the black king as he ran for his life.

"Check!" Sam screamed with such force that spittle flew from his lips, landing defiantly in the face of Abel. His white rook now stared in the face of the terrified black king, who quickly dodged to the side. The white queen entered from the far side of the board, laughing as the fat desperate king could only take one short step at a time in order to avert death. Such is the curse of royalty.

"Check!!" Sam now rose to his feet, relishing in his impending victory, resulting in another single cowardly step from the black king. The white rook took position to block the escape. Death was inevitable, and the smell of fear was palpable coming from the board and Abel Cain alike. One last step, to avoid the deadly noose. At last the white queen took her prize and drove her dagger into the heart of the black king. Dark blood covered the square as she withdrew her blade.

"Checkmate!!!" Sam erupted. He jumped and danced as he relished in his victory.

"Noooooo!!!!!" Abel shrieked. It was not a human sound, but a blend of animal cries being slaughtered on the altar. It pierced the night and was heard above the reveling din of Bourbon Street. All of New Orleans felt the anger and despair of Abel's defeat. Abel rose from his milk crate and kicked the board off of its perch on the bucket. Cries came from the chess pieces as they were scattered across the sidewalk. Abel then crushed them under his feet amidst more anguished screams.

Sam witnessed this tantrum with cool detachment. Clearly, Abel was not used to losing, and his previous gentlemanly manners were now replaced with childlike rage. Finally, Abel stopped his unsportsmanlike behavior and stood quietly, taking in deep breaths of the humid night air.

"Go now and enjoy the short time you have left on this earth. We may yet meet again for a rematch," Abel said.

Sam turned and walked in the direction of the Great Mississippi River and found the trolley station that took him back to his hotel. He was exhausted from the day's events and dropped onto the bed, falling asleep immediately.

In the morning Sam woke with no hangover at all, a surprising gift from Abel Cain. He ate a hearty breakfast and began responding to his messages and emails. Apparently, many of his former customers, and a few new ones as well, were struggling with the poor quality of the new Chinese plumbing fixtures. Failures were running rampant, and they were all requesting replacements from Sam's company, begging for immediate deliveries no matter the cost. Sam smiled to himself, relishing in his good fortune. Once at the airport he decided to upgrade to first class for the trip home to Indianapolis. As Sam settled into his comfortable seat, and the flight attendant brought him a glass of chilled champagne, the thought occurred to him that he had better start teaching his son to play chess, just in case.

THE VORAGO
By Ellery D. Margay

The place was cursed, the Apache claimed—haunted by the restless spirits of those who'd fallen from its treacherous edge to meet their doom upon the jagged rocks below. It was not quite a canyon, for it was neither long nor particularly wide; it was a gash, an open wound in the surface of the earth, and by night so palpably sinister in appearance that even the miners—pragmatic, straight-thinking men not usually given to such superstitions—had come to believe that misfortune preyed on all who strayed too close. It had no official name; to the residents of Silver, Arizona, it was known simply as the Vorago.

By my estimation, it was neither haunted nor unlucky; it was my refuge, my mute confidant—and it was, in part, to spite these absurd and antiquated notions that I returned every sundown, seeking solace at its dusty rim. Countless hours I'd spent perched at the edge of that precipice, whiskey bottle in hand, feet swinging freely over open air—for in the sheer recklessness of that action, I found both thrill and comfort. Perhaps I would someday muster the courage to leap; at present, I was content with the mere possibility.

The night in question had begun like any other. I rested upon my favorite stone, an enormous slab of granite that jutted precariously from the cliff face, breathing the crisp December air and thinking the thoughts I had diligently suppressed throughout the watchful light of day—thoughts of Aurelie. Twenty-six months had elapsed since last I'd seen my beloved's face—twenty-six wretched months!—yet, embalmed in the fluid of memory, her image held inviolate, immune to the ravages of time. At first I'd wished only to forget, and to that end I'd crossed half a continent, abandoning my life's work and fleeing New Orleans, where, through the haze of grief, every dark-haired girl had been my Aurelie. Now I cherished each memory, each detail of our years together, for each was a priceless jewel—and it was here, in the silence, that I polished them.

Taking a final draught of whiskey, I hurled the empty bottle into the chasm where it shattered far below with a pleasing crash; then I stood rather tipsily and whistled for Jeopardy, the odd-eyed paint who'd been loaned to me upon my arrival in this godforsaken wasteland. A queer animal was Jeopardy. Possessed of both singular beauty and abhorrently bad manners, he displayed an irksome penchant for wandering off at the most inconvenient of times. In the distance a nighthawk called, but I detected neither hoof beats nor equine silhouette upon the horizon.

I did, however, spy a light. It did not seem terribly far off—though, Lord knows, it is difficult to tell in the vastness of the desert night—and it appeared to be drawing nearer, bobbing slowly along in the fashion of a lantern held by a human hand. The presence of another living thing so near the Vorago was a rare and curious event, and I reasoned that anyone imbued with the mad gall or pressing purpose for such a venture might best be avoided; it would be wise to turn immediately for home, giving the light and its bearer a wide berth. But, alas, my foolish soul is governed not by wisdom but by curiosity—the insistent and perverse need to *know*—and so I waited, with a hand upon the pistol at my belt and an increasing lack of confidence in my aim.

As I stood in the eerie stillness, eyes fixed upon the light, a shiver of dread crept over me and with it the niggling sense that something was *wrong* about it, unnatural even, though I was unable to discern precisely what. Perhaps it was the sickly colorlessness of the light—its brazen lack of the golden overtones commonly associated with candles and their ilk—or perhaps it was the fact that it was moving in an unwavering, now unmistakable, line toward me.

Gradually, from that single sphere of cold white light, emerged the figure of a man, scarcely visible through the blinding rays of the lantern he carried. Without a pause, he glided through the cumbrous thicket of sagebrush to the rim of the Vorago, and then made his way gingerly along it. As he drew near, I observed that he did not seem to be armed, but my relief soon turned to puzzlement at his appearance: he was smartly— indeed, almost formally!—attired in a manner quite incongruous with his rugged surroundings. His shoes gleamed with freshly polished luster, both hair and mustache were immaculately groomed, and his suit was of a style and fineness more befitting an elegant opera house than the dust-blown, weed-choked perimeter of a rough-hewn mining town like Silver.

Yet the most disquieting thing about this peculiar personage was his color, or what might better be described as a lack thereof, for he resembled nothing so much as a tintype photograph come to life—gray!—every inch of him gray as slate!—all but his face and hands, which, by the light of the lantern, glowed a luminous white.

"Good evening," he called. "A very pleasant one, is it not?" It was a disarmingly mellow voice, accented with the familiar undulating cadence of the Deep South. Perhaps he had not come unbidden.

"Good evening to you," I replied. "Are you a guest of Mr. Corbet? He didn't say he was expecting company."

The somber white features gave a near imperceivable twitch of amusement. "Indeed not," he said, "and I doubt I'd be invited in for a sherry should he learn that I'm here."

I was fixing to inquire as to why, if they were on less than amicable terms, he had chosen to wander about Mr. Corbet's property at such an un-businesslike hour, but I held my tongue. He'd drawn very near—there were not three feet between us—and while his voice had remained unerringly calm, there was something in his overall mien that seemed paradoxically at odds with this impression—something that spoke of obsession, of judgment, and absolutes. He was small and slight of build, and, despite the ashy pallor of his hair, no older than thirty; yet there was a sense of gravity about him, and in his sharp gray eyes a focused intensity that made one want to stand up straighter.

"It's true that Mr. Corbet is a difficult fellow to keep peace with," I said.

"Especially, I would imagine, for his dependents."

"I am not his dependent, if that's what you're insinuating."

"Are you not Francis Marche, the young nephew of Mr. Morris Corbet?"

"The very same."

"And are you not currently residing—sans employment—under your uncle's roof, and therefore under his miserly old thumb?"

"I beg your pardon? What entitles you to make such vulgar suppositions?"

"I meant no insult to you, Mr. Marche. In fact, you'll find that I am sympathetic to your predicament. But I've forgotten my manners! Allow me to introduce myself: my name is Bartholomew Isles, and I have a proposition for you—a terribly appealing proposition, and at a most propitious time, as you shall soon learn."

"And is this proposition one of such infamy that it must be discussed in the dark at the ends of the earth?"

"Some may call it infamy, young sir; I call it justice. It is my aim to see Mr. Morris Corbet dead by the end of the week. I have every faith that you are the man to accomplish this, and you shall be amply rewarded for your troubles."

"Me?" I laughed. "You expect me to murder my benefactor, the dear uncle who has shown me nothing but generosity?"

Bartholomew Isles waved a hand as though shooing away a fly. "Shall we dispense with these cumbersome pretenses? You despise your uncle; we both know this."

"Do not presume to know me, sir," I warned, my choler rising. "I should have no reason to hate my uncle, nor any right to take his life. Susannah would be devastated."

"Susannah! The way he treats that child is abominable. She'll flourish once the yoke of his tyranny is lifted from her pretty young shoulders."

"Is that your quarrel with her father? I would never have taken you for a thwarted suitor."

"What a scandalous suggestion! If our negotiations are to remain harmonious, you'd best not repeat it. Now, regarding your reward—"

"I don't want it! There is no sum on earth that would make a murderer of me."

"My dear young fellow...Who said anything about *money*? You shall have that which your heart most desires."

"You could never deliver what you suggest...for it no longer exists. Kindly take your propositions elsewhere. Silver is replete with scoundrels who would gladly carry out such unsavory work for a pint and a turn at the cat-house."

"As you wish," said Isles, smiling genially. He then gave one sharp whistle, and, to my acute vexation, Jeopardy appeared, swishing his tail and looking pleased with himself.

"Good night to you," I said, turning to mount my wayward paint.

"Good night, Mr. Marche. We won't meet again, but payment will be prompt once the task is complete—and if you should require a token of good faith, look to the persimmon tree."

Keen to terminate the encounter, which had left me greatly discomfited, I made no reply; I kicked Jeopardy, rather more savagely than intended, and we sprang headlong into the welcoming darkness. More than once I glanced over my shoulder, half-expecting to find the ghastly white light bobbing along in pursuit, but, to my bemusement, both man and lantern had vanished. I was pondering this phenomenon and listening, with conditioned abstraction, to the cacophonous racket of cracks and splinters beneath Jeopardy's hooves, when I was struck by an epiphany: Bartholomew Isles had passed through identical terrain—a morass of dry sagebrush and long-deceased cacti—without so much as snapping a twig.

The hour was not quite as advanced as I'd imagined, for as I approached Nepenthe House, the estate of my uncle, a tentative glow still streamed from the dining room windows. Nightfall rendered the structure nearly invisible—an angular black bulk against an expanse of star-dappled sky—and this was just as well, for in the unforgiving glare of day it was a sight capable of arousing—in even the most stoic of Southern hearts—a melancholic twinge of nostalgia. Designed in faithful homage to the lost glory of the Corbet's River Road house, it had, in a little over ten years, fallen into a deplorable state of disrepair. Relentless wind-borne sands had scoured its outer walls near bare, and the stately Doric columns that fronted its capacious veranda were riddled with long, spidery fissures. It reminded one of the weathered face of an old woman, who had, in youth, been exceedingly lovely.

In the dining room, my little cousin Susannah sat alone, her youthful features softly illuminated by the flame of a single lamp. There was a half-eaten slice of cake on the table and a fretful crease in her brow.

"Francis!" she cried. "Come and have dessert with me. Daphne has made a divine lemon pound cake."

"Perhaps later, dear. I need a word with your father; is he in his study?"

"Yes, but you'd best not trouble him; he's in a foul temper."

"Was there a quarrel?"

"Yes," she admitted. "Oh, Francis…do I look terrible in this dress? Maggie May gave it to me—she knows I don't own anything so fine—and I want to keep it, but Father said I look like a prostitute! Is it true, Francis?"

She rose and gave a shy twirl. The gown in question—a yellow, many-ruffled thing—dwarfed her diminutive frame in a way reminiscent of a child taking liberties with her mother's wardrobe. Though Susannah was nearing two-and-twenty, she remained little and lithe as a woodland nymph, and one might have been forgiven for presuming that the wide gray eyes, the delicate chin, the honey-colored curls, belonged to a much younger girl. Since she'd come of age, her guileless beauty had inspired innumerable marriage proposals and calf-eyed declarations of love—much to the consternation of my uncle who had no intent to relinquish the hand of his only daughter.

"Sue," I said, "you are far too sweet to be a prostitute. Ignore your father; he is a bitter, curmudgeonly old bore."

My uncle did not greet me as I entered his study; his beady black gaze shifted momentarily in my direction then returned to the tumbler of bourbon he held.

"I won't disturb you long, Mr. Corbet," I began, "but I must ask you a question."

"Then quit prevaricating and ask me, boy." He leaned back in his chair, regarding me with unrepentant antipathy.

Physically, Morris Corbet was not the most imposing of men; his stature was ordinary, his shoulders visibly slumped, and all across his glistening pate was spattered a profusion of raised, purplish spots—a feature for which I felt a disproportionate sense of revulsion. An uninformed stranger might look upon him with pity rather than fear; but when in his cups, as he often was, his temper turned volatile and his olive-like eyes took on a decidedly malevolent gleam.

"Very well," I said. "Do you know a Bartholomew Isles?"

A frightful expression crossed his face—one of simultaneous confusion and rage. He leapt from his chair, cheeks crimson, and pounded the surface of his desk with both palms.

"*Where* did you hear that name?" he demanded.

"Won't you tell me what history you have with this Isles?"

"That is no concern of yours. You'll divulge where you heard that name you miserable young whiffler, or—"

"I heard it from the man himself, of course. He's in town—and I don't believe he means you well."

"Well, *that* is quite impossible," he sneered. "Whomever you've met is an impostor, likely one of my competitors hell-bent on driving me into the madhouse. You're to speak of this no further; mention that accursed name in the presence of my daughter and you'll be made to regret it!"

"What would you do, uncle? Throw me penniless into the desert?"

"That I will soon do nonetheless if you don't begin to earn your keep."

"Silver has no need of a French chef," I lamented, "and I've been trained for no other vocation."

"Hogwash! There is no excuse for such idleness. At your age, I was master of a plantation. Then when the war came and everything was lost, do you think I sat on my laurels waiting for a helping hand? Certainly not! I came out here, and I *made* this life; I knew nothing of banking— now mine is the largest bank in town! So you see, Francis, I'm baffled by your uselessness. You could at the very least teach that silly, addlebrained girl of mine to cook. As it happens, she'll be preparing our supper tomorrow evening; you will assist her."

"Perhaps," I said, "if I can find the time."

On my word, I had every intention of completing the requested task, but such was my loathing for my uncle that I was unable to resist needling him a bit. This loathing was not, as may be supposed, a result of his temper, his miserliness, or his flagrant lack of anything resembling human sentiment—though neither his friends nor enemies would dispute the veracity of this depiction—but rather due to the fact that I found myself humiliatingly dependent upon his grudging hospitality and his oft-mercurial goodwill.

It was no secret that lingering reverence for his late wife, Isadora—my aunt by blood—was his sole motivation for permitting me to remain at Nepenthe. Of late, my welcome had worn thin, yet still, I could summon not an ounce of ambition, and the leaden paralysis of grief is not an ailment readily explained to a man who'd worked while his wife lay dying. Aye, I hated Morris Corbet, and often wished for his demise; but in such cases, the margin between wish and act is wide indeed.

That night I could not sleep for thoughts of the persimmon tree. That seemingly unremarkable shrub stood against the east wall of the library, and I had passed it on countless occasions, oblivious to what secrets it concealed. Now in my drunken fancy, a fixation had formed—over and over I heard the words of the man in gray: "Look to the persimmon tree," and, compelled by an overriding urge to do just that, I rose, fetched a candle, and crept downstairs.

The tree had belonged to my aunt. Having somehow transported it all the way from Louisiana, she had, by all accounts, been fanatically protective of it. Now it grew—or rather lived, for it was far too root-bound to expand in size—in an enormous earthenware pot beside the French doors that opened onto the back veranda. Here it was guarded by the watchful dark eyes of its mistress, for upon the wall opposite hung a life-size portrait of the good lady herself.

"My apologies, Aunt Isadora," I whispered. Then I began my inspection. Observing nothing unusual in the tree's exterior, I moved on to its subterranean portions. I brought a poker from the hearth and made several insertions, alert to any resistance that might suggest a buried object. My task was obstructed by a multitude of roots, and I was nearly ready to concede defeat when I struck something unyielding with a tinny, metallic clang. As it was nearly a foot beneath the soil, there was nothing for it but to upend the hapless tree and liberate it from its pot.

When, after much feverish digging, I'd managed to excavate my prize, I could scarcely tell what it was I held; it appeared to have once been a small box, now so disfigured by rust as to be quite unopenable. I pocketed it, and then began re-potting the tree; and I was completely engrossed in this task when I was startled clear out of my wits by a voice. "What you be doin' wi' dat po' tree Missuh Francis?" Behind me, hands on her hips, stood Daphne, the estate's caretaker and cook.

"Daphne," I said, "you don't intend you tell Mr. Corbet about this, do you?"

"Well, I s'pose not…but what *is* you doin' down here in the dark?"

"I'm afraid I can't tell you—not just now. But Daphne…you've been with this family a long time, haven't you?"

"Yessuh, since yo' aunt were just a girl."

"Have you ever heard of Bartholomew Isles?"

At this, her eyes grew wide as saucers. "Where you hear dat name?"

"Aha! So you know of him?"

"Course I know 'im. He were Miz Isadora's betrothed befo' she ever did meet Mr. Corbet—and I never did see two folks so in love! They was always playin' the pianuh together…always playin' Miz Susannah's namesake song."

"Susannah…is Susannah?" In my weary intellect, the glimmer of a thought had emerged, one that defied articulation.

Daphne was quick to intuit my meaning. "Yessuh," she said. "Susannah ain't never been Mr. Corbet's chile, but don't tell nobody I said it."

"But…what happened? Why didn't my aunt marry Mr. Isles?"

"He was killed…a week befo' de weddin'—and dey say he shot hisself, but I *know* he ain't. It was dat heartless old devil, Mr. Corbet. He'd been comin' round, pesterin' Miz Isadora; he wanted her for hisself, and he wud never let anotha' man wed her."

"Good God, Daphne! Are you certain? That is, are you certain Mr. Isles was truly dead?"

"Yessuh, I is, 'cause aft'ward he come back—we all seen 'im! He haunted de grounds for years, always showin' hisself de second week o' December, same week he was killed—and dat devil Mr. Corbet din't know no peace—not 'til we come out here an' leave de spook behin'."

By this time, I was feeling very queer, so I excused myself and went upstairs. It seemed I had met a ghost, and at this, my logical mind rebelled most grievously. Yet the events in question—my own encounter with Isles, the reaction of my uncle, and the testimony of Daphne, who'd never been known to fib—seemed more compatible with a paranormal explanation than an earthly one, and I was not so foolish as to discount the evidence of my own eyes.

Once alone, I brought the rusted box from my pocket, and, with the aid of a slim knife, coaxed it open. Inside, nestled in folds of decaying silk, lay two rings—both gold and in startlingly pure condition. The first was a thick unadorned band, which, from the inscription along its inner surface, I deduced to have been my aunt's wedding ring. The second was set with a round, faceted gem of a pale red hue. It too was inscribed: *B loves I.* A promise ring, perhaps.

I returned my new-found keepsakes to their box and stashed it in a drawer. Then, chilled, blurry-eyed, yet still oddly wakeful, I dosed myself with laudanum—a recourse I avow is not my wont—and sunk directly into an undisturbed slumber.

And, oh, how I dreamed; I was in New Orleans once again, in the cluttered studio on Rue Canal. The shutters had been thrown open, and there, bathed in the noonday sun, stood Aurelie, clad in a gown of defiant black and white. Propped on an easel before her was a painting—her latest masterpiece—and she was studying it with evident displeasure. She looked precisely as she had on our final day together, even including the indigo paint that stained her fingernails—but when at length she turned to me, she did not ask whether I thought a third figure might balance the composition, as she had in fact done. She fixed me with her fay, unearthly stare—for the eyes of Aurelie were not like those of other mortals; I was convinced they had the capacity to see through one's fleshy exterior to the naked soul beneath—and when she spoke, there was desperation in her voice. "Do it," she said. "Do it for me."

I awoke with a start and a sense of impending failure that would harry me the rest of the day; I knew of what she spoke, and although she was now but a phantom, there was no wish I could deny her without dreadful self-reproach. As evening fell, I fled to the Vorago and endeavored to drown my nerves in whiskey, but it brought me no solace, for all the while I remained vigilant, alert to the appearance of a ghostly white lantern.

Upon returning home, I discovered both my uncle and my cousin seated in the dining room; I had once again abandoned poor Susannah, and, as the air was fouled with a most unappetizing odor, it seemed she had cooked supper on her own. In her culinary choices, my dear little cousin displayed a distressing lack of the senses most fundamental to an able cook: those of taste and smell.

"Am I late for supper?" I asked, seating myself.

"You certainly are, you whey-faced young wastrel," said my uncle. "Once again, you've shirked the only duty for which you have practical use."

"It's alright, Francis," said Susannah. "I've done fine on my own, and we haven't eaten yet; the pies are in the oven."

I was questioning how any *pie*, regardless of its contents, could produce such an unholy stench, when Daphne arrived to serve us. The crust was hard as plaster and the filling tasted precisely as its aroma had portended. I glanced at my uncle, fearful that his choleric temperament would not permit him to swallow politely as I had, and my worry was well-founded for he promptly regurgitated the first mouthful.

"What is it?" he demanded. "What on God's green earth have you tried to feed us?"

"There are potatoes," said Susannah, her voice atremble, "walnuts, gooseberries, turbot—"

"Turbot! And where, pray tell, did you obtain this turbot?"

"The pantry…there were several jars—"

With one abrupt movement, Morris Corbet sent his pie careening to the floor amidst a crashing spray of crumbs and grease. Susannah leapt to her feet in fright, clutching at the skirt of her dress. Among the yellow ruffles, there showed several large, spreading oil stains.

"You worthless imbecile! That turbot is older than you!" shouted Mr. Corbet. "It is vile—unfit for human nourishment—and that is precisely why it remains in the pantry. I'm thankful your mother isn't here to witness such incompetence—she'd be ashamed!"

For one so gentle, Susannah rarely wept, but in the face of such vitriol, her great soft eyes brimmed with tears.

"I…I'm sorry, Father. I didn't mean to disappoint you." With that, she turned and shuffled from the room—stiffly, as if stunned—and as I watched her retreating form, something was ignited in a forgotten corner of my long-dormant heart; an icy flicker of rage. Like a drug, it rushed through my veins, banishing my apathy and sending my moral compass awhirl—and I grew giddy with the stuff, giddy and perilously bold.

"You must go after her, Mr. Corbet," I declared. "Go after her immediately and apologize. Truly, sir, I would not treat my dog the way you treat that girl, and if you won't amend your ways then you alone are responsible for the consequences."

"Consequences, eh? If I were ten years younger, boy, I'd make you regret your smart words, but as it happens, you're to make yourself useful instead. I've found you a position at the bank—the unskilled sort, of course—and you'll begin working off your debt come Monday."

So drunk was I on whiskey and hatred that I merely laughed—a hideous torrent of maniacal, hedonistic glee. It was as if some foreign entity had taken possession of my psyche and implanted it with the basest and most murderous of impulses; at that moment, I wanted very badly to harm my uncle, but there are some lines which no decent man must cross—not, at least, without risk of permanent alteration to his soul—and I must not allow rage to make me its puppet.

I stood and made for the door, but my uncle's fulminations pursued me. "It's been two years, boy! Just how long will you go on festering over that whore you were fool enough to marry?"

"Aurelie was never a whore," I snapped. "She was an artist—the most refined and cultured of ladies!"

There was an air of bloated triumph about his detestable, speckled countenance, as if by provoking my ire, he had somehow bested me.

"At heart, all women are whores, Francis…no matter how refined."

"Very well," I said coolly. "If that is what you believe, so be it." And I knew then that Bartholomew Isles had spoken the truth: ere the week was through, Morris Corbet would be dead.

Later that evening, I knocked at the door of Susannah's room. "Let me in, little cousin," I pleaded. "I have something that may lift your spirits."

Upon entering, I found her seated at the edge of the bed in a tattered dressing gown; soaking in a wash basin beside her was the prized yellow dress.

"Hold out your hand," I said, and into it, I dropped Isadora's gold rings.

"Oh!" she gasped, "Mother's rings! That is her wedding ring and the other is a hessonite ruby. I hadn't seen them since the war! Father threatened to sell them, so Mother hid them away." She then implored me to reveal how I'd come by them, but I refused, promising to do so at a later date.

"I don't deserve to keep such treasures," she cried. "I'm a disgrace to her memory."

"Nonsense. Tomorrow I'll help you cook supper—as I ought to have done before—and all will be made right."

True to my word, I devoted much of the following day to Susannah's culinary tutelage. We concocted a fine mound of pie dough; then, as the pantry presented a woeful dearth of ingredients, I crept into the library and gathered every ripe persimmon. Susannah prepared the filling—over-spicing it as I had feared— but her lattice tops were cut with unexpected symmetry.

As suppertime approached and the pies baked golden, compulsion wrestled with reason; the murder of my uncle would be neither justifiable nor rational, yet I found myself overwhelmed by an insurmountable urge to do so, and to act this very night without delay. I was, however, still perplexed as to the method of said act; I had no stomach for violence.

While retrieving the bubbling pies from the oven, an idea arose. I requested that Susannah choose a bottle of wine from the cellar, and in her absence, I dashed upstairs and fetched the laudanum from the medicine chest. When it comes to decisions, my little cousin is like molasses in winter, and by the time she'd returned toting a dusty bottle of Burgundy, I had, with the aid of a small funnel, emptied the vial's contents into the pie filling.

Regret descended when, at length, we'd gathered at the table and Morris Corbet cut into his pie; the flavor of laudanum is not easily disguised—he'd taste it and immediately discern its contents! And yet, I mused, he was not as habituated to this substance as I, being, as he'd once stated, rather sensitive to its compounds. Perhaps he would merely detect a vague unpleasantness without guessing its source.

To my surprise, he swallowed the first bite with no hesitation, and took a lengthy swig of Burgundy—clearly having imbibed much already.

"It's an improvement," he pronounced. "It's very bitter—I assume the fruit was unripe—but it is edible, and I'm famished."

Susannah and I looked on—she, with pride; I, with horror—as Morris Corbet devoured the remainder of the pie and two more glasses of wine, and I was nearly convinced that my effort had been futile when at last his eyelids began to flag.

"I think...I'll retire to bed," he muttered—and he fell abruptly asleep in his chair.

"He's overindulged again," sighed Susannah. "Shall we have a game of checkers in the library?"

Two excruciating hours crawled by ere she wearied of the game, and I was left alone to assess the situation. In the dining room, my uncle remained upright at the table, appearing not to have stirred—but the characteristic flush of wine had been supplanted by a bluish pallor. When at last I summoned the courage to touch him, I drew back, aghast; he was not yet cold, but I detected no pulse.

My panic at that moment was absolute. What precisely I had expected was unclear, as were my reasons for having committed an act so wholly at odds with my greater nature. I had been compelled, launched like a bullet from a gun, and I knew not whether the trigger hand had been that of Bartholomew Isles or some demon from my own soul. Now, however, was no time for such reflection, if I wished to avoid the gallows. I fetched paper and ink from my uncle's study and penned a quick note. It read thusly:

> *Sue,*
>
> *When I woke your father, he became angry and left the house in a huff. Since he is still very drunk, I worry for his safety and have gone out to bring him home.*
>
> *-F*

I did not expect Susannah to wake. The note was intended chiefly for the eyes of Silver's sheriff, who, in being a conveniently linear-minded fellow, would be apt to dub my uncle's death an accident if only it appeared as such. As his vices were no secret, few would find it far-fetched if he should be discovered at the bottom of a cliff after a night of misadventure.

Morris Corbet had not been a large man, but his weight seemed to have increased tenfold, and I won't describe what frenzied methods were employed in the transport and subsequent fastening of his earthly remains onto the back of the understandably reluctant Jeopardy. As we waded into the moonlit expanse of sagebrush, I grew as skittish as my steed; my senses tingled with that intangible terror one experiences while being observed by unseen eyes, and I cast about continually, searching the horizon for a pale white light.

Gradually I fell to ruminating. Through the daze of guilt and shock, I could not help but concede that, once again, Isles had been correct: unfettered by Morris Corbet's tyrannical penny-pinching presence, Susannah would indeed flourish. At last she would be free to wed; free to entertain; free to fill the pantry with delicacies, or to purchase jewels and gowns of ostentatious splendor—as befitted a beautiful young lady of means. She would mourn—bitterly, no doubt—for the man who'd raised her, but I saw sunshine in her future where before there had been none.

Soon the Vorago opened before me like a river of ink, black and impenetrable, as if slashed into the land by some devilish claw solely for the disposal of sins. I led Jeopardy to its extreme edge and set about unbinding the unwholesome burden from the saddle, fumbling over the knots, for my hands had grown numb from the cold. Suddenly, from far below, came a clear, sharp whistle; and Jeopardy, always the traitor, wrenched his neck from my grasp and trotted briskly toward the summons.

"Get back here, you painted fiend!" I shouted, scrambling to follow. He had strayed onto my favorite sitting stone—a precarious position for a beast of his weight—and now stood swishing his tail and turning his great rabbit-like ears to and fro. From this spot, he mulishly refused to budge, so it was here that I once again set to untying—and the objectionable task was all but complete when there arose the most alarming sound one can imagine when poised above a chasm: the crack and grind of shifting stone.

For one panicked moment I fancied that the very jaws of Hell had opened beneath to consume me, and I was not much relieved when the stars and the horizon and the solid rock on which I stood gave a sickening lurch, revealing the fatal truth; the stone, beneath the combined bulk of a horse and two men, had finally broken free of the cliff face. Many nights I'd spent flirting with Death; at last my affections were returned. No sooner had I grasped this than I was falling, plummeting backward into those cold pitchy depths, the moon and the star-spattered sky reeling above in rapid retreat. Then, with a jolt, the darkness descended.

How long I lay swathed in oblivion remains unknown, but presently I became aware of a light; and as consciousness returned—slowly, as when waking from a dream—I perceived that said light seemed to emanate from a figure perched atop a nearby rock—that of a young woman in a gown of defiant black and white. My heart leapt, for the very shape of her—the slender waist, the mane of coal-black hair, the proud curve of the neck and shoulders—was familiar as the streets of my childhood, yet still I dared not hope, not till that exultant moment when at last I glimpsed her face; it was Aurelie, and in her hand a pale white lantern.

THE GRUNCH
By Bret Valdez

"Maxim?" I questioned to clarify. He replied in a sexy Creole twang, correcting me, "Yes, but it's accented. Max-*EEM*." I melted at the smile spread across his handsome face. His eyes were a deep emerald green, and his dirty blond hair made them all the more prominent. I quickly collected myself from my gawking and wiped the palm of my hand off on my jeans, offering it for him to shake. He took it and held it firmly, but not too hard.

"I'm Laura," I flashed him a bright smile before introducing my friends. "This is Eric," I motioned behind me and paused while they shook hands. "And this is Nicole." There was an awkward silence after the introductions, and I was no good at ice breakers, so I got right to business.

"So, I'm the photographer," and, pointing to the Nikon hanging from my neck with the huge zoom lens, added "duh," and a giggle. "Eric is the videographer, and Nicole is the writer." There was a smile in my voice, not just because he was handsome, but to make him feel comfortable. We may have been from Seattle, but we weren't wimpy city folk. We were hikers and mountain climbers, well-accustomed to the outdoors, and I'd grown up in Southern Florida, where swamps and marshes weren't uncommon.

Together, we worked on projects about the planet; some pieces for local wildlife and expedition magazines, footage used in televised news segments, and specials highlighting the beauty of the Pacific Northwest. We filmed and documented everything, in hopes of someday having our own documentary or docu-series. That was the long-term goal; for now, we were freelance.

With all of us feeling stagnant, though, I thought a change of scenery was in order: something new and exciting. New Orleans seemed just right. How much farther could we get from the peaks, valleys, and waterfalls of Washington and Oregon? The sea-level, humid, swampy bayous of

147

Louisiana would contrast our work in the Northwest nicely. We were immediately roused by the idea of traipsing through dangerous marshlands with deadly alligators and poisonous snakes. Of course, for our own safety, we thought it best to hire a "swamp guide," someone who knew the hazards, what to look for, and how to keep us safe.

We met at a local diner, where the white walls were dirtied by rain and debris, and the thick air smelled of fish fry. This particular diner, Maxim had told me on the phone, was famous for freshly caught fish, shrimp, and crawdad. The simple blue and white sign read DIANNE'S FISH & GUMBO, and below it was a lit marquee letter with black plastic sides you sometimes see at movie theaters. It proudly stated: FROM NATURES KITCHEN TO OURS, and in smaller print $5 GUMBO B0WL ALL DAY. The "o" in "bowl" was replaced with a zero, as though they'd run out of the letter.

Gathering our traveling bags over our shoulders, Nicole, Eric, and I followed Maxim to the outside seating area, which was covered by an awning, made of rippled aluminum, to protect patrons from the elements.

"Do you live around here?" I asked Maxim.

"Aw, no, no. I met you in the middle. I live further south," he indicated.

"Were you born here in New Orleans?" I continued.

"Yeah, I'm here since I was born, 'bout 34 years now. You like it?" Maxim volunteered.

"It's hot!" He laughed at me, and I nudged him for it. "Nah, it's beautiful down here, and I love the architecture. I was born in Florida, so I'm allowed to complain about the heat." He looked over at me, and I winked. "It's these city folk back here you gotta worry about," I teased the lollygags behind us.

Once we were under the cover of the awning, we shrugged our sacks off our backs and chose a picnic table.

"Y'all want anything? Some coffee? They make real good funnel cake…" Maxim offered.

Everyone shook their heads, and I, not wanting to appear rude, said, "I could use some coffee."

"Comin' right up, *manmzèl*," he ticked his head at me, winked and smiled as he turned and opened a screen door to step inside, Southern hospitality on full display.

I let out a relaxed sigh. "He's so sweet."

"Yeah, sweet on you," Nicole razzed. I knocked her in the shoulder playfully, and tried to hide my blush.

"Ho-kay," I exhaled, and opened up the map Eric passed me. I read over the plans, and then checked the equipment. Once we set course for the dark, dank swamp, we wouldn't be able to turn back for forgotten items. "You guys check on battery, please? And Eric, make sure you've got the backup film for your camera." I was issuing orders while I dug through my own bag, noticing I didn't have the things I needed. "Shit. Nicole, do you have the batteries?"

"No, I don't," she held her hands up, displaying her notepad and tablet. "Eric?"

He was determinedly shuffling through his bag, his brows furrowed as he searched, more frantically as time progressed. There came a huge sigh of relief, first from him, and then from us as he pulled out the velvet pouch which held the batteries and cards for my camera. He tossed the pouch to me, and showed off the box of extra 35mm film for his Motion Camera. It wasn't the huge bulky kind you're probably thinking of; in the technology age, they'd become more and more portable. Still, I was glad film wasn't my thing—I wanted nothing to do with lugging that around. We began assembling our equipment, while Nicole was already writing notes in her spiral notebook.

"So, what do you guys think?" I tossed my head toward the diner, and Maxim. "He's super nice. He was when we spoke on the phone, too. Can you guys understand him?" I asked with a giggle; his accent was quite thick, and he'd also used a couple Creole words.

"He's very cordial. You can tell he's from the South," offered Nicole, still scribbling notes, head in her scratch pad. She took her plaid button-up blouse off, revealing a coral tank top, and tied it around her bag. The temperature was climbing to uncomfortable degrees.

"I think you already have a crush on him," teased Eric. He stuck his tongue out playfully, but then flicked it up and down gratuitously. I reached across the table to smack him in the arm, which he pretended hurt. Eric and I tried to force something once, but it just wasn't there. Not for me, at least. I think it was for him, though. Unless we were working, it was a little awkward between us, especially alone.

Maxim exited the diner and handed a hot Styrofoam cup to me. I thanked him, and passed him the map when he sat down. He searched it, and began explaining the path we could take. He was all about warnings, making sure we knew the hazards explicitly. Using his thick, coarse fingers, he showed us an area of woods we could enter that would take us to swampland. His gold watch glistened in the late-morning sunlight. It was already 11:29. I sipped my black coffee quickly, impatiently.

"Well," I announced, launching myself up off my seat and drumming my hands on the table. "Let's go get eaten!"

Maxim drove my jeep with me riding shotgun. It was about a half-hour drive to the entry point of the woods, and he didn't like our taste in music, so I agreed to let him put on country radio. He listened to much more classic country, though, which was something at least. Not that I had anything against country music, having spent a lot of time in Florida. But, *having spent a lot of time in Florida*...I kind of had something against country music.

As we got closer to the swamp, the pungent smell of boggy mud tainted the air. We began to gag and cough away the stench while Maxim laughed. There was an orchestra of bullfrogs and cicadas as we zoomed down an empty stretch of dirt road. I realized I hadn't seen another vehicle for miles. The sun burned my eyes even through my dark tinted sunglasses, and my right arm, exposed to the rays filtering in through the window, felt scalded.

I looked in the rearview mirror, where I could see Nicole writing, as always. I admired her commitment. She could write about anything and make you think she absolutely loved the topic. She had mused to me on the drive down that she didn't know what she'd write about in a swamp, but she could probably think of something. If anything, she acquiesced that she could provide a literary documentation of our excursion, to accompany my photographs and Eric's film.

The drive took about an hour before we arrived at a completely—and eerily—nondescript entrance to the woods that Maxim said would lead us to the swamp. I looked around in circles, and could see no signs of humanity. Tall, yellowed grass, dead from the sun, surrounded the area. Peering at the edge of the woods, I saw no tracks or visible trail leading into the trees. Something wasn't sitting right. I hoped there was cell reception, so that if this guy ended up trying to kill us I could leave him a harsh review on Yelp.

"Maxim, will you go ahead and find a safe path for us while we get equipped?" I requested. "We just need to adjust our settings." He agreed and immediately started into the tall grass along the edge of the cypress trees. He poked his way around with a long wooden shaft, pointed at one end. He carried three identical spears, strapped to his back. My eyes switched from him to Eric, and then to Nicole, neither of whom seemed the least bit worried. I wasn't either; just thinking the worst, as I tended to do. A gust of wind came, and felt refreshing against my sweating skin. An array of noise played, from the croaking of frogs to heavy clicking sounds, presumably from movement through the trees.

I looked through my Nikon and took some test shots. I took a few of Maxim as he walked cautiously through the thick grass. I snapped a few of Nicole, who leaned against the jeep watching Maxim, using her hand as a visor over her eyes. Adjusting my settings and zoom, I took three of Eric: one of him making a goofy face, another of him pointing his film camera at me, as he also adjusted his settings, and finally a close-up of his profile as he looked behind us at the heat soaked dirt road we'd just beamed down. Beads of sweat pooled in his hair and on his upper lip, and plenty more dripped freely down his cheek and jaw, eventually falling onto his shirt.

"'K, set. You good?" Eric tossed the small boom mic up from one hand to the other, and Nicole brushed the dirt from the road off her face. I looked them each in the eyes, and they nodded at me, signaling they were all set.

"All right, Maxim, here we come." I wanted to alert him so the footfalls didn't startle him. The tall grass was itchy against my bare arms, but my legs were covered in pants and swamp boots that rose all the way up the thigh, but could fold down to the calf, if need be. The three of us had stopped at an outdoor gear store upon entering New Orleans and picked up a few necessities, one being mosquito repellent, which I figured would come in handy sooner rather than later.

Maxim watched as we made our way cautiously through the thick, tall grass, wary of our steps. Standing at the edge of the wood, he held some branches out of the way so that we could enter with ease. I thanked him, and turned to Eric.

"It's a lot darker in here. How's your lighting?" I asked, even as I adjusted my own settings to accommodate the different brightness and hue under the cover of the cypress canopies. He fidgeted with his equipment a moment before signaling me with his forefinger to walk. "Nicole?"

"My notebook doesn't require any settings, Laura. I'm good." I could tell she was a bit irritable, probably from the heat. I didn't take it personally. If anything, I wanted to commiserate with her and tell her we'd have an ice cold beer waiting for us on the other side.

A good thirteen-minute trek into the woods hadn't revealed any swamp, but Maxim narrated the way, and told us we were approaching the stretch of swamp that would take us about seven miles deep into the forest. The acrid smell of the bayou was burning my nostrils, so I knew we were closing in. My camera was at the ready, but other than trees and shadows, there wasn't much worth photographing yet.

Finally, at the twenty-five-minute mark, we reached the edge of the swamp. "Ten," I announced, my breath shallow and sapped, and sat down on the dry ground for a rest and water break. We'd each brought two large insulated thermoses full of water. Maxim joined us, leaning against the bark of a tree. The humidity was so thick and the air so hot, it was like inhaling steam rather than oxygen, and it took a while for us to catch our breath. I felt gluttonous with the ice cold water, not wanting to stop it refreshing me, lubricating my irritated throat and cooling my core temperature. Everything in me was screaming *"more, more!"* but I knew I had to conserve for the rest of the journey.

Peeking into the swamp from my vantage at the base of a tree, I could see the sunlight was scant, and it was rather dark. The number of cypress trees seemed to double, and the leafy roof blocked out most of the illumination. What little light seeped through had an eerie green opacity. I reached for my camera, while swatting away gnats and mosquitoes, to capture it. Maxim was nosing around the bound of the swamp, using long, javelin-like spears to test the firmness of the ground. They looked hand-crafted, with thick, apparently sturdy whips of wood and a leathery twine wrapped around the middle for grip. The spear on the end was simply sharpened to a steep point.

"Protection?" I asked plainly.

"I brought one for each-a ya. Anything come atcha you can poke 'em good. Also if we have to walk in the water they good to poke in front of you, make sure you ain't gon' step on nothin'.'" I really hoped we wouldn't have to tread swamp water.

Eric walked around slowly, swiveling this way and that, getting steady shots of the entrance of the swamp, pointing his camera up at the sun rays filtering through the leaves, and down at the bright green duckweed that topped the water.

"Do you think we'll run into any alligators?" I asked inquisitively, and maybe with a little trepid excitement.

"Oh yeah, we gon' see some. You just keep you a distance, and they won't bother you." He paused to regard me before continuing: "Snakes is what you oughtta be thinkin' 'bout, *manmzèl*. You said you was from Florida?" I nodded. "Then you know about a cottonmouth. You know, a water moccasin. They about the deadliest thing you gon' see. They keep to themselves, but the trouble wit dem is they camouflage, and they look just like a part of the muck or a stick."

I shivered at the thought of sharing time with a snake of any kind. It wasn't my idea of convivial. The cottonmouth was not a popular breed, that's for sure. One of the most venomous, they're feared down south almost as much as the rattlesnake.

I stood and stretched out the places my muscles had settled, letting them know it was time to wake up. Maxim handed us each a spear, and we admired them and practiced poking inanimate objects. I took a quick photograph of Nicole, because she looked hysterical as the spear was nearly double her height. As we passed the threshold of forest to swamp, I looked behind me, just in case it was the last safe place I ever was.

* * *

The scorching heat of the day seemed to increase as we journeyed deeper into the muggy swamp. Eric had removed his shirt completely, and I'd doused him in mosquito repellent. I'd sprayed myself, Nicole, and

Maxim down at the same time. Even still, I found myself swatting at bugs. It was absolutely teeming with the pesky insects.

The green tinted sunlight cast itself on the surface of the water, which, fortunately, had remained still, save a few splashes that startled me and sent me pulling back my spear. Maxim reassured me it was more than likely frogs or fish. We hadn't yet had to go into the water—the path of dry land seemed to go on for as far as I could see. However, the farther we walked, the narrower the earth got. It was only a matter of time before we lost this luxury.

The ambiance of crickets chirping and frogs croaking was relaxing. I found myself almost lulled. No one spoke, as Eric was utilizing the boom microphone to capture the sound for his film. Now and then, Maxim would alert us to something and talk to the camera about what we were seeing—mushrooms, lizards, etcetera, as if he were the host of his own wildlife show.

Farther down the path, as it narrowed even more, I photographed a collection of raised roots in the water that Maxim had called "knees." They looked like small stumps, but were actually, as he explained, a natural growth of the cypress trees' roots to collect oxygen, as the trees themselves were rooted underwater.

His hiss caught me by surprise. "Ohh! Hey, hey, hey, hey," he said softly, as if to comfort us. He bent himself at the waist and knees, his arms spread wide, in a protective stance. He motioned slowly straight ahead of us, where an alligator was lazily crawling across the dirt from one side of the water to the other. Eric and I focused our cameras intently at the creature, though I didn't look away from it to adjust the shot. My jaw had instinctually gone slack, as I took in the size of the gator.

"Now that's a mama. The males don't get that big. We gotta be careful of nests, naw. If we walk up on her eggs, she gon' 'ttack. They leave you alone usually, but they territorial. Especially if they got babies." I appreciated the warning, but I don't think any of us planned on taking a nap in an alligator nest. I swallowed hard against the back of my dry throat in a frozen horror. Twenty seconds later and we might have been in the very path of that beast. The fragility and incompetence of us against that made it finite how deep over our own heads we were. We stayed back until we saw it—her—slide into the greenish-black water, still so slow and intimidating. Once she was out of sight, we continued.

We came across an area where there was no path anymore, just random, tiny islands of dry land. We had to pass through thickets of some kind of bush to get there. Spears at the ready, we stepped cautiously into the precarious water, which wasn't deep enough to put our wading boots under the surface. We followed Maxim's lead, poking ahead of us into the water, about five feet from our footing.

We finally reached another stretch of land, where we could afford to sit and rest. I went to take a seat against a tree with exposed roots when I saw something move. A large, girthy black snake slithered away slowly and then stopped. I could see from its triangular head and white markings on its lower mouth that it was a cottonmouth.

"*Shhhh, sh, sh, sh, sh….*" Maxim sounded after I let out an accidental, pitiful sound of fear. I slowly angled my spear in the event I needed to use it against the deadly serpent. He pulled me by my upper arm from behind, frightening me, and I let out a scream. I dropped the spear, and I panicked, running away from the scene with high steps. Eric caught me in his arms and comforted me, and looked on as Maxim worked himself away from the snake, backing up slowly with no sudden movements. It sat coiled, its head perpendicular from the ground, flicking its forked tongue into the air.

Nicole tugged at my shirt from behind, and I looked back to see that she too was panic-stricken. Of the three of us, she was the least outdoorsy, and I felt terrible for bringing her here. I was afraid of this place, and we were out of our element. We embraced each other for comfort, and I whispered an apology in her ear that her nod accepted.

"Maxim, I think we're done. This was a terrible idea. We," I looked at my friends for confirmation and nodded, "we wanna go back." He seemed disappointed, but he agreed we'd bitten off more than we could chew. He was off on some tangent about how people are made to survive the areas they're born around, but all I could focus on was leaving. Maxim handed me back the spear I'd dropped, and we turned to head back the way we came.

But, looking into the eyes of the swamp's most dangerous predator, we quickly realized we were trapped. The huge alligator from earlier had followed us, and she lay in wait just below the water's surface; focusing on us, remaining still, but with intent. A warning. A challenge.

"Maxim. Oh, God. Maxim, what do we do? Maxim!" I hissed through my teeth, but he was frozen. Tears fell from my eyes, and I shuddered. I backed away slowly, pulling on Eric, while Nicole pulled on me. "Maxim," I spoke evenly.

"We can't outrun her. We in a standoff. Look out there to the right, in the wood. How far does that water go out yonder?" His question sounded flat, like a statement.

"Thirty, maybe forty feet," Eric replied.

"Y'all ready to get wet?"

"You've got to be kidding me. We can't get into the water with an alligator stalking us from behind, Maxim!" I was nearly frenzied, practically convulsing with fright. Nicole's hand shook in mine as we continued backing up slowly.

"Y'all start movin' that way. Get y'all sticks out and hold 'em horizontal. Dip each end in with each step, like you was paddlin' a canoe. I'll distract her, make sure she don't come, and I'll holler at you if she does," his direction was somehow both reassuring and petrifying. It felt like finality.

"Thank you," I said, weakly. I watched him stare down the gator as we walked backward toward the scummy green water.

Eric insisted he take the lead. The water slowly rose above our boots, then our hips, and our waist. Nicole was almost up to her neck when I looked back at her. She had the disadvantage of being much shorter. Every time I caught my foot on a stick under the water, I wanted to surrender, resign myself to swamp food. But an odd calm had come over me, and apparently all three of us, as we traversed the murky water, which had about 5% visibility. When the spear was tipped down into it, it couldn't be seen almost instantly after entering.

Finally, we reached an area where we could leave the water, and cross the rest of the way on the tree roots, and the "knees," as Maxim had told us. I let Nicole go ahead of me, putting me at the end of the pack. Ahead, I could see that rather than land, it was actually some sort of makeshift walkway, made out of wooden planks and poles. It looked old and beat up, and I questioned if it could hold any of our weight. First, though, we had to make it there.

I urged Nicole to take it slow, and to hold my hand from behind and Eric's ahead of her, in case there was a root too far for her to step to. She had the flexibility to stretch from knee to knee, though, and she took on the obstacle course with fair ease, only getting caught up twice, where she used our arms to carry her over a longer step. I hadn't realized how precarious this was, as I looked down after Nicole had crossed over to Eric successfully, and noticed that if I were to wobble and fall, I would probably take one of the roots to the chest or the back. I focused my steps and worked out the best way to cross, until eventually, I reached over to Eric who picked me up and swung me into the shallow water just before the walkway.

We worked out a plan to cross the warped boards more safely, with me leading, standing at one end of the beams, Eric in the middle, and Nicole on the back, balancing our weight so as not to put too much pressure on the ailing wood. Still, it creaked and cracked now and then, causing us to freeze in place.

The sun was almost completely hidden here. It was pitch black in some places, and the only light source was on Eric's camera. He turned it on and aimed it ahead of us. There were about six more planks to cross. I noticed the sounds of the swamp had gone strangely silent. The chorus of crickets and frogs had almost completely ceased.

Another board crossed, and we took a moment to survey our

surroundings. The quiet seemed to be troubling us all. Our breathing, which had grown ragged with the increased physical exertion, slowed altogether, and we looked at each other knowingly. I took Nicole's hand as the beam of white light from Eric's camera looked out at the water. No signs of life.

Like clockwork, a noise shot past my ear that sounded like something moving with speed. It hit the water with a puny splash. I gasped in shock and spun my head from Nicole to Eric. Another. We huddled together and stayed low. Was it bats? No, they wouldn't be flying into the water…What was that sound? Eric took the lead on the planks, hunched over. He panned the light behind us and a shocking crash of leaves sounded. I screamed at the sudden intrusion into the silence. Something large was moving behind us. My eyes stung with fear, and I reached ahead of me and hooked my finger around Eric's belt loop.

Thwop. This time the sound landed into something; a thick, wet sound. I felt Nicole's hand leave mine, and, in what felt like slow motion, I turned to see her reach for her neck, a dark liquid leaking down her throat. Eric shone his light on her, and her brown eyes were brimmed with terror. I imagined the last thing she saw was the same thing in my own eyes, as her small body fell forward into the black water, with a hard splash.

I was screaming but I couldn't hear anything. The light moved from Nicole's lifeless body floating in the swamp, surrounded by duckweed, to my face, and back. In the unnerving silence, all I could hear was the sound of my exaggerated pulse. I was utterly still, afraid to move.

"Laura!" I heard Eric shouting, "Laura, go!" I looked at him, and his eyes were wild and protective, telling me things he couldn't put together in this moment of terror. I moved but I felt slow. Eric had his hands on my head, softly cupping my right temple. I reached up and felt a wooden thing lodged there, the same as the thing in Nicole's neck. I fumbled with it: it felt like a dart. "Laura," he was exasperated now. He grabbed my whole body, shifting me in front of him on the walkway, and pushed me to where I had a tree against my back.

"Eric," my right eye stung from the hot blood dripping down my face. "Can I take it out?" I tried hard to focus. I became methodical. He looked at me but said nothing, just worked on catching his breath. He too was hidden in front of a tree, from whatever was attacking us from behind. I tugged loosely on the dart and felt a throb of pain shoot through my head. Fortunately, it had just grazed me. In searing hot pain, my eyes clenched so tight they felt bruised and my mouth gaped open as I struggled for breath. Again, my hearing seemed impaired, but came to once I focused.

Before I could react, a dark figure at the start of the weathered walkway came hurtling through the night towards us. I couldn't scream. I braced myself, and felt myself being ripped from my stooped position against the tree. It was Maxim. He pulled me along with him, though I felt limp. He positioned himself where his side was exposed to the darts, shielding me. Once I'd made sense of what was happening, I found my footing and wrapped my arm around his waist as I ran with him. "Eric!" I cried. He didn't answer. "Eric! Eric! Eric!" I shouted his name frantically until I heard his footfalls behind us.

Suddenly, a flash of stark white flew past my field of vision, bringing me and Maxim to a crashing halt, sliding off the broken walkway into the water, where I caught my breath just before my head sunk beneath the surface. I screamed underwater until, disoriented, I found the surface again. "What the fuck was that?!" I screamed over and over again. "What the fuck was that?!" It had broken the last plank. I was in such a state of shock, without any assistance I was certain I would have forfeit and given up out of sheer terror.

Maxim carried my weight out of the water and up onto the embankment, but didn't stop. There were peculiar noises all around us: hard clicking sounds, gruff huffing that sounded animalistic, and hard steps in the earth like the gallop of a horse. My hair was free of its ponytail and kept falling in my face. I wondered if we were running through a herd of deer being chased by an alligator. I tried to stay focused, but I felt checked out, mentally.

Finally, Maxim found a divot in the thicket of roots of the cypress trees where we could hide, and we hurried into the snug spot. I looked back for Eric, but he wasn't there. I listened intently, but heard nothing or no one, except the sound of Maxim's and my own breathing. "Eric," I whispered hoarsely. He shrugged, reclining his head against the base of the tree. "Maxim, what...what just happened?" He was silent. I angled myself so that I could face him rather than sit next to him. "Maxim!" I exclaimed in a hush. "What was that?"

He took a couple swallows before talking. "Them the Grunch."

"The *what*?"

"They a N'Owlins old wives tale. They say they was some albino kin that was ostracized from society so they moved on into the woods off ole Grunch Road." I was dumbfounded. I felt the tickle of laughter in the back of my throat and the throbbing of anger in my flushed face. I looked on, quizzically. "They's all kinds of stories 'bout dem. They say they was half human, half goat. They say they was demons. Wudn't nobody that thought it was true, though." He looked at me apologetically, a sorrow in his eyes. "They real, though. And they mean us harm."

"Eric," I said again, watching his eyes as they looked back at the broken walkway. I turned around to see what he saw. His camera lay on the last plank before it was broken, the light glitching in and out, maybe from crashing hard on the wood, or from water damage. "Are we gonna die?"

He didn't answer. He remained stone-faced, his eyes fearful, and avoidant. I sat back further into the bundle of tree roots, where I'd once feared a snake. I listened to the sounds of the woods, the rustling of trees, the cracking of branches, and still, the absent croaks of frogs. I shuddered, crying into my folded arms, which hugged my knees to my chest.

Click click click. The sound was farther away the longer we waited. Maybe Maxim thought those things would retreat; tire of hunting us, and we could escape. But we were so deep in the swamp, where would we go?

"We can't stay here, Maxim," I whispered, my voice husky from dryness and screaming. He looked out of the line of trees, left and right, and tucked himself back in. He seemed to be busy with thought. Every time I blinked, I felt a sting of pain from the muscles pulling at my puncture wound. I tried wrapping my mind around what was happening. Some kind of albino human-goat hybrid shot us with darts, tried to ram us off a walkway, in the middle of a Louisiana swamp. This all could have very well been a ridiculous hallucination of heat exhaustion and dehydration if it weren't for what I saw next.

Click click click. Closer this time.

A large shadow loomed, the figure illuminated by the light of Eric's camera. I didn't dare look. I watched as the shadow grew larger as it drew nearer and nearer, the intensity of fear flickering with each strobe of the malfunctioning camera light. Finally, the creature stepped into view, and I shoved both hands against my mouth to keep from screaming. It was white, marble white, except when the light shone on it. In the light, the surface of its skin appeared iridescent, like an oil slick. Its feet were hooved, and perhaps most disturbingly, its knees bent back. The monstrosity leaned forward onto its hands, which were cloven, and lifted its legs, balancing its weight on thickly muscled forearms.

Click click click.

The sound I'd been hearing was from the creature standing on its hands and clicking its hooves together. I clinched my eyes closed, my chest so heavy with horror it felt like punching a bruise just to breathe. I kept my head ducked in my arms, praying it passed without seeing us.

When I thought it had gone, I picked my head up slowly, and looked up my forehead, using my peripheral vision. I didn't see anything. I then raised my eyes, but still didn't have the courage to poke my head out enough to get a good look around. I looked at Maxim, who seemed placidly afraid, and was sunk so deeply into the tree roots it was as if he'd braided himself into them. The creature was gone, and I wanted to run. Maxim looked me in the eyes with some implication, my mouth quivering from keeping in a scream or a wail that was killing me inside. I nodded to him and grabbed his hand, and we lifted ourselves from our cocoon inside the roots. I needed to run. I didn't know where, but if I was going to die anyway, I wanted to at least try.

Maxim stopped and pulled me behind the shield of a tree, where he displayed his spear to me, and I nodded. I'd lost mine. "We're gonna run. Straight down this path. There's no obstructions in my line of sight. As soon as you touch the ground, you *run*, got it?" There was a flutter in my whisper, as I put on my bravest face. We grabbed hands and stepped up onto the ground raised before us.

"Laura!" I let loose the scream that had been choking me when Eric came running toward us. I was stunned, and with terror in my eyes, I thought of nothing else to say.

"Run!" I screamed in length, as if willing myself. We were off, and our feet beating the ground was a welcome sound as our tired legs carried us as fast as we could go. It was quickly halted, though. From our left, a huge, white beast with glowing red eyes charged at us, the way a goat might charge a challenging male. I shrunk myself from its path and tripped over Maxim, and we took a tumble. I looked behind us to see that the Grunch had rammed itself into Eric, and his body went flying high into the canopy of branches, until it made an audible crunch sound as it landed. I let a cry escape my covered mouth.

The Grunch turned on its haunches back toward Maxim and me. We'd climbed to our feet, and I was horrified to see that the face was human-like, with a long, broad nose and thick jaw. It stood seven to eight feet, even with its knees bent backward. I turned to run, screaming bloody hell. Maxim matched me in step, as we both lurched our bodies forward, all while looking back, to see the creature galloping on cloven hand and hoof. When it caught up to us, Maxim swung the spear at it, smacking it in the head with a satisfying crack. It slowed the creature down.

We just kept running. The swamp looked as though it had ended, and we found ourselves on a beaten path through the trees, heavily coated with Spanish moss. I didn't bother looking back, anymore. I didn't need to. Ahead of us, three, then four, then seven, then twelve more of the beasts, varying in size, stepped into the path. Maxim and I fumbled our way into a right turn, running through the branches and thickets, outrunning a future that was already grim.

A scream escaped when I tripped into a slide, as the ground beneath me began to slope. I held my arms over my face as I tumbled and fell hard on my back, knocking the wind out of me. I clawed and heeled at the dirt, desperate to find purchase. "Max—" I tried to shout for him but was cut short when my head hit a rock.

The taste of blood and dirt hung on my lips as I finally stopped the tumble and began sliding on my stomach. Looking behind me, I could see the end of the ridge leading to a drop off, and desperately reached for anything to keep me from falling. I wrapped my fingers in the roots of a small tree that I knew would not hold me for long. Maxim cried out, but his scream was stifled by a hard splash as he hit the water below. I shouted for him, but he was motionless as a wave of white bodies converged on him. I tore my eyes away in horror, my face stinging with tears. My hand tightly grasped the unsteady root. I took a deep breath of resignation and looked down to see dozens of horrifying red eyes, now fixed on me.

ABOUT THE WRITERS

Cassandra Arnold is an English/Australian retired humanitarian physician. She currently lives in Calgary, Canada, with her engineer partner, an indoor worm farm, and long winters in which to explore and create imaginary worlds that she hopes will somehow make this one a better place to be. Read more about Cassandra on her website at Cassandra.Arnold.com.

Brad P. Christy is the author of the following short stories: "Miseryland," "Angel Dust," "Krampus: the Summoning," "T'was the Fifth of December," "The Things We do for Love," and "Cape Hadel." His poem, "A Friday So Black", was featured on *Literary Escapism*, he writes for *Ghost Night Review*, and was a finalist in the Writers' League of Texas 2014 Manuscript Contest. He is a member of the Writers' League of Texas, and holds a degree in Creative Writing and English. He now resides in the Pacific Northwest with his wife.

Erin Crocker was brought up in El Dorado Springs, MO and moved to Fredericksburg, VA in 2007, where she graduated from Germanna Community College with honors and later earned a Bachelor's in English, Linguistics, and Communications from Mary Washington University. She published her first novel, *Synchronicity* in late 2016 and is currently working on the sequel, *Menoetius,* due out this summer. Erin currently resides in Fredericksburg with her husband, six children, four chickens, and three puppies. Find more of Erin's work on AuthorErinCrocker.com.

Pamela Q. Fernandes is a practicing doctor by day and writer by night. She's a big fan of Alfred Hitchcock thrillers and loves books that keep her up all night. When not practicing medicine or writing, Pamela learns Mandy Moore's "Only Hope" on the piano. She's been trying to play it unsuccessfully for the past five years. She writes romantic suspense, Christian non-fiction and speculative fiction. You can read her work at PamelaQFernandes.com/books or reach her on Twitter @PamelaQFerns.

Klara Gomez immigrated from Havana, Cuba, in her late teens and now lives in Miami Beach, Florida. She's passionate about writing fiction, playing classical piano, and teaching general music to hundreds of students at her elementary school.

Joshua James Jordan writes speculative fiction to the chagrin of his wife and two children. He misplaced his debut novel at the Acme House off of Bourbon Street. If you find it, please return it. You can get in touch via Twitter @_JJ_Jordan or go to his website www.JoshuaJamesJordan.com.

Hillary Lyon lives in southern Arizona, where she is the founder of and editor for Subsynchronous Press. Her stories have appeared recently in *Black Petals, 365 Tomorrows, Night to Dawn, Eternal Haunted Summer* and numerous horror anthologies. Since childhood, she's loved all things frisson-y. HillaryLyon.Wordpress.com.

Ellery D. Margay is a freelance food and fiction writer who currently resides in a crooked cabin in the California redwoods. When not dreaming up tales and occasional poetry, he can be found sampling and reviewing the newest restaurants and wandering the world in search of weirdness, wonder, and misadventure. For more news on Ellery's work, visit his Facebook: Facebook.com/ShadowScribbler

P.L. McMillan is a creator of fiction featuring the murderous, the macabre, and the monstrous. She is dedicated to exploring the very darkest corners of her imagination, and is compelled to share these journeys with the world. She has been previously published in *Sanitarium* and *Neat Magazine*, as well as in Fundead's first anthology: *Shadows in Salem*.

Laurie Moran is a lover of the macabre, quirky, and cute, and she wishes it were Halloween every day. When she isn't writing or editing for FunDead Publications, she likes to make costumes and tiny cemeteries. Find her at FunDeadPublications.com and on Instagram as @thecemeterrarium.

Jonathan D. Nichols has been writing for eight years, and has always been huge into horror. Jonathan was in the military and spent over a year stationed away from this family, where he began writing and hasn't been able to stop since. Jonathan has previous published works in *Tome Magazine*, *Blood Moon Rising Magazine*, and has been featured in several anthologies.

Richard Pastor is a writer from California's Central Coast. His short novels and stories can be found in popular publications and online on Amazon Books. His last two novels, *A Texas Cowboy in Tuscany* and *South Swell* were well received by many. He is new to the occult genre but has always been fascinated with the opportunity each writer has to explore their imaginations without any boundaries to hold them back.

Nathan Pettigrew was born and raised an hour south of New Orleans, and lives with his pet rabbits in the Tampa Bay area. His story "Dog Killer" was named among the top 4 finalists of the *Writer's Digest* 8th annual Popular Fiction Awards for the Crime category, and appears in *State of Horror: Louisiana Vol. II*. Other stories are featured in the award-winning pages of *Thuglit*, and *DarkMedia Original Fiction and Poetry*. Visit Nathan at *Solarcide.com*, or on Twitter @NathanBorn2010.

Corrine Phillips, a nocturnal creature who sleeps by day and writes by night, never made it to Transylvania so she settled for Pennsylvania. A passion for fairy tales, science-fiction, horror, and Halloween continuously simmers in her cauldron and often boils over into her writing. Read more at Corrinelua78.Wordpress.com.

Brian Malachy Quinn currently teaches Physics at the University of Akron and in his free time writes and creates art. He is the author of *Astronomy: A Computational Approach*, Van-Griner 2010, and ghost writer of a book on wealth management. His gold standard for short story horror is Poe's "Fall of the House of Usher," and he enjoys writing specifically historic horror in which he has to learn about a certain by-gone period. His art can be found at: www.BrianQuinnStudio.com.

J. Benjamin Sanders, Jr. is a freelance writer who lives outside of Dallas and is currently in the midst of remodeling sixty-year-old Tudor house, along with his wife and two rescued dogs, one an insane Jack Russell terrier. He also has a deep interest in Irish/Celtic history and mythology (He named his dog Cuchullain), and comparative religion. His short stories have appeared *Sanitarium Magazine*, in A Lee Martinez's anthology *Strange Afterlives*, and in *Mysterical E*. He has been a member of the Dallas Fort Worth Writer's Workshop for several years, where he has been shamed and abused into honing his craft by a group of merciless critiquers.

Jonathan Shipley is a Fort Worth writer of fantasy, science fiction, and horror who ranges from traditional fantasy to vampires to futuristic space opera. Although he self-identifies as a novelist, it is short fiction where he has enjoyed success with sales of over eighty stories. He was a contributing author to the *After Death* anthology that won the 2014 Bram Stoker award, as well as a finalist for the 2014 Washington Science Fiction Association's Small Press Award. He maintains a web presence at ShipleySciFi.com where you can find a full list of his publications.

D.J. Tyrer is the person behind *Atlantean Publishing*, which has just released its twentieth-anniversary anthology, *A Terrible Thing* (available from Amazon). DJ has been widely published in anthologies and magazines around the world, including *Chilling Horror Short Stories* (Flame Tree), *State of Horror: Illinois* (Charon Coin Press), *Steampunk Cthulhu* (Chaosium), and *Sorcery & Sanctity: A Homage to Arthur Machen* (Hieroglyphics Press), and issues of *Black Girl Magic, Weirdbook,* and *Ravenwood Quarterly*. In addition, DJ has a novella available in paperback and on the Kindle, *The Yellow House* (Dunhams Manor). DJ Tyrer's website is at DJTyrer.Blogspot.co.uk/

Bret Valdez is an independent writer, horror film aficionado, and, unfortunately, a native Floridian. His literary influences include Stephen King, Edgar Allen Poe, and Theresa Caputo, The Long Island Medium. He is currently hard(ish) at work on his debut novel. Bret has been involved in the beta process of several writers, and consistently supports those new to releasing their work. You can follow him on Facebook at Facebook.com/ByBretValdez or @ByBretValdez on Twitter.

ABOUT FUNDEAD PUBLICATIONS

FunDead Publications is located in Salem, Massachusetts, a city which has provided endless inspiration to writers of every genre for hundreds of years. Established by Amber Newberry in late 2015, FunDead released its first collection, *Shadows in Salem*, in October of 2016. Since then, FunDead has published a Christmas anthology, *O Horrid Night*, and regularly posts new writers on their blog. Devoted to providing a space for scribblers new to publishing, as well as veterans of independent and traditional means, Amber Newberry hopes to keep the age old art of story-telling alive and well in The Witch City.

With a love for horror, gothic fiction, and all things macabre, FunDead brings a little joy to those who prefer the dark side. *Night in New Orleans* is the first print release of 2017, to be followed by a Salem-inspired poetry collection in the summer, and a Halloween-themed sister anthology to *Shadows in Salem* for the fall.

For more info and to find out how to submit your work, visit
FunDeadPublications.com

WHERE TO FIND FUNDEAD BOOKS

Online

FunDeadShop.com
Amazon.com
BarnesandNoble.com

eBooks Available for Kindle

Shopping on the Northshore

Wicked Good Books in Salem, MA
Cabot Street Books and Cards in Beverly, MA
Black Veil Studio of Tattoo and Art in Beverly, MA

Thank you so much for your support, your reviews are greatly appreciated, and we'd love to hear what you think of our anthologies!

We Love You to Death,
The FunDead Team

Made in the USA
San Bernardino, CA
24 June 2017